Jamis shouldn't be here in the dark with a beautiful woman

Not with the yearning for simple touch coursing through him. The need. The want for Natalie's warm hands on his skin. He should've been turned off by her too-good-to-be-true nature. Instead, he couldn't tear his eyes away from her lips.

Go, Jamis. For her sake. Get as far away as you can.

One of his favorite smells, wood smoke, emanated from her hair. He wished he could bury his face in those long blond curls and breathe her in.

"Why are you hiding on Mirabelle?" she whispered.

No one had ever asked him that. "I'm not a nice man, Natalie. The world is a much better place with me out of the way, unable to harm."

"I think you're wrong. I think inside here," she said, pressing a fingertip to his chest, "there's a good man hiding away."

Dear Reader,

As Harlequin's sixtieth anniversary year comes to a close, I think we can safely say it's been a smashing success. For one thing, romance readership is up as more people are coming to appreciate the genre's positive and uplifting stories. All the press has been exciting, too. Between national news specials and newspaper articles, it seemed we couldn't turn around without hearing or reading good things about Harlequin. All I can say is *it's about time!*

So here we are at the third in my Mirabelle Island series. Jamis's story is going to take you to the secluded northwest end of the island, although once Natalie shows up it won't seem nearly as quiet. If you've already read about Noah and Sophie and Erica and Garrett, I'm hoping Mirabelle is starting to feel a lot like your favorite vacation spot!

As you look toward 2010, keep an eye out for my upcoming books. In the next Mirabelle story someone from Missy Charms's mysterious past is going to come back and haunt her. And Kate Dillon, Maggie's youngest sister from *Finding Mr. Right*, is going to have a wild and suspenseful ride with none other than Riley, her bodyguard!

I love hearing from readers, so stop by my Web site at helenbrenna.com and drop me an e-mail, or send a note to P.O. Box 24107, Minneapolis, MN 55424. I can't wait to find out which Mirabelle story is your favorite.

Hope your New Year is happy, healthy and peaceful!

Helen Brenna

Then Comes Baby
Helen Brenna

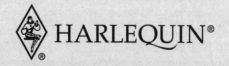

HARLEQUIN®

TORONTO • NEW YORK • LONDON
AMSTERDAM • PARIS • SYDNEY • HAMBURG
STOCKHOLM • ATHENS • TOKYO • MILAN • MADRID
PRAGUE • WARSAW • BUDAPEST • AUCKLAND

Recycling programs
for this product may
not exist in your area.

ISBN-13: 978-0-373-71606-7

THEN COMES BABY

Copyright © 2009 by Helen Brenna.

ABOUT THE AUTHOR

Helen Brenna grew up in a small town in central Minnesota, the seventh of eight children. Although she never dreamed of writing books, she's always been a voracious reader of romances. So after taking a break from her accounting career, she tried her hand at writing the romances she loves to read. Since her first book was published in 2007, she's won Romance Writers of America's prestigious RITA® Award, an *RT Book Reviews* Reviewer's Choice award and Virginia Romance Writers' HOLT Medallion. Helen still lives in Minnesota with her husband, two children and far too many pets. She'd love hearing from you. E-mail her at helenbrenna@comcast.net or send mail to P.O. Box 24107, Minneapolis, MN 55424. Visit her Web site at www.helenbrenna.com or chat with Helen and other authors at RidingWithTheTopDown.blogspot.com.

Books by Helen Brenna

HARLEQUIN SUPERROMANCE

1403—TREASURE
1425—DAD FOR LIFE
1519—FINDING MR. RIGHT
1582—FIRST COME TWINS*
1594—NEXT COMES LOVE*

*An Island to Remember

HARLEQUIN NASCAR

PEAK PERFORMANCE
FROM THE OUTSIDE

For Rosalie Jensen Brenna,
the best mother-in-law in the world!

Acknowledgments

Harlequin employs many truly wonderful people, and I'm proud to say that some of the best of the best are those who put their hearts and energies into the Superromance line.

Thanks to all of you who make my books possible, who answer my silly questions time and time again, and who are always professional and supportive, especially Wanda Ottewell, Victoria Curran, Alana Ruoso, Megan Long, Maureen Stead, Lola Speranza, Alicia Wong and Jane Hoogenberk.

Most importantly, heartfelt thanks to my editor Johanna Raisanen for her insight, patience and never-ending faith in my stories.

I couldn't do this without all of you!

CHAPTER ONE

"DADDY, I'M SCARED."

"It'll be all right, sweetheart." Neil stood frozen, listening. "I think it's gone."

Had he caused all this? Neil wracked his brain for another explanation, but there was none. That tunnel in the Ellora caves had been sealed off for a reason, and as usual he'd ignored all the warnings. If only he could turn back the clock. If only he'd never gone to India in the first place. But this was exactly what he'd asked for, wasn't it? Excitement. The unplanned and unknown.

They both heard it at the same time, that god-awful deep-chested cat growl. Katy screamed, and Neil reacted, pumping buckshot through the bedroom door again and again. This time he had to have killed that panther demon.

Jamis Quinn's hands stilled over his computer keyboard. On rereading what he'd written, he couldn't help but chuckle. "Don't get too cocky there, Neil, buddy. Things always seem to get worse before they get better."

"Get back, Katy," Neil whispered. Nudging his daughter behind him, he went to the door. The paint-chipped, shot-up wood barely hung from the hinges. He pulled on the knob, cracked the door open. Red. That's all he could see. Red

floor. Red walls. Blood? It couldn't be. That thing had no flesh, no substance.

Then he noticed bare feet and jean-clad legs, motionless on the floor. He hadn't killed the panther demon. He'd shot— "Oh, dear God! Colleen!"

"Mommy!" His daughter darted through the doorway.

"Katy, no!" There was that growling hiss again, coming from the living room. "Get back! It's still here." He jumped into the hall, putting himself between Katy and that… Rakshasas, that's what the Hindu locals had called it.

"Katy, run! Go to the Turners!"

"But Mommy—"

"Go! I want you out of here. Now!"

She scrambled down the hall, into the bedroom and outside through the window.

Neil cocked his shotgun, pumped off several shots, reloaded and shot again before the black panther spirit leaped and engulfed him like a cool, syrupy wave. The force pushed him back against the wall, but Neil could feel it dying, feel its heat draining away. He had to do something. Before it was too late. If it consumed his energy, the damned thing would revive itself and live to kill again. That was what'd happened with Wayne.

Well, that wasn't going to fly again. Not as long as Neil had a breath in his body.

"Take this, you son of a bitch." Neil pointed the gun at his own chest and fired. He fell to the floor next to Colleen and reached for her hand. "I'm sorry, baby."

"Oops. Too bad, buddy." If he didn't talk to himself, Jamis could go weeks without hearing the sound of his own voice. "Everyone, and I do mean everyone, is fair game. That's what you get for killing your wife."

"You always said one of these days I was going to get myself into something I couldn't handle," Neil whispered. "Well, I sure as hell did it this time."
The End.

"That was a perfect scene." Jamis filled his chest with a breath of air and slowly exhaled. "A perfect ending."

He took a swig of cold, black coffee, proofread the last chapter of his manuscript, and e-mailed it off to his agent. How many books was that? Fifteen? Yeah, that sounded about right. Now what? Book sixteen, of course. But that could wait until tomorrow. He was taking the rest of the day off.

Leaning back, he contemplated the choppy waters of Lake Superior's Chequamegon Bay from the desk in his loft office. A cool, early June breeze blew in through the window he'd opened that morning, and wonderfully complete silence fell over his blessedly isolated Mirabelle Island home.

That is, until a hopeful whine escaped from the tricolored mutt lying impatiently at the top of the steps. Jamis glanced at Snickers, whose fluffy black, brown and white tail swayed tentatively. "So you think it's time to celebrate finishing the book, huh? Red wine and a T-bone? I get the steak, you get the bone. My thoughts, exactly."

So what if it was only two o'clock in the afternoon? Feeling uncharacteristically cheerful, Jamis stood and followed Snickers, who was racing down the stairs and into the kitchen. Looking at the log cabin with its marble countertops, leather furnishings and big-screen TV, it was hard to imagine the place had been built close to eighty years ago. When he'd first bought it four years ago, the roof leaked, a family of raccoons had been nesting in the loft where his office was now, and a good gust of wind would have been as likely to blow rain as snow through the cracks in the windows.

Except for the massive fieldstone fireplace, Jamis had practically gutted the entire interior. He'd hired someone to update the wiring, plumbing and insulation, but had done the majority of the finishing work himself. Though he hadn't been much of a cook when he'd first moved here, he'd never regretted adding the center island stove and countertop that looked out over the great room, the woods and the lake beyond.

He stood there now, slicing the last of the mushrooms he planned to sauté, when his phone rang. "Figures." Caller ID displayed his agent's name. "Hello, Stephen." Jamis put the call on speakerphone, cracked open a bottle of cabernet sauvignon and poured out a generous glass. "You read it that quickly?"

"What do you think? You sent me everything but the last chapter last week," Stephen said. "I had to find out what was going to happen."

"And?"

"I can't believe you killed Neil. I liked him."

"He deserved it." Jamis was normally hard-pressed to find anyone truly worthy of life, himself included.

"Why?"

"He was a selfish idiot." Jamis tossed the last mushroom toward Snickers, who snatched the morsel out of the air and gulped it down without chewing. "He should've known that killing a monster of his own creation wouldn't be easy." He took a sip of wine. *Full flavor, not overly tannic, decent finish.*

Stephen sighed. "Who am I to argue? You're on a roll. Your editor thinks this one's going to get you back on the list."

Many years ago when his career had been on the upswing, he'd hit the *New York Times* bestseller list several books in a row. But that had been before his life had fallen apart. Since then he'd done a damned good job of burning bridges and every big publisher refused to work with him. Save this last one.

"I just need to write," Jamis whispered. This crap building up inside him had to manifest itself somehow. "At the moment it seems preferable to serial killing."

An uneasy silence hung on the line. "Honestly, Jamis, sometimes I don't know whether or not you're kidding."

"It sucks to be you, doesn't it?"

"Your publisher will up your advance on your current contract if you'll come out and play."

"A signing?"

"One-shot deal. You name the time and the place."

"No." Jamis tossed the T-bone onto his stovetop grill, the mushrooms in a pan of melted butter and garlic, and flipped on the cooking fan.

"But that's—"

"I said no."

"Jamis—"

"We've been over this before." He hadn't stepped off this island in four years. He wasn't about to leave for a damned his-skin-crawled-thinking-about-it book signing.

"It'd be in your best interests—"

"It's the one thing I will not give on, Stephen."

"Well, I had to try. You're contracted to give them the next book in three months. You have to make that deadline, or else—"

"It's a wildfire, tsunami and earthquake all rolled into one. I know, I know." He'd been in this business long enough to understand that a writer's success was due, in part at least, to momentum. Lose it and you might as well give it up. Starting over was worse than never having begun.

"You going to have the next book finished by September thirtieth?"

"No problem."

The summer months were his most productive. Fall, winter and spring, he could roam Mirabelle's shoreline, even the town square, to his heart's content and rarely encounter a living soul. But from June through August, with tourists crawling all over the town, Jamis kept his in-town excursions to a bare minimum, giving him all the time in the world to sit at his desk and write.

Snickers ran over to the porch windows, jumped onto his favorite chair, an oversize corduroy-covered monstrosity, and stared outside, cocking his head. Probably a squirrel.

"You're long overdue for a vacation. Why don't you take a trip somewhere? A few weeks off might do you some good."

Vacation? He had no intention of ever leaving this island. They'd be carrying him off in a long pine box. "You want that book by September thirtieth, I gotta get to work."

"Are you cooking? I can barely hear you."

He flipped off the noisy fan and what sounded like voices and a boat motor penetrated the thick walls of his cabin. People? Here? Highly improbable. There were only two private homes nestled within the more than five square miles of undeveloped Wisconsin state parkland on the northwest side of Mirabelle Island. His cabin was one and the other was an old Victorian that had been built in the 1950s to match the quaint architecture of the rest of the island. That house, a few hundred feet away, was owned by an old woman who spent only summers on Mirabelle.

Snickers let out a short bark.

Jamis walked out onto his four-season porch, glanced out the window and down the steep and rocky hillside to the Lake Superior shoreline. Through the new spring foliage now thick on the trees he barely made out the shape of a boat. It looked as if a small barge had anchored near the shore and had swung out a gangway to the dock. Several men were carrying boxes up to the old woman's house, and by the sheer number of them, it looked as if whoever was here, was here to stay.

"Good God," he muttered.

"Jamis, you there?" Stephen's voice came across the speaker on the phone. "What's the matter?"

Snickers sat in front of him and whined.

"Looks like someone's moving in next door."

"What happened to the old woman who used to live there?"

"I have no idea."

"Well, let's hope these new people are quiet."

No one could be as quiet as the previous occupant. Jamis barely ever heard a peep out of her. Occasionally, she'd have a guest or two, and he'd hear a door slamming or a garbage can clanging, but that had been the extent of it. She'd kept completely to herself. In fact, now that he thought about it, he wasn't sure he'd even seen her last summer.

"I gotta go," he said.

"This won't interfere with the new book, will it?"

"Have I ever once missed a deadline?" Jamis disconnected the call, and shut off the T-bone and mushrooms before going out onto his deck. Snickers raced down the steps, through the yard and toward the activity next door.

The events of the past several weeks finally made sense. He'd woken late one morning to Snickers barking frantically at the door. But when Jamis had looked outside there'd been no one around, although a boat similar to the barge now anchored below had been pulling away from the shore. A few days later, coming home from a lengthy trip to town for various errands and copious amounts of groceries, he'd passed the new police chief, Garrett Taylor, on the main road. Taylor, apparently a part-time construction handyman, had been pulling a small trailer filled with tools and supplies behind his golf cart. Jamis should've guessed then that something was up.

Now he walked through the shaded woods, stepped over the poison ivy and past the heavy ferns toward the old woman's house. There had to be at least four men carrying boxes from the water's edge.

"You got that end?" one of the men hollered.

"You betcha."

"Damn, this is a steep hill."

There was no practical way to move that much stuff from Mirabelle's town center to this side of the island. The path from the main road had to be close to a mile long and barely wide enough for golf carts, the only motorized vehicles allowed on the island.

"Who's moving in?" Jamis asked one of the men passing by and loaded down with a large, cardboard box.

"Don't know for sure." He nodded toward a woman standing on the wide back porch and directing traffic. "Ask her."

"All the boxes have the rooms marked," she said to the moving men.

That spindly wood sprite was in charge? Impossible. In tight, low-rise jeans and a short-sleeved orange T-shirt, she looked barely old enough to have graduated from college.

"Bedrooms one through four are upstairs," she went on. "The numbers are on the door. Bedroom five is on the main floor." With wavy blond hair, wide, heavily lashed eyes and a tall slender frame, all that honey needed was a wand to look like a modern-day princess from a kid's movie. *Wholesome,* there was no other word for her.

"Excuse me." He stepped toward the porch. "This house belongs to a *quiet* old woman." He'd no sooner closed his mouth than he realized how odd the comment sounded, but he'd be damned before he'd explain.

"Hi," she said. Then she smiled, lighting up her face and making the deepest blue eyes he'd ever seen almost dance, and wholesome turned to lively, pretty to beautiful. "Yeah, my grandmother used to live here. Sweet, wasn't she?"

"I wouldn't know." He'd never once spoken with the old woman. "What're you doing here?"

The wattage of her dazzling smile dimmed. Much better. "Grandma passed away a few months ago, and I inherited her house." She came into the yard and Snickers raced toward her. "Well, aren't you the cutest thing in the whole wide world?" She squatted and rubbed the dog's ears.

Snickers showed his appreciation by planting a big sloppy one on her mouth. *Disgusting.* How could she let him do that?

"Is he your dog?" she asked, looking up at him.

"Yeah."

"What's his name?"

"Snickers." Was he really having this conversation?

"And you look like a candy bar, too," she cooed and scratched the dog's neck, then she stood and held out her hand. "I'm Natalie Steeger. Nice to meet you."

Feeling distinctly dazed, Jamis shook her hand before the distant rumbling of golf carts coming through the woods distracted them both.

"Oh, goodie," she said, grinning. "Here they come."

Oh, goodie. "Here who come?"

"The kids."

Kids. As in more than one?

"I know it's crazy having them come on moving day, but I wanted them to feel a part of this." She motioned to the activity around her. "You know, help with the unpacking decisions. Get vested in everything happening here."

"What, exactly, *is* happening here?"

"I'm starting a summer camp for kids."

"You're kidding." Surely, his heart stopped midbeat. "Did Stephen put you up to this?"

"Stephen who?"

Holy hell. A camp for kids.

Man, did that bring back a whole host of bad memories. That's what Jamis's too-busy-for-their-only-child parents had done to get rid of him for three of the most miserable summers of his adolescence. His mother had thought she'd been doing him a favor sending him to the plushest, most expensive camp in the country. But somehow spoiled-rotten rich kids running untamed through the woods at all hours, not to mention bullying and pranking, hadn't been Jamis's idea of fun.

This had to be a dream. His imagination often took bad, even worse turns. *Any minute now,* Jamis told himself, *you're gonna wake up and this is all going to disappear. In fact, now would be a very good time. Wake up, Jamis!*

"Are you okay?" She reached out and rubbed his arm in a comforting, soothing way.

Jamis forgot all about the noise, the movers and the cool breeze blowing up from the water. He hadn't been touched by another human being in four years. That wasn't counting the casual brushing of fingertips at the post office or grocery store, the doctor and dentist appointments.

Those were impersonal in nature and didn't matter. This contact was genuine. Her hand was still firmly on his arm. He glanced into her sapphire eyes and felt the first stirrings of arousal since he couldn't remember when.

Holy hell was right.

"Hey." She was staring up at him, concerned, yes, but aware. Aware of him, definitely, as a man.

"I'm fine." He backed away.

The disturbing moment passed as quickly as it had descended when three golf carts, loaded down with kids of varying ages, emerged from the woods and pulled into a clearing near the house. Ron Setterberg, the owner of the Mirabelle Island rental business, was leading with the first cart and teenagers, a boy and a girl Jamis had never seen before, were driving the other two.

"Isn't this great?" the princess said, smiling again. "This summer, we're starting small. Only eight kids. But next summer, who knows? Maybe twenty."

As he stopped his cart, Ron nodded at him. Jamis gave a short wave, words entirely deserting him. "Let me know if you need anything else, Natalie." Ron waited until the kids climbed off his cart and then turned and headed back to town.

"Will do, Ron. Thanks."

The kids jumped down from the other two carts. "What do you want us to do?" asked the oldest girl.

"Can you take the younger kids into the house and get everyone familiar with everything?"

"Sure," said the oldest boy as they all filed past him.

Snickers, of course, had to run up to every single one of them, sniffing and licking hands and begging for pets.

"That's Galen and Samantha." She pointed to the teenagers. "Arianna, Chase, Blake and Ella are the middle four." She put her hand on her hips when one of the boys tried tripping the young fellow in front of him. "Chase, behave, please. Ryan and Toni are the two youngest."

The littlest girl, who lifted her hands away from an inquisitive and wet-nosed Snickers and who couldn't have been more than seven or eight, was the last to walk by Jamis. She had chubby cheeks and long curly hair the color of which almost perfectly matched her big, brown eyes, just like…

No, he wouldn't—couldn't—go there. This wasn't a dream. It was an outright nightmare. Jamis shook his head and laughed out loud. He'd have been hard-pressed to write this scene better himself. It was perfect, down to every last minute detail. He deserved nothing less than this.

Welcome, Jamis, to your own personal horror story.

CHAPTER TWO

"ARE YOU OKAY?" Natalie asked. For the life of her, she couldn't figure out what this man was laughing about. The almost hysterical quality to the sound of his voice made her want to invite him in for a cup of cocoa or give him a back rub. His relaxed state of dress, black T-shirt and loose-fitting khakis belied the fact that he was obviously stressed about something.

"Wonderful. Never been better." Instantly, every speck of humor disappeared from his handsome but troubled face. His long, dark hair and scruffy beard made him look desperately in need of some grooming, but his clothes were clean, his skin was clear and healthy and she could smell the scent of some musky men's shampoo on his shiny hair. And if muscular arms were any indication, he was in excellent physical shape. "Snickers, come." He turned and headed toward the woods.

"Hey!" Natalie called. "You didn't tell me your name."

"Jamis Quinn."

The name he'd thrown over his shoulder didn't sound familiar, but there was something about the severe, angular features of his face that reminded her of someone. Her first look into his toffee-brown eyes had confirmed it, but how could she have ever forgotten that mockingly superior gaze of his?

"Wait a minute!" She caught up with him and stepped directly in his path, forcing him to stop. "My grandma was in a nursing home for a while before she died, so it's been some time since I've been on Mirabelle. Are you living in the old log cabin?" The safety of the kids was priority and this guy seemed, though attractive in a potent woodsman sort of way, a bit strange.

"Yep. Can I go now?"

That was when it came to her. "I know! You're that writer, aren't you? What's his name?" Though Natalie had never read a single one of his books, let alone watched one of the movies based on his horrific stories, a person would've had to have her head buried in the sand to not recognize him.

"Quinn Roberts," he said. "Yeah, congratulations."

Handsome, sexy even, but definitely odd. Someone who wrote such distasteful stuff would have to be somewhat touched. What she couldn't understand was why in the world so many people enjoyed his books. "Do you live out here by yourself?" she asked.

"Yep."

"All year-round?"

"Yep."

"Even in the winter?"

"Didn't I just answer that question?" He glanced down at her, his furrowed brow openly expressing his impatience.

The idea of anyone staying on this island when the windchill frequently hit twenty below zero and the only way to the mainland was by snowmobile or helicopter seemed crazy to her. Even her grandmother had always moved to her Minneapolis home during the winter months.

"I happen to like peace and quiet. Can I go now?" His left eyebrow rose in a cocky sort of way as he glared at her, and she was left with the distinct impression he'd like nothing better than for her to disappear into thin air.

"Sure. Sorry. Didn't mean to keep you." Natalie watched him stomp through the woods with his dog leading the way. He didn't seem like a very happy man. "Good to meet you!" she called after him.

"Yeah, right." He kept walking, head down.

Maybe she shouldn't have touched him. She did that all the time, touched everything in stores or outside, people and things. She couldn't help it. Most folks didn't mind, but then most folks weren't charged up like Jamis Quinn. He'd felt tense, his muscles flexed as if he were poised to run off any second. Only he hadn't wanted to run, at least not at first. Initially, she was sure he'd welcomed the feeling of her hand on his skin. There'd been something in his eyes that made her want to reach up and knead his shoulder, but then he'd pulled away.

Stop it, Natalie. Remember what happened the last time? If you're attracted to this guy, he's bound to be a loser.

"Nat!" Samantha called from an open, upstairs window. "Everyone's fighting up here. We need help figuring out the bedrooms."

"I'm coming!" Natalie spun toward the back door. It was a good thing that last week Chief Taylor had come by to make sure the house was in working order, and that the movers had brought out all the furniture and arranged everything exactly to her specifications. All she and the kids had to do was unpack boxes and settle in.

"I am *not* sharing a room." Galen stuck his head out another window.

"Who died and made you king of the world?" Sam said, tossing her ponytailed light brown hair.

"No one." Galen smirked. "I always have been."

"Hold on," Natalie said. "I've got a chart." She grabbed her clipboard and ran upstairs to find kids zipping through the halls like wild animals, yelling and fighting. "Chase, no pushing," she said. "Blake, let go of your brother's arm. Arianna, don't snap at your sister."

Everyone ignored her. She watched them for a moment, her worries building. What had she gotten herself into? She'd thought she could handle this, having worked with kids her entire adult life, first as a camp counselor in the summers during college, and then as a social worker. Maybe she'd been kidding herself. Maybe she couldn't make a difference in the world. Old tapes fast-forwarded through her mind. Maybe she wasn't smart enough, caring enough, organized enough. Maybe—

No. She closed her eyes and focused. *You will not let in those doubts.* She could do this. She *would* do this. Instead of sitting at her old social services desk day in and day out, hands tied by bureaucratic red tape, she was finally going to be directly impacting lives. She'd even gone so far as to take a leave of absence from work to bring her ideas for a baby boot camp to life. She was going to turn these kids around. They were all going home at the end of the summer feeling better about themselves and believing they could make a difference in their own lives. But first she had to get control.

She stood in the hall, put two fingers in her mouth and let a whistle rip. Everyone stopped in his or her tracks. "Attention!" She pointed to the spot in front of her. "Let's all make a circle and have a quick meeting."

"I don't wanna."

"Do we have to?"

"Where's my bedroom?"

Time to get tough. "Do I need to remind all of you why

you're here?" she asked softly, looking into each child's face, one at a time. Every single one of these kids was on track to either flunk out of school or get kicked out for disciplinary issues. Her camp was their last chance.

Finally, although the kids complained, one by one, everyone except Galen gathered around. She had to hand it to that boy. He'd mastered the sullen James Dean act to a tee, arms crossed, head tilted just so, lips curved in a sardonic smile, but Natalie wasn't about to force anything on him. He'd had enough of that in his short life. Eventually, he'd come around.

"Okay, here's the deal. All your stuff is in boxes with your name on it in your assigned room. There are four bedrooms up here," Natalie said. "Galen and Samantha are the oldest and they're camp employees, so they get the two smaller bedrooms at the back of the house." She pointed down the hall. "Galen, you're in room number three. Sam, you're in four." The teenagers each looked at the other kids with smug expressions. "Galen and Sam? Remember, this is a summer job for you two."

"I know," Sam agreed.

"Whatever," Galen said, shoving his hands inside the pockets of his baggy jeans.

"So as part of your job, you two help the other kids make up their beds, put away their clothes and then you can take care of your own rooms."

"Got it," Sam said.

Galen nodded, looking bored to tears.

"Arianna, Ella and Toni, this is your bedroom over here. Chase, Blake and Ryan, you three are over here." They started to turn. "Wait a second." She leaned in, putting her arm around Ryan's too-bony shoulder. She was going to have to put some meat on this boy before the end of summer. "What do we need to do to make this the best summer ever?"

One of them groaned. "Ah, not this again!"

The others, of course, followed suit.

"I hate this!"

"Totally lame!"

Natalie didn't care. She'd take all the ridicule this world could dish out if she could instill hope in one child. One tiny drop in a pond could make far-reaching waves. "Close your eyes," she said. "Wish it, see it, make it happen." Sooner or later, they were all going to believe. She stepped away. "Okay, let's get settled! And there's a surprise for every one of you on your beds!"

Most of them didn't have the appropriate clothing for sometimes-chilly Mirabelle, so she'd bought them all new fleece jackets, sweatshirts, tennis shoes and several outfits. Knowing the teenagers would be more selective about styles, she'd given Galen and Sam a clothing allowance when she'd first offered them the job, and they'd had plenty of time to shop before leaving Minnesota, but from the size of Galen's small pack, though, she wondered if he hadn't pocketed the money.

As the little ones raced into their rooms, Natalie grinned. "I'll be downstairs if you need me."

She bounded down the steps and stopped outside the entryway to the old-fashioned kitchen, feeling suddenly nostalgic. With the white painted cabinets, yellow Formica countertops, black-and-white checkered floor and large, sturdy oak table at its center point, the room was exactly as Natalie remembered. Well, except for the cardboard boxes stacked on every flat surface.

The first time she'd come to Mirabelle with her adoptive parents and five older brothers and sisters, Natalie had been ten years old. Those two weeks with her new family had forever altered the course of her life. She'd been able to count on a bed to sleep in at night, warm covers and, every single day, enough food to eat.

Her favorite meal had been breakfast. With all the fresh air and activity on the island, she'd wake up starving every morning. She and her new brothers and sisters would all crowd around the big oak table waiting for Grandma's secret recipe French toast. When Grandma said secret, she meant secret. Through the years, no one had managed to finagle it out of her. Before Grammy had died, though, and with her entire family encircling her hospital bed, she'd singled out Natalie and whispered, "Orange zest. And Grand Marnier liqueur."

The old woman had known the urge to pay it all back ran even more deeply within Natalie than any of the other adopted grandchildren. That's why she'd willed to Natalie this house here on Mirabelle, as well as her home in Minneapolis, and enough money to cover expenses for at least a year. Rather than feeling slighted, Natalie's brothers and sisters and their adoptive parents, all of whom still lived relatively close to one another in the Twin Cities area, had encouraged Natalie to make the best of this opportunity.

So with everyone's blessings she'd taken it from there. She'd not only put together a comprehensive curriculum and filled out mounds of paperwork in order to get this camp licensed and approved by the state, she was also working on getting donations and grants to fund future camps. It all seemed a small price to pay to give a few kids a summer to remember the rest of their lives, a summer of hope.

Natalie looked around the house, boxes stacked all around, and smiled. "Thanks, Grammy, for making my dream come true."

A few hours later, the bedrooms had all been set up with Natalie having to negotiate only two disputes, the majority of the kitchen boxes had been emptied, the kids were alternating between playing outside and making chocolate chip cookies, and a dinner of pork chops and rice was bubbling away in a large slow cooker. She stepped out onto the back porch, already on her way to being exhausted. It was both exciting and frightening. For three months, she was going to be alone with eight kids. Well, except for that strange, but ruggedly sexy man living a hundred or so yards away.

She peered through the craggy red oaks and sugar maples with their new spring leaves and discerned the outline of Jamis Quinn's cabin. He had to feel cut off out here by himself, through the long, cold winters when more than half the island headed south as soon as the last tourist left at the end of every summer. That man had to be lonely.

Okay, stop. You're taking a break from men, remember?

She had the worst luck of any woman she knew with regard to men and relationships. Every guy she'd ever dated turned out to be a total jerk.

But there was no harm in being neighborly. Right?

Grabbing a plate of chocolate chip cookies, she stepped off the porch. "Come on, kids, let's go visit our new neighbor."

"I CAN'T BELIEVE THIS is happening." With his phone on speaker, Jamis paced the floor of his kitchen, his celebratory meal completely forgotten. Except for the wine. He'd downed that first glass while dialing his attorney's number, a man who also happened to be an old friend, and had immediately poured himself another. Too bad he'd quit stocking hard liquor in the cabin after losing a couple weeks his first winter here. A shot or five of tequila would make this situation, if not acceptable, at least more palatable.

"Jamis, relax," Chuck Romney said. He might be Charles to his fellow partners in the largest, most reputable law firm in downtown Minneapolis, but he'd always be Chuck to his old college party buddies. "Maybe it won't be as bad as you think."

"She's starting a summer camp for kids."

"This is a joke, right?"

"So you had no clue this was in the works?"

"None."

"You were supposed to be watching for that house going up for sale. What happened?"

"The property never went on the market," Chuck explained. "The woman inherited the estate from her grandmother when she died. What was I supposed to do?"

"What did you do?"

"I made a few inquiries with the attorneys handling the estate, asked if the new owner might be willing to sell and got shot down."

"That's not good enough."

"If she doesn't want to sell, Jamis, there's nothing I can do."

"Then you're fired."

"Yeah, so what else is new?" Chuck said, unmoved. "I've got a novel idea. Why don't *you* move and leave this poor woman alone? There has to be some uninhabited private island in Wisconsin. You could buy your own piece of rock and never have to worry about this again."

Jamis glanced around his house and broke into a cold sweat thinking of what it would take to pack up his loft office. Every wall was lined with built-in bookcases stuffed to the gills with research books, manuals and such. When he'd remodeled this old dog of a log cabin, he'd hired electrical engineers and computer technicians to connect him to the world via satellite. Everything was wireless, including his TV, network, speakers and Internet connections. He could work on his laptop in any room in the house, out on his porch and deck, even down by the lakeshore. It'd taken him no less than a year to get this house set up so that he'd never be able to find an excuse to leave Mirabelle.

There was no good reason that woman or her camp needed to be on this island. Jamis, on the other hand, had every reason to keep himself away from the rest of the world. Away from her and her kids.

"I have a book due in three months," he whispered, his mouth suddenly dust dry. If he was late with this publisher, he'll have burned his last shaky bridge. What would he do if he couldn't write, couldn't sell his books? "She needs to move."

"Good luck with that."

"Don't people have to get licenses or something for that many kids in one house?" Frustrated, he pounded his hand onto the granite countertop. "You know like pets?"

"There are all kinds of laws that apply to organizations that care for children. If you want me to, I'll check into it and make sure she covered her bases."

"Do that. Find something that'll close her down." He took a deep breath, calming himself.

"Jamis, maybe it's not such a bad thing that you have neighbors. Maybe this is good—"

"When's the last time you read one of my books?"

There was a short pause on the line. "No offense, Jamis, but you know they're not my cup of tea."

"That's what I'm talking about. Would you want to live next to me?"

"Yeah. I would."

"You have to say that. You're my friend."

"Well, at least you'll admit to the friend part. For God's sake, Jamis, come back for a weekend at least. Let's have lunch."

How long had it been since Jamis had had a beer with a buddy at a bar? Went to a football game? Asked a woman to dance? "Can't do that, Chuck. I need her gone."

Chuck sighed. "I'll see what I can do."

Jamis disconnected the call and stared out the window toward that house. It felt strange knowing there were people, live human beings, no less than a hundred yards through those trees. Not for long, if he had anything to say about it.

His stomach grumbled and he went to his kitchen to see if any part of his meal was salvageable. The steak was tough as a hockey puck, but it'd fill his stomach. He took the plate to his computer and set to work answering the e-mails he'd left unanswered for the past several weeks while he'd finished this last book.

A strange noise sounded downstairs. *What the—?* Was that a knock? On his door? That's something he didn't hear every day. Or ever, for that matter. Could he ignore it? Pretend like he was… out?

"Hello!" a voice sounded from outside.

Dammit.

He pounded across the hardwood floor and yanked open the door. With a couple kids piled up behind her, that woman—what was her name again?—stood outside.

"We brought you cookies," she said, holding out a plate covered in plastic wrap.

"Cookies." Was she serious?

"Homemade. Chocolate chip. Can we come in?"

"No."

As if she hadn't heard him, Natalie, that was her name, took a step toward him. "Oh, goodness, look what you've done to this place." She stepped close, too close, and he was forced to back away. "This cabin used to be a ramshackle dump. My brothers and sisters and I used to play hide-and-seek in here. I can't believe the changes you've made. It's gorgeous."

While the other kids stayed outside, yelling at each other and roughhousing and jumping from one large rock to the next in his yard, the littlest girl stuck close behind Natalie and cautiously eyed Jamis with those too-big brown eyes.

"This is Toni."

Not names again. No, no, no. He really, really didn't want to know, let alone remember. "Can you just…go?"

She glanced up at him, no anger, only concern. "I'm sorry. I…"

"Look. It's not you. It's me. I came to this island for peace and quiet. Believe it or not, that's the way I like it. So…could you not…bother me? I won't bother you, either. Not a word. Pretend like I don't exist."

At first, she looked confused, then, as understanding dawned, supremely and frustratingly undaunted. "I can see you need some space."

Yeah. Try five miles of it.

She set the plate of cookies on the side table by the door. "Come on, Toni." She turned the girl around and went outside. "Kids, let's go."

Jamis watched the kids run willy-nilly through the woods, feeling something curiously bordering on regret. "I haven't always been this way," he whispered.

Years and years ago in Minneapolis, he'd lived like everyone else, worked and went to coffee shops and parties. Some people—okay, only a few—had even liked him, once upon a time. He'd been so normal, in fact, that those first years of being alone here on Mirabelle had nearly killed him. That'd been the outcome he'd been after, he supposed. Instead, he'd simply adapted over time and become comfortable with the silence. Now, Jamis couldn't imagine life any other way.

Oh, for crying out loud. His thoughts were jerked back to the present. She was taking the group straight through the poison ivy. *They are not your problem. Do not get involved.* Why should he care if every single one of them developed a horrible, itchy, miserable rash?

At the edge of the forest the smallest girl looked back over her shoulder. When she saw him watching them, she scurried forward and, apparently frightened of him, grasped for Natalie's hand. Smart girl. Kids somehow always managed to see the truth inside a person.

Something long dormant stirred inside him. Compassion, sensitivity, humanity? Impossible. Jamis no longer felt those emotions.

He glanced at the plate of cookies, grabbed one and took a big bite. Cringing, he spit the mouthful into his hand. Had the woman used an entire box of baking soda or just half?

"That has to be the worst thing I've ever tasted." He tossed the remainder of the cookie to Snickers. The dog caught the thing in midair, dropped it to the floor and sniffed at it disdainfully.

"Unbelievable." Jamis shook his head. On second thought, maybe he'd get lucky and those kids would starve to death. *Yeah, that'd get rid of 'em. Or drowning. Carbon monoxide poisoning would work, too. Aliens. Evil spirits. Water demons.*

Suddenly he realized what he was doing. Again.

Stop it! Geez, Jamis! Don't you ever learn?

I take it back. I take it all back. Every single word.

Disgusted with himself, he glanced down at Snickers. "Let's go for a run, pup. A *long* one."

CHAPTER THREE

THE NEXT DAY AROUND lunchtime, creativity having eluded him all morning, Jamis glanced into his refrigerator. Pickles, ketchup, mustard and mayo. *Yum. That'd make a spectacular meal.* Closing the door, he muttered to himself, "You've put it off long enough." He didn't relish the idea of going into town and bumping elbows with the tourist crowds, but his cupboards, too, were just about bare.

The decision made, he grabbed the package he needed to mail, his backpack, a baseball cap and a pair of sunglasses and set off on the path through the woods to the road into town. Familiar with the once-a-week ritual for groceries and mail, Snickers led the way into town until a white-tailed deer leaped onto the road and Jamis stopped. "Snickers. Sit."

The dog plopped his butt down by Jamis's side and Jamis grabbed his collar to make sure the silly mutt didn't run after the deer and get his skull kicked in. They both watched as a string of three female deer ran in front of them and disappeared into the woods. Afterward, they continued on their way with chickadees and finches chirping in the trees.

About a five-mile walk down a paved, heavily wooded and narrow road, he walked fast, considering it part of his workout for the day. It normally took him about an hour one-way. He could have his groceries and mail delivered directly to his house, but that would require conversing with these islanders, something he tried to keep to a minimum. He left them alone and they left him alone. The arrangement had worked out very well for years.

His first sight of civilization was the Mirabelle Island Inn, and as soon as its red-tiled roof became visible, his stomach took a tumble. People. Talking, laughing, breathing. This summer seemed busier than last. In fact, he had to walk on the cobblestone street to avoid the crowds on the sidewalk. The damned pool and golf course they'd built last year were wreaking havoc on his once-quiet island.

On reaching Newman's Grocery, Jamis stopped. Snickers immediately sat on Jamis's left and looked up at him, waiting. He knew the drill. Jamis hooked a leash to Snickers's collar and tied him to the lamppost. Out in the woods, Snickers could run untethered to his heart's content, but in town the leash became a necessity.

"Stay," Jamis said to Snickers, putting out his hand palm forward. "I'll be back soon."

Jamis slipped on the hat and sunglasses and walked into the store. One time, not long after he'd moved to Mirabelle, a reader had recognized him and made a fuss. "It's Quinn Roberts," she'd screamed, practically swooning. "I'm your biggest fan." Blah, blah, blah, blah, blah. Jamis had ignored the woman, but a crowd had gathered. In the end, he'd left his grocery cart and run, not walked, out of the building. He'd even skipped the post office that day, the only part of this routine he halfway enjoyed.

In the produce department, he selected his usual fruits and vegetables and glanced around. What was going on here? There seemed to be a bigger selection of items. Fresh artichokes. More varieties of chilies. Arugula. Vine-ripened tomatoes. The meat department was carrying a new brand

of Italian sausage that looked amazing. Some organic se-
lections had been added in frozen foods, so he decided to
try a few things. And the variety of cheese was outstanding. There appeared to be one upside to Mirabelle's
newfound popularity.

While waiting in the checkout line, several tourists eyed
him, but he refused to look at them. After paying and
stuffing his groceries into his pack, he collected Snickers
and walked to the post office, a couple blocks inland off
Main. Tying the dog to another lamppost, he entered the
small brick building to the sound of a soft chiming.

The usual clerk, a woman with short salt-and-pepper
hair, came to the counter, looking as cantankerous as ever.
She had to be close to retirement and acted as if the event
couldn't come quick enough. No matter the time or day of
the week, this woman treated him as if he'd just disturbed
her lunch hour. Without a word, she stared at him from the
other side of the counter.

"I'm here to pick up my mail," he said.

"Your name?"

She did this every time, and every time he chose to
ignore her. Today, she'd finally gotten to him. "You gotta
be kidding me."

"Name."

"Jamis…Quinn," he said, punctuating every syllable.

"Identification."

He glared at her, wishing there was something, anything, he could do to mess with her, but there wasn't. He'd
tried on numerous past occasions to ruffle her feathers and
had more than once left completely disappointed. Nothing
fazed this woman. If he didn't show her his driver's license,
he wasn't going to get his mail. No ifs, ands or buts. He
flipped out his wallet.

After taking her time studying his ID, she slowly walked into the back room, returned what seemed an eternity later with a stack of envelopes, papers and flyers all banded together and tossed it on the counter toward him.

"I need to mail this package," he said, setting a large padded envelope between them.

"Is there anything liquid, perishable or flammable inside?"

"What do you think?"

The only thing he'd ever sent out of this post office had been paper. Every manuscript he'd ever written he mailed to his mother. Why, he couldn't say. Although she never read any of his books, every time he finished one he had to send it to her. Most likely he was still looking for some crumb of acknowledgment from her, but he wasn't holding his breath.

The postal clerk cocked her head at him. "I think if you don't answer my question, I won't mail your package."

"No. There is nothing liquid, perishable or flammable in the damned thing."

She put the package on her scale and came up with a charge. He flipped out his credit card to pay.

"May I see your ID, please?"

He laughed. "You're funny, you know that?"

"Just doing my job."

"I already showed you my ID. Besides which, I've been coming here once a week for years picking up my mail and mailing packages, so you know very well who I am."

"Correction. You've been coming here once a week for *four* years and have never once said thank you or please."

She had him there. "What's your name?"

"Sally McGregor," she said with virtually the same intonation as he'd used with her.

"Well, Sally, you're right." He snapped up his credit

card. At this point, not drawing out his ID again was a matter of principle. "Can I *please* pay with cash?" He threw a ten spot onto the counter. *"Thank you."*

Jamis took his receipt and left the building. That had been one of the longest face-to-face conversations he'd had with any islander since coming to Mirabelle, and it was, in a strange way, invigorating.

With early summer sunshine beating down on his shoulders, he collected Snickers and headed for his next stop. He was almost there when he noticed his new nemesis, brood in tow, ready to spread her good cheer down Main Street. Damned, if Natalie Steeger didn't seem to know every single person she passed on the sidewalk. It was just his luck that she'd stopped not far from Henderson's, and he with a long list of drugstore items yet to be purchased.

Slipping his sunglasses back on, he pulled his hat lower on his brow. With any luck, he'd get out of Dodge without her noticing him.

"THIS IS PRETTY," ARIANNA announced as they approached Mirabelle's town center.

"Horses!" Toni said as an old-fashioned carriage rolled by them on Island Drive.

"I bet they have a bomb candy shop," Chase said, nudging his brother.

After morning chores and lunch, Natalie had decided to bring the kids into town to explore. A sense of community was important in a child's life, at least it had been in hers, and there was no better place than Mirabelle for feeling connected. As long as she'd been on Mirabelle, she'd never felt alone. Getting Galen involved, though, straggling as he was at the back of their pack and looking extremely disinterested, was going to take some concentrated effort.

Before reaching Main Street, she'd noticed the town was much busier than she remembered the last time she'd visited her grandmother, so they'd parked their bikes and walked. Now, as the children followed her down the cobblestone street, she realized not much had changed in the two years since she'd been here, although everything looked somehow brighter and fresher.

Whether it was new coats of paint or changes in colors, she wasn't sure, but the green and white striped awnings marking most businesses looked new and fresh. The American flags hanging from every other old-fashioned black lamppost and the gold and black signs on every street corner listing the shops on the upcoming block were nice new touches.

"It feels like we're in an old movie," Toni whispered to Sam, who was holding hands with her and Ryan.

"Weird," Sam murmured, looking around. "There really aren't any cars?"

"Nope," Natalie said. "Except for the emergency equipment."

Ryan picked up a penny lying on the sidewalk and quietly stuffed it in his pocket.

"Can we go sailing sometime?" Blake asked as they passed by the marina.

"Sure," Natalie said. "The plan is to take in everything Mirabelle has to offer at some point during the summer. Kayaking, windsurfing, horseback riding. We're going to work hard and play hard."

That met with murmurs of approval. Galen appeared to be keenly interested in the sailboats, kayaks and windsurfer boards in the bay, and Natalie smiled to herself. He'd get there.

As they continued down Main, Natalie glanced up a side

street and noticed a man leaving the post office. The way he moved, with purpose and confidence, felt familiar, although a baseball cap and dark sunglasses shaded his face. Then she saw the dog tied to the lamppost and knew she'd been right. Her new neighbors, Jamis and Snickers, had also come to town.

She was about to head toward them, when she met up with her first islander. "Hey, Doc." She waved as she approached Doc Welinsky, a tall, always jovial fellow who seemed much older than she remembered.

He pulled up short and studied her. "Well, if it isn't little Natalie Steeger. Only you're not so little anymore. How the heck are you?"

"Very well, thank you."

His smile disappeared. "Sorry, about your grandmother."

"Thanks, but if I live to ninety-seven, I'm going to guess I'll be ready to go. We can't all live forever." In her peripheral vision she noticed Jamis slinking into the drugstore, obviously hoping to avoid her.

"Ain't that the truth?" Doc turned pensive. "I've actually been thinking about retiring."

For as long as Natalie had been coming to the island, he'd been Mirabelle's only doctor. "What'll they do without you?"

He shrugged. "Time for some new blood."

A tourist bumped her shoulder and passed on without pardoning herself. "Why is it so busy in town?" Natalie asked.

"We put in a golf course and a couple swimming pools up on the hill."

"No kidding?" The pool would be another activity for the kids. "Doc, I'd like to introduce you to my summer kids." She went down the line, introducing everyone. "This is Doc Welinsky."

"Hey, kids." He gave them all his thumbs-up.

"I've set up a camp at Grandma's house."

"Yep, I remember hearing about that." An oddly concerned look had passed over his features as the kids moved down the street and stopped in front of the drugstore to pet Snickers. "There was quite a discussion at the town council meeting when you first applied."

"There was?"

"Oh, yes. There were a few folks who weren't too sure about opening up the island to…" he said, pausing, "an undesirable element."

"Undesirable? These kids?"

"Well, they come from some pretty tough neighborhoods, don't they?"

"Yes, but none of them are troublemakers." Yet.

"Well, it'll probably take some time to convince some of the more stubborn islanders, but I wish you the best of luck, Natalie."

"Thank you," Natalie said, but Doc's comments had definitely colored the day for her. She'd had no idea that some of the islanders had been against her camp.

She rejoined her kids and they all went into the drugstore. Bob Henderson was standing at one of the cash registers. He glanced up and opened his arms and hugged Natalie as if she were a long-lost child. "Natalie! It's so good to see you."

"Good to see you, too, Bob."

"We heard through the town council that you were opening a camp for kids out at your grandmother's place," Bob said. "Boy, that created quite a stir."

"That's what I've heard."

"Well, you know how some of the Mirabelle folk hate changes." He smiled and whispered, "But I thought I'd better give you fair warning."

"Thanks. But Doc already beat you to it."

"He did, huh? Well, I'm gonna guess he's looking out for you, too. How's it going?"

"So far, so good. Let me introduce you to everyone. Kids, this is Bob Henderson. I worked for him and his wife every summer all through high school and college."

"And she spoiled us, she did. Haven't found as good a clerk ever since."

Galen picked up a magazine off the rack and pretended to be flipping through it. With Sam craning her neck down the makeup aisle, it was clear even her attention was wandering. "Everyone up for some ice cream?"

"Yeah!"

"Sweet."

"I'll meet you kids at Mrs. Miller's ice cream and candy shop, 'kay? Galen and Sam, you guys are in charge. Keep everyone together." She handed them some cash.

"Will do," Sam said.

After they'd left, Bob said, "That crew looks like a lot of work."

"They're all good kids at heart. They'll be working a lot this summer, but should have plenty of fun times, too. I think the time away from the city will do them all some good."

"If you need any help, you let me or Marsha know." A customer came to the register. "She'll be disappointed she missed you."

"I'll be here all summer." Natalie turned to go and spotted her new neighbor in the hair care aisle, head down and searching the shelves. He was a tall man and in surprisingly good physical shape for a writer. She would've expected someone who made up stories all day at his computer to have rounded shoulders, pasty white skin and a potbelly.

Wearing sunglasses and a hat, even inside the store, Jamis appeared to be hiding. She flashed on his reaction yesterday when she and the kids had brought him cookies. *Pretend like I don't exist,* he'd said. As if. The man had a presence that simply couldn't be ignored, despite being either totally antisocial or extremely shy. Good thing she was neither.

She spun around and meandered toward him, flashing her brightest smile. "Fancy meeting you here."

Jamis glanced up, but wouldn't hold eye contact. Not that she could see much of his eyes through the dark lenses of his glasses. "Yeah," he said, sounding infinitely bored. "What do you know?"

"We missed you at our campfire last night," she said, hoping to start a normal conversation.

"I doubt that." He tossed a bottle of shampoo into his basket and then moved to the first-aid aisle.

"We'd love for you to join us some time. Really," she said, trailing after him and grasping for common ground. "S'mores. Popcorn. Hot dogs. You name it, I'll make sure we've got it for you."

Ignoring her, he grabbed several items off the shelf, tossed them into his basket and moved to the next aisle, passing a section of books and magazines.

Books. That was the ticket.

Searching amidst the varied covers, she spotted his name toward the bottom of the display. "I've been thinking I should read one of your books." She picked up a cover that caught her eye. "How 'bout this one?"

His gaze swung toward her. "Um. No. You won't like that one."

"What about this one?" She grabbed the next paperback in line and held it out.

"You do know I write horror stories?"

She nodded. "It'll be good for me to expand my horizons." *In more ways than one.* Her gaze automatically flew to his mouth. She'd never kissed a man with a mustache, let alone a beard. *Stop it, stop it, stop it!* As if reading her mind, he reached up and ran a hand down his cheek, smoothing his whiskers. Would they feel as soft as they looked?

"Yes," he whispered.

Startled, she sucked in a breath and blinked up at him. "What did you say?"

"I said, yes. On second thought, maybe you should read one of my books."

"Oh." She swallowed, relieved that her thoughts hadn't been quite so transparent. "Then which one would you recommend?"

As he studied her, she couldn't be sure, but it seemed the barest hint of a smile worked the edges of his mouth. "This one." He picked up the title *Lock and Load* at the end of the row. "Knock yourself out." That time, the smile on his face and in his voice was unmistakable, and it was a surprisingly pleasing sound.

"Thanks."

"No problem." He headed to the checkout counter and without so much as a backward glance was out of the store within minutes.

By the time she'd finished with her own purchases and went outside, both Jamis and Snickers were long gone. More than a little disappointed, she moved on to her next stop, Mrs. Miller's ice cream and candy shop. "Hi, Mrs. Miller!" Natalie sailed through the front entrance with a smile on her face. "I see you've met my camp kids."

"So that's where these kids came from." Mrs. Miller frowned.

"I'm sorry. Have there been problems?"

"No, not yet, but maybe next time you should all come in together so you can keep an eye on them."

"All right, I'll do that." She turned to her kids. "Well, guys, if you know what you want, tell one of the clerks." There were several college-aged kids behind the counter scooping up ice cream.

Every one of her kids hesitated. A couple dug into the pockets of their shorts. "And I'm buying!" Natalie quickly added. "So get whatever you want."

While the younger ones were ordering, Galen and Sam were talking to several teenagers, both boys and girls, sitting near the far corner. "Come to the pizza place Friday night," one of the boys said. "Hang out. Play some foosball."

Yes! Natalie did an internal happy dance. Sam and Galen were already making friends. This was working out perfectly.

After they left Mrs. Miller's, Natalie said, "Last stop is the gift shop." She wanted to touch base with the owner of the store, a very nice young woman who had agreed to take on consignment everything they made at her camp. Natalie had spoken with her on the phone several times and met her once or twice while visiting her grandmother. They'd connected immediately.

Walking a couple of blocks down Main, she stopped outside the gift shop's interesting window display. Instead of the standard Midwestern collection of painted wooden loons and coatracks made out of deer hooves, there were candles and incense, handmade jewelry, books on astrology and tarot cards and new age CDs.

"Last stop, guys," Natalie said. "You can come inside if you promise not to touch anything. Okay?"

Their mouths full of ice cream, they all nodded or murmured in agreement. A soft chime sounded as she opened the door to Missy Charms's shop and everyone filed inside. A row of wind chimes for sale tinkled in the warm breeze blowing in from outside. The scent of something spicy and warm hit Natalie's nostrils and she noticed a stick of incense burning at the front counter. There were tourists in the store, a mother and daughter, flicking through a stand of T-shirts.

A sign up front declared customers could Buy with a Free Conscience. Every product in the store was guaranteed as either free trade or made in the U.S.A. Natalie loved this place.

With the sound of beads parting, a young woman's familiar face appeared from the back room. "Natalie! You're here!"

"Hey, Missy!"

Galen came alive the moment Missy appeared. But then with curly blond hair, green eyes and the angular face of an elf princess, there probably weren't many men who didn't immediately notice the woman.

"I see you brought your whole group with you." Missy glanced around.

"Yep."

"Well, I need to meet them." She charged up to each child and introduced herself. At least Missy didn't have any reservations about these kids. "You guys need to get cracking. It's been so busy already this summer that my inventory is flying off the shelves."

"We've started the ball rolling and should have something for you by next week. Right, kids?"

"Right," everyone except Sam agreed.

She was enthralled with a stand of necklaces on the front counter. "Missy, can I make jewelry for you?"

"Boy, can you ever. Hold on a minute." Missy went into her back room and came out a moment later with a small box. "Here are a few samples and all the supplies you need to make bracelets, necklaces and amulets." She leaned toward Sam and whispered, "If Natalie ever gives you some free time away, I'll teach you how to bless the feathers."

"Awesome," Sam whispered, putting the box in her pack.

The younger kids were getting restless. "We need to get going." Natalie turned. "See you next week, Missy."

As the kids all filed outside, Missy grabbed Natalie's arm. "You got a sec?"

"Sure," Natalie said. "Sam and Galen, why don't you two go get the bikes and take the younger kids back to the house? I'll catch up with you in a few minutes, okay?"

"Come on, guys." Sam led the way for the younger kids and, with a last glance at Missy, Galen took up the rear.

The moment they were out of earshot, Missy said, "Call me sometime soon. You can come into town and have dinner with me and a couple of friends."

"Oh, I don't know." Natalie shook her head. It wouldn't be right for her to just take off. "I should be with the kids."

"Twenty-four-seven out on that lonely end of the island with eight kids and no adults to keep you company? You're going to burn out, honey."

That's something Natalie hadn't given a lot of thought. "You're probably right."

"You're paying Sam and Galen, aren't you? Let them take care of the kids now and then. You're going to need some adult time."

"But you're forgetting." Natalie grinned. "I've got Jamis Quinn for company."

Missy laughed.

"What do you know about him?"

"Very little. He's a tough man to read."

"He seems very private. And quiet."

"So unlike you."

"Seriously. You must know something about him."

"I've never talked with the man." Missy sighed. "But I hear things about him and the blue aura I see around him when he comes to town is quite an enigma."

"Why?"

"Blue usually signifies a person who's extremely balanced and relaxed."

"Doesn't sound like the Jamis I've met."

"Exactly."

"So tell me—" Natalie smiled at Missy "—what color is my aura?"

"Mostly turquoise. Dynamic, energetic. People want to follow you, Nat. You're perfect for these kids." She squeezed Natalie's hands and then grinned. "And now that I think about it, blue goes awfully well with turquoise."

"Oh, no." Natalie shook her head.

"I thought you liked flings. Minimum time commitment for maximum fun? Three months and you'll be leaving Mirabelle. Doesn't get any better than that."

Leaving the fling before the fling could leave her. That was—used to be—right up Natalie's alley. "I've sworn off all men."

"I'll believe that when I see it."

"I'm serious. I haven't dated anyone for…three whole months."

Missy laughed.

"Okay, so I'm trying. You would, too, if you had the kind of luck I do with men. Things will be going fine and then all of a sudden a major deal-breaker pops up out of nowhere." She shook her head. "I just want to be friends with Jamis. Nothing more. Nothing less."

"Then you'd better watch out for that gray shadow I sometimes see surrounding him."

"Meaning?"

"He has an unpredictable dark side," Missy said. "I have a feeling a friendship with Jamis might get you more than you bargain for."

CHAPTER FOUR

As THE SUN DIPPED lower on the seemingly endless Lake Superior horizon, Jamis paddled his kayak to Mirabelle's rocky shoreline. He'd circled one of the outer lying Apostle Islands before heading home, so it'd been an acceptable workout. Stowing the kayak away, he headed up the steep hill to his cabin. After a shower and a cold beef sandwich, the silence was getting to him. He put on an alternative rock CD and, with Snickers close on his heels, went out onto his deck, cold beer in hand.

He wasn't entirely comfortable relaxing after having had, so far, such an unproductive writing week. Unproductive? It'd been disastrous. With all the comings and goings next door, he hadn't written anything except e-mails. But he needed to unwind and the beer tasted good on this warm evening.

Doing his best to ignore the Victorian, he took a swig from the cold bottle, followed quickly by two more and glanced out over the lake to watch the sun sink below the horizon. Quickly now, it slipped lower and lower still until finally disappearing completely. Dusk, quiet and heavy, settled over the lake. From here he could see for close to five miles on a clear night. Most nights he contemplated the serenity of the uninhabited islands to the north, but tonight it was the flickering lights of the mainland that grabbed his attention.

Lights from homes and businesses where life was taking place. People making dinner. Running children to various activities. Reading. TV. Talking. Laughing.

As if he'd conjured the images in his mind, voices low and indecipherable came to him on the light breeze. But these were real. He glanced toward the sound and saw fire-light flickering in the distance. Miss Camp Director and her rug rats were having another campfire.

Snickers glanced up at Jamis as if asking permission to join the group. "Sorry, Snicks. Not our game."

Closing his eyes, Jamis listened to his music and let his mind wander. Ideas for a new book were bound to come to him. Any time now. Now would be good. Perfect setting for creativity to burst forth. *Right...hold it...hold it...now!*

A little squeak of a whine pierced his thoughts. Next a tail swishing on the surface of the wood deck. Then a whimper.

Jamis opened his eyes. The dog immediately stood and pawed at Jamis's leg, clearly hoping for an invitation. "Okay. Up you go."

He jumped onto Jamis's lap and settled. Jamis scratched under the dog's collar and behind his ears and Snickers threw his head back onto Jamis's chest and breathed a heavy and contented sigh.

"Tell me something, Snick," Jamis whispered. "Do you ever miss them?"

As if the memories were too much for him, the dog hopped back down to the deck and wagged his tail expectantly. "All right. Fine. Go." Jamis nodded toward the woods. "Go on. Get out of here."

The dog scampered quickly down the steps and trampled through the woods. Jamis knew the moment he'd reached them.

"Snickers!" It was her voice, Natalie's, filled with

sincere joy. "Isn't he the cutest thing? Watch out for the fire. His tail!"

Then it seemed as if the whole group joined in squealing, talking, laughing.

"Snickers, lie down."

"His nose is wet."

"And cold."

"Kisses. Kisses." Natalie blubbered on and on. "I love you, too. Yes, I do. Lie down. Good boy."

Jamis would've bet anything Snickers was lying at Natalie's feet, but he wondered if the little girl was still frightened of the dog. Curiosity getting the better of him, Jamis moved silently through the forest until he could see them and make out the quieter bits of their conversation. The moment he saw Natalie's face lit by the fire, he stopped. He wouldn't have thought it possible. He'd thought sunlight and blue skies would put her wholesome beauty at its best advantage. But he couldn't have been more wrong.

She might look like an angel in daylight, but at night with golden firelight flickering in her eyes and shadows dancing around her, that innocent angel had turned into a sultry and mysterious she-devil. The angles of her face. The shape of her shoulders. Her lips.

Five long years he'd been without a woman. For the first year after Katherine had left him, he'd been sorely tempted by anything with long legs, but hadn't wanted to add any more fuel to her flame. These past four years, he could not have cared less. He'd seen women in town, some pretty, some gorgeous, some on the beach in bikinis baring a lot of skin, but not once had he regretted isolating himself. Not once had he imagined touching a woman's skin, her lips, her waist, her…

With a hard-on pressing against his jeans, he closed his eyes. *You have no right to step into her world. Your touch would at best taint her, at worst destroy her.* But he could watch, couldn't he? From a distance.

He leaned up against the nearby tree. She'd made a fire pit, arranging a ring of rocks around a nice-size blaze and a couple of fallen logs for seating. Although he was just out of the ring of light, he could see their faces, illuminated by the red-orange glow of the fire. It was chilly tonight and they all sat close. All of them except for the teenage boy.

Snick was indeed at Natalie's feet, but she was sitting on a log and out of reach. The youngest girl, on the other hand, was sitting on a folded blanket, her legs crossed. She was inching away from the dog, but the more she tried to get away from him, the more pathetically he begged for her attention. First a nose to her hand. Then a lick on a finger. Then a whole head nudged slowly under her arm.

He rested his chin on her leg and waited, his tail thumping expectantly every time she glanced down at him. Finally, she tentatively touched his forehead and Jamis could've sworn he heard the dog sigh with delight.

"So where were we?" Natalie asked. "Oh, yeah. Highs and lows this week. Arianna, it's your turn."

"My grandma gave me and Ella both ten dollars for spending money," the one who must be named Arianna said. "She's never given us money before."

"That's pretty exciting," Natalie said.

"But," the girl went on, her voice a little sad, "it has to last for the whole summer."

"I didn't get any money," said one of the boys.

"Me, neither."

"Who's got the chocolate chips cookies?"

"You've already had two."

"So?"

"Hey, hey. I made them for everyone. Pass them around." That was Natalie. "As for money this summer, you'll all have the chance to earn some when we sell our crafts in town. The nicer they look, the more money you'll make. It'll be your money. You'll get to decide how much to save and how much to spend."

What kind of camp was this?

"Toni, how 'bout you?" Natalie asked. "Is there anything you'd like to share?"

"Hmm." The little girl made a small sound. "I guess my high was coming here. And my low." She paused. "I don't know."

"It couldn't have been easy leaving another foster home," Natalie said, nudging her.

Foster home?

"I'm used to it," the little girl said.

The circle around the fire fell silent.

"Anyone missing home yet?"

"Are you serious?"

"As if."

"Galen? Do you have anything you'd like to share?"

"No."

"You sure?"

"Trust me. No one around this fire wants to hear what I have to say."

"Get off it, Galen." That sounded like the teenage girl. "Every single one of us was handed a shitty deal. What makes you think you're so special?"

The circle around the fire turned quiet again.

"Okay. You want to hear my high for the week?" He paused. "That was when my mom kicked me out of the house. She locked all the windows and put chains on the doors. I had to break one of my bedroom windows to get some clothes for this stupid camp."

He threw a piece of wood onto the fire. "By the time I get back from this camp, I won't have anything to come back *to*. Even if she is still living in that dump, she'll have sold all my shit. You know what happened to that money you gave me for some clothes, Natalie? My mom stole it." He looked away. "That enough sharing for you guys?"

Great. This was a camp for disadvantaged kids. Just what Jamis needed next door, a do-gooder and her do-goodees.

"Galen," Natalie said. "For the summer you can forget about what's happening at home. What's important for you right now is what's happening here."

The boy grunted and looked away. "Whatever."

"I'd like each of you to think about what you'd like to get out of this summer," Natalie said. "You don't have to share it with me or anyone else, but after you've spent some time thinking about it, I want you to visualize those hopes coming true." She closed her eyes and Jamis couldn't keep from staring at her face, at the conviction and determination lit by the flames of the fire. "See it. Wish it. Make it happen."

Holy hell. She believed. So many people dallied with the concept of making your wishes come true, but Natalie truly believed. She understood.

"This summer is going to change all of us," she whispered. "I believe."

He'd never told anyone what he'd done. He'd simply packed up and left, holing himself up in his cabin on Mirabelle and letting Chuck handle everything else, selling his furniture, art, cars and houses. Suddenly, Jamis felt chilled, as if his heart had stopped pumping warmth to every extremity.

He didn't belong out here at their campfire. He didn't deserve to be sharing this night with good and decent people.

As quietly as possible, he turned to head home. Snickers, naturally, chose that moment to hike into the woods and head directly for Jamis. The moment the dog found him, he barked and jumped up.

"Jamis?" Natalie said. "Is that you out there?"

Jamis froze and waited.

"What if it's a wolf," one of the younger boys said, his voice laced with a wickedly mischievous undertone. "Or a bear?"

"Stop it, Chase," Natalie said. "Snickers? Who's out there?"

"Do raccoons eat dogs?" the littlest girl asked, nervously looking over her shoulder.

"Could be a coyote," another one of the boys teased.

He had to show himself, or risk scaring the whole crew. "It's me," Jamis said, moving through the brush and stepping into the firelight. "Sorry to interrupt. I was looking for the dog."

"Jamis!" Natalie said. "Join us. We have more cocoa." She held up a thermos.

"No, that's okay." Suddenly, he wished he was alone out here with Natalie. The firelight, the moon, the stars. Talk about a glutton for punishment.

"Jamis, are there wolves here?" the littlest asked, looking up at him.

Her small voice clutching at his emotions, he refused to let her name settle in his mind, let alone his heart. "No," he whispered. "No wolves or bears on the island."

"You sure?" asked one of the older girls.

"Positive. We only have deer. There's nothing in these woods that would hurt you." As far as he knew. Wolves and bear had been known to cross the ice during the winter looking for food, but since there'd been no sightings all these years there was no point in frightening the kids.

"Sit down. Join us." Natalie smiled at him. "I'll make you a s'more."

He glanced around at the young faces illuminated in the flickering firelight and felt something chip away at the frozen shell of his heart. There seemed to be no turning back. "A s'more sounds nice." He sat on the ground next to Snickers.

"Why do you live out here?" one of the boys asked. "All alone?"

"Because I like it." Jamis watched Natalie put a marshmallow at the end of her stick and set it over the fire.

"Don't you get lonely?" the girl next to him asked.

"I've got Snickers."

"Jamis is a writer." Natalie turned the marshmallow.

He wished she hadn't said that.

"What do you write?" the oldest girl asked, suddenly interested in the conversation.

"Books."

"What kind of books?" the little girl asked.

"They're…horror stories."

The boys grinned and nodded.

"Dude," one said.

"Sweet," said another.

"Any of them ever been made into movies?" the oldest boy asked.

"Yeah. A couple."

"No shit? Which ones?"

"I don't remember."

"How can you not remember?"

"I know," Natalie said. *"Bring the Night. Nothing to Lose. Lock and Load."*

"You're Quinn Roberts!" said the oldest boy. "Awesome. I've read most of your books."

The marshmallow Natalie roasted was a toasty brown. She stuck it between two graham crackers and chocolate and handed it to him.

"Suddenly, I'm not very hungry." He held it out.

"I'll take it!" One of the younger boys reached out his hand.

"Why did they change the ending on *Lock and Load?*"

"No spoilers!" Natalie announced. "I plan on reading the book."

He was counting on it. That story was just what she needed to put him in perspective, and then maybe she'd rethink having her camp next to a madman. He glanced at the teenager. "I don't know. Never saw it."

"You don't watch your own movies?"

He shook his head. "Don't read my own books, either." Once he sent the manuscripts off to his agent, he never wanted to revisit those characters or their pathetic lives again.

"Where do you come up with your ideas?" the teenage girl asked.

He didn't want to talk about this. Him. His books. "I don't know. They're just there. In my head." Except for now. Now he could really use an idea.

"I've read your books, too," the girl said. "There's almost a spiritual quality to some of them. Like your last one, *House of Reign.*"

Spiritual quality? He almost laughed. *That was a good one.* Across the fire he caught Natalie's gaze and he quickly looked away. Writing about a man whose life was destroyed even as his every wish came true had damned near killed Jamis.

"You know it's getting late," Natalie said, glancing at her watch. "Time for bed, guys."

A few of the kids groaned. A few yawned in quiet acceptance. The little girl glanced at Jamis. "Will you and Snickers walk us up to our house?"

The request took him by surprise, and before Jamis could refuse, Snickers was already following the other kids. Now he had no choice. "Yeah, I'll walk you up," he said, standing. "Snickers needs to stretch his legs before we go to bed." His heart almost stopped when the girl reached out and laced her small fingers through his. The small hand. Warm and soft. He looked down at her and immediately regretted ever having come outside in the first place tonight.

While he was pulled along down the path, Natalie put out the fire. By the time they reached the steps of the Victorian, she'd caught up with them. As all the kids ran into the house, she called, "Everyone brush your teeth and get ready for bed. I'll be up in a minute to say good-night."

The interior lights flicked on and footsteps pounded up the stairs as she turned to Jamis. Suddenly his hand felt empty and cold. He shouldn't be here, in the dark with a beautiful woman. Not with the yearning for simple touch he felt coursing through him. The need. The want for her warm hands on his skin. He should've been turned off by her too-good-to-be-true nature, instead he couldn't seem to tear his eyes away from her lips.

Go, Jamis. For her sake. Get as far away as you can. "Good night, Natalie." He spun away. "Snickers, come."

"Jamis?"

He turned, held himself back. One of his favorite smells, wood smoke, emanated from her hair along with something else, something sweet like chocolate. He wished he could bury his face in the long blond curls and breathe her in.

"Why are you hiding on Mirabelle?" she whispered.

No one had ever asked him that. He supposed everyone had assumed he was despondent after the accident. He had been, but there was a bigger reason. A reason he wasn't sure he could share. Not now. Maybe not ever. "Who says I'm hiding?"

She came down the steps and met him in the grass. "Me."

"I'm not a nice man, Natalie. The world is a much better place with me out of the way."

"I think you're wrong. I think inside here," she said, pressing a fingertip to his chest, "there's a good man hiding away."

It was all he could do to keep from stepping forward and leaning into her touch. He grabbed her fingers and held them for a moment before noticing a face, one of the kids, peering out from the window and watching. Slowly, he pushed her hand away. "You might know what's inside most men, but not me," he said softly. "Have you read my book yet?"

"No."

"Do it. Then you'll get a glimpse of the real Jamis Quinn."

And then you'll despise me, want nothing to do with me, and the world's balance will be set right again.

JAMIS'S BOOK SAT ON Natalie's bedside table, as yet unopened. Every night since she'd started this camp, thoroughly exhausted, she'd all but collapsed onto the bed. Tonight, though, curiosity had kept her awake. She sat up with her laptop in front of her and stared at the newspaper headline on the screen, tears pooling in her eyes.

Author Quinn Roberts's Wife and Children Killed

Having searched and pored through everything she
could find on the Internet regarding Jamis after she'd gotten
ready for bed, she'd finally found details of a horrific car
accident in an old online article. Now that she read the
headline, she remembered all those years ago having heard
something about the incident, but not bothering to pay attention to the details.

Now she read that his children, Caitlin and Justin, ages
three and one, had been killed at the scene. Their mother,
Katherine, had made it to the hospital before succumbing to
her extensive internal injuries. Jamis had suffered a concussion as well as a broken arm and leg, three broken ribs and a
lacerated liver. His children had been little more than babies.

Although no charges were expected, sketchy accounts
claimed icy road conditions may have played a role in a
semitrailer carrying heavy equipment broadsiding the
Quinn vehicle in the middle of a busy intersection. The
truck driver had walked away with only minor injuries. The
only survivors from the Mercedes had been Jamis and a
lucky little puppy, a tricolored mutt.

Snickers.

Oh, Jamis.

Flicking off the lamp, she snuggled under the covers and
glanced out the open window and through the woods. A
lone light shone through the trees. He was still awake.
Instinct had her wanting to run over to his cabin right then
and there to comfort and heal him. Make that damaged man
whole again. Only she had to admit, if only to herself, that
there was something else going on inside her, something
not entirely altruistic.

When she'd touched his chest earlier that night after

he'd walked them back from the fire, the urge to kiss him had welled up from some deep and primal place inside her and that urge had little to do with taking care of Jamis and nothing at all to do with wanting to be neighborly. She could feel it, her own heavy yearning. She wanted Jamis for herself. She wanted to feel his hands on her body, his mouth on her lips. Closing her eyes, she sighed.

A girl couldn't be all good all of the time. Apparently, Jamis wasn't the only one with a dark side.

CHAPTER FIVE

"OKAY, DAD." CHASE groaned into the phone after dinner a few nights later. "Yes, we're behaving. I swear. Ask Natalie."

Natalie stood by the sink helping Ella dry the dishes Arianna was washing and listened to the one-sided conversation in case there was anything with which the boys might need help. Both boys looked forward to what they'd hoped would be twice-weekly conversations with their dad over the summer, but after a few minutes they were antsy to get moving. Arianna and Ella, on the other hand, had proved they could stay on the phone for hours in their conversations with their grandmother.

"Okay. Okay. Here's Blake." Chase handed the phone to his brother.

"Hey, Dad, how's it going?" Blake leaned up against the wall. "I'm good, good." Then he went into a long and excited explanation of everything he'd been doing since their last conversation.

"Your dad doing okay?" Natalie asked Chase.

"Yeah. He's mad at himself."

She nodded, understanding. After two DWIs, their dad had stayed sober for more than five years, then he'd fallen off the wagon at a buddy's wedding and got his third offense and a ninety-day jail term. The wedding had been no excuse, and losing his boys for the summer was, hopefully, going to be what it took to keep him on the straight and narrow. At least Natalie prayed it would be enough, given the boys' mother was no longer involved in their lives.

"Nat," Chase said, "can I have something to eat?"

"We just finished dinner." Natalie put a stack of clean plates into the cupboard.

"I'm still hungry."

"All right. Something healthy. Grab the grapes leftover from lunch."

He dug around inside the refrigerator for a few minutes and then wandered into the living room, passing Sam and Galen on their way into the kitchen. They hung around, looking as if they were at loose ends. Finally, Galen said, "It's Friday."

"Yes, it is." Natalie glanced at them. They seemed to be waiting for something. Then it hit her. "Oh, goodness! I almost forgot our agreement. You guys have the night off, and I need to give you paychecks!"

"Yes!"

"Cool!"

Galen and Sam connected fists in the air.

Natalie ran back to her bedroom, grabbed the two payroll checks she'd left on her desk by her laptop, and hurried back out to the kitchen. "Okay," she said, handing them envelopes. "The kitchen is clean and the supper dishes are done. You two are on your own."

The teenagers glanced at each other.

"Want to go into town?" Galen asked.

"Totally! Let me change first." She took off upstairs and came down a short while later. "The sink is clogged again."

"I'll take a look at it," Natalie said, studying Sam. Something had changed. Clothes? No. Hair? Yep, that was it. She'd forsaken the ever-present ponytail to let her light brown hair hang long and straight halfway down her back. And she was wearing makeup. With hazel eyes and pleasing features, Sam was naturally pretty, but the mascara, blush and lip gloss, not to mention a full, almost womanly figure, made her look easily several years older than Galen, despite the fact that she was actually a couple months younger than him.

Even Galen had done a double take when Sam came into the kitchen. "Dustin and Chad said they'd be at the pizza place," he said, recovering quickly.

"Sounds good."

"Blake's off the phone," Arianna said. "Can we call Grandma now?"

"Absolutely. And then when you two are done we're going to have some popcorn and watch a movie."

As Galen and Sam shot through the back door, Natalie followed them outside, not a little envious of them having a night without a single responsibility. They'd been here less than a week, but the concentrated time with eight kids was forcing Natalie to accept that Missy had most definitely been right. She was going to need a break every now and again.

"Hey, guys!" she called. "Be home by eleven, okay?"

"Whatever."

"No, not whatever, Galen. Eleven. And take the golf cart, so you can see your way home in the dark."

"Good idea."

"Do you have your cell phones?"

They both nodded.

"And one more thing." They both looked up at her, clearly anxious to be on their way. "Have fun."

Feeling an odd mixture of both excitement and apprehension, Natalie watched them drive the cart out of the yard and disappear within minutes on the path through the thick woods. *Don't worry,* she reassured herself. Sam and Galen are from a big city. What trouble could befall them on Mirabelle?

"QUIT KICKING ME!" The next morning Arianna glared across the kitchen table at Chase.

"I'm not even touching you!" Chase said.

"There!" she said. "What was that?"

Day and night. Night and day. The kids were constantly after each other, and Natalie could feel her normal patience waning more and more every day. "Blake?" she said softly.

The other twin, looking innocent as all get-out, glanced at her. "What? I'm not doing anything."

She'd been up and about since the crack of dawn getting organized for the day. There wasn't much these kids were going to sneak by her. "Keep your feet to yourself, Blake, or you'll be doing the breakfast dishes alone this morning."

"Fine," he grumbled, apparently unconcerned about having gotten caught attempting to get his twin in trouble.

"Um, Natalie?" Toni said. "Is there any cold cereal?"

"You don't like the pancakes?"

Quietly, the little girl shook her head.

A quick inspection of the table showed Galen, Blake and Chase in various stages of devouring everything on their plates, Samantha forsaking everything else for a yogurt and apple, and Arianna and Ella picking at the food on their plates. This scenario had been virtually the same for most of their meals this past week as they set about establishing routines and getting settled. In the past, Natalie had managed to survive on her own without being much of a cook, but things were different now that she was responsible for all these kids.

"Okay," she said. "I can see things are going to have to

change. After breakfast, I want each of you to write out three suggestions for meals and set them on the counter by the phone."

"Why?"

"Do we have to?"

"If you want food you like to eat, yes," Natalie said. "And I can see we need a rule about meals."

Everyone groaned except for Galen. That boy had been nearly impossible to awaken that morning and with his longish black hair still sticking out this way and that it was obvious he'd merely thrown on jeans and a shirt before stumbling down the stairs.

"Not another rule," someone murmured.

"If you don't like what's being served or are still hungry after a meal," Natalie said, glancing in particular at the growing boys, "the options are cold cereal or PB and J, but you have to prepare it yourself. You don't like the rules, you can go home. Anyone want to go home?" She looked at each and every one of them.

Everyone except Galen shook his or her head.

Going home for the twins, Chase and Blake, meant dealing with a father in jail. For Arianna and Ella, it was a mother who couldn't be found and a grandmother who was going through drug and alcohol treatment. Toni, Ryan and Sam would be going back to foster care homes. And for Galen, it meant a mother with unacknowledged substance abuse problems.

Natalie had painstakingly selected every one of them from a group of more than fifty applications, looking for kids whose profiles implied a high risk for problems, but a probability for success with the summer program she'd outlined. While Natalie was loathe to send any of them back before she'd gotten a chance to instill a small amount of hope in each one's heart, she wasn't going to sacrifice the success of the entire camp for any one individual.

The only one in the group who hadn't matched her profile was Galen. His school counselors, principals and teachers had all told her he wouldn't make it. They saw a young man with a bad attitude who was going to end up in trouble with the law, just like his mother. Natalie saw a boy with a possible learning disability trying desperately to find his way, a boy who hid his frailty behind a mask of defiance. Somehow, she had to find a way to get through to him.

"Okay, let's review the schedule we developed these past few days," she said. "Breakfast is at eight every morning, lunch at noon, dinner at six. Lights out at nine for everyone except Sam and Galen. After breakfast is chore time."

Because of their home lives, all of these kids spent far too much time alone. The more life skills she could instill in them, the higher their self-esteem and the better they'd fare once they went back home.

"After chores, we'll do some sort of fun activity and then free time until lunch. After lunch, we'll be making crafts to sell at the gift shop in town, and, if everyone behaves, we'll be taking in all of Mirabelle's charms over the course of the summer."

"What does that mean?" Arianna asked.

"Well, this summer isn't going to be all work and no play. We'll be making field trips into town at least once a week, and taking advantage of all that Mirabelle has to offer. Horseback riding, sailing, fishing, golfing."

"Horses!" the girls squealed.

"Fishing. Cool," was the consensus from the boys.

"All kinds of fun stuff." Natalie smiled. "So let's all work together this summer, and if you're ever not sure what you're supposed to be doing, look at the whiteboard on the pantry door. I'll do a new one every week with rotating chores and activities."

Toni raised her hand.

"Yes, Toni?"

"What's a pantry?"

Natalie was explaining it was the room next to the stove where their food was stored when the phone rang. Sam hopped up to answer the call. "It's for you, Natalie."

She stood and took the phone, and the boys finished with breakfast and wandered toward the living room. "Ah, ah, ah!" she said, covering the mouthpiece of the phone. "After meals, no one leaves the kitchen without first taking his or her own dishes to the sink. And then chores, people."

Another round of groans sounded, but the boys turned back. She pointed to the pantry door. "When in doubt, refer to the whiteboard."

"Ha-ha, Chase. You have to wash dishes," Blake taunted.

"So! You have to wash tomorrow."

"Yeah, but—"

Deciding to let them hash it out themselves, Natalie went inside the pantry with the phone and closed the door. "Sorry about that. Natalie here."

A man chuckled over the line. "It's Roger." Her grand-mother's longtime attorney and now Natalie's. "Sounds like you have your hands full."

"We're still ironing out some details. We'll get there."

"I thought you might want a heads-up on something."

"Shoot." She leaned against one of the shelves and felt it wobble. The board was warped. That was going to have to get fixed.

"I got wind of someone making inquiries with the city

of Mirabelle and various departments with the state of Wisconsin with regard to the filings for your camp."

"Who?"

He sighed. "An attorney here in town who just happens to represent your neighbor."

"Jamis? Why would he care?"

"If I were to guess, I'd say he's looking for a way to shut you down."

"Well, that's just sil—" She stopped. "You're right. He's not at all happy about our presence on this end of the island. Can he make us leave?"

"All the proper paperwork has been filed and approved, but, in my experience, if a person looks hard enough, he can usually find some kind of loophole, especially if he has a good attorney. Jamis Quinn could make your life miserable."

He could try. "Thanks, Roger. Let me know if anything else comes to your attention."

"By the way, we filed those grant requests for you."

"Oh, good. Do you think I'll get enough to fund this camp for next year?"

"I think you've got a good chance, Natalie. There are several agencies very excited about what you're doing. But it wouldn't hurt to solicit some private donations. Send me some information and I'll get it out to our list of donors."

"Thanks, Roger." She hung up the phone. So Jamis wanted her and the kids gone, huh? Well, there was only one thing for it. She was going to have to change his mind.

NADA. ZIP. ZILCH.

Jamis stared at his blank computer screen. This morning and every morning since Miss Chipper had taken over next door, he had nothing. Normally, starting a new book was a piece of cake. Long before he typed the words *Chapter*

One a concept for a story would have effortlessly laid itself out for him. Sometimes in a dream a fully formed opener would come to him. Other times, a kernel of a scene would hit him while he was running or lifting weights. He could be brushing his teeth and a line of dialogue would hit him. Cooking a pasta dish he might feel a character's name hot on his tongue. Or out on the water kayaking, an overall concept would come to him, giving him something to work out in his mind as he worked out his body.

Unfortunately, the only story his brain seemed receptive to developing these days was a bloody mass murder at a small-town orphanage. And for good reason. Natalie seemed to have made it her personal mission to feed him.

Earlier in the week, she'd brought over a hunk of cake, undercooked and mushy in the center. Jamis had gone back to his computer in the hopes of starting his new book, but it wasn't happening. He'd finally surrendered and had put on his wetsuit, dragged his kayak down to the frigid water and paddled his way around several of the islands as fast as he could.

A few days later, it was homemade ice cream she and her kids had churned by hand in her grandmother's machine. That particular treat hadn't tasted half-bad, but how could anyone screw up sugar, strawberries and cream? Again, after attempting unsuccessfully to return to work, he'd finally gone outside and chopped half a cord of firewood.

After she'd needed bay leaves for a soup he could only hope he wasn't going to have to sample, he hadn't bothered returning to his computer. He'd gone straight to his work-out room and pumped weights until every single one of his muscles had failed.

The biggest problem was that as that woman grew more irritating, she also seemed to grow more beautiful.

She would stand on his porch with sunlight glinting off her hair, a bright smile on her pretty pink lips, and a twinkle in her sea-blue eyes. In spite of everything, there was something indomitable about her that he couldn't help but respect. What in the world had possessed her to organize a summer camp for kids? What was the point? What made her tick? And why in God's name did she give a rat's ass about him?

He glanced at his watch and was surprised she hadn't been over to his house yet today. *Great.* He shook his head, disgusted with himself. Now he was actually waiting for her to make an appearance on his doorstep.

Snickers whined.

"What?"

The dog's ears arched expectantly.

"No." Jamis scowled. "You cannot go over to her house."

Another whine, and this one was accompanied by a swish of the tail.

"It's *not* Snickers time. Snickers time is *after* lunch."

Resigned, the dog laid his head on his paws. He continued looking up at Jamis with those forlorn brown eyes, and the memory of the morning Snickers had come into his life came back to Jamis in a rush. The smells, the sounds.

"Daddy, that's him," his three-year-old daughter, Caitlin, had declared in her sweet little voice. "He looks like a candy bar." She'd stuck her chubby fingers through the cage at the pound and singled Snickers out from a litter of puppies.

He'd tried steering her toward a tough pit bull, a Rottweiler, even a lab mix, but no. She'd wanted this puny mutt. A scruffy-haired mishmash of white, black and caramel, the animal folk had guessed he was part hound and part Border collie. When they'd gotten him out of the cage, Justin, not quite a year, had toddled over, grabbed the puppy by his ears and planted a sloppy wet kiss on his furry forehead, and it had been a done deal.

At the time, Jamis had thought it would help his children with the rough patch they were going through with the impending divorce. Instead, Snickers had been the reason for yet another fight, another bargaining point for the lawyers, another excuse for Katherine to wheedle more money from Jamis. Now the poor dog served only as a constant reminder of the two lowest points in Jamis's life.

"Come here, Snick." Jamis patted his lap. The dog hopped up and Jamis scratched him good and hard on his neck and ears. "Good boy." He kissed his forehead and let him hop to the floor. Snickers's ears perked up and he cocked his head toward the window.

"No!" The sound of a girl's voice came through the open office window. "I'm not going to ask him. You ask him."

"No way." That was a different kid, a boy.

Snickers ran down the steps and, without a single bark, sat at the door, waiting.

"This is so jacked." That voice belonged to an older boy, perhaps the teenager.

"Then you ask him."

A knock sounded on the front screen door.

"Unbelievable." Shaking his head, Jamis pushed away from his desk yet another time and went slowly down the steps. The outline of several heads standing on his porch took shape. He opened the solid oak door and stood in front of the screened storm door, not bothering to invite them in. "What?"

Snickers pawed excitedly at the door as several of the camp kids of varying ages and sexes stared up at Jamis. "Do you have any marbles?" asked the littlest girl.

Was this a joke? Jamis stared at each one of them, in

turn, debating. No, they were serious. "Why?" He heard himself asking the question as if disembodied from the idiot he'd suddenly become. What purpose could possibly be served by engaging them in conversation?

"We're on a scavenger hunt," said the middle boy who looked to be about twelve. "The first team to get all the items on Natalie's list gets breakfast in bed tomorrow morning."

So Miss Chipper had started up with her camp activities, huh?

"The other team is beating us," said the youngest girl.

Jamis glanced at the teenage boy, who was shaking his head and rolling his eyes. "Yeah, I got marbles. Come on in." He'd gone nuts. Certifiably so. All this time alone on this island had finally done the trick. "How many do you need?"

He opened the door and Snickers happily scurried around the kids, sniffing every one of them and pushing his wet nose into their hands. The kids stepped inside, the littlest one keeping her cautious eyes on the dog. One look at the big-screen TV and the teenager's attitude went from bored to calculating in seconds. Jamis could practically see his wheels turning looking for the angle that would get him viewing time on that screen.

"Just two," said the teenager.

Jamis went to a vase on the table by the window, pulled out the arrangement of dried grasses and dug out a couple of the clear acrylic marbles at the base used to hold the arrangement in place. "Will these do?"

"Sure. Why not?" The oldest boy took them. "So...do you have satellite?"

"Yeah."

"Sweet."

Shoving the dried grasses back into the vase, Jamis set it down. "Yeah, it is. You can go now." He ushered them outside and closed the door while they were still standing on his porch.

He'd taken several steps up to his computer when his doorbell rang. He paused, considering his options. Would they get the hint if he didn't answer? Snickers whined and his tail swished back and forth on the rug. The bell rang again and was followed by a quiet knock.

He spun around and threw open the door. "Now what?" He'd barely kept himself from yelling.

This time Miss Chipper herself was standing on his porch. "Hi, Jamis."

Today, her hair had a brighter honey-gold sheen, as if she'd been in the sun, and her lips looked wet, as if she'd just licked them. And if that wasn't enough to tempt him, there was always the way that strappy tank top clung to her too-full-for-that-body set of breasts. From nowhere, he was struck with the sudden urge to pull her into his arms and kiss her senseless, but then he'd more than likely end up senseless as well, and where would that leave them?

"We'd like to invite you over for dinner tonight." She bent and scratched Snickers behind the ears. "And you, buddy."

"He has other plans. So do I."

"Tomorrow night?"

"Plans."

"Any night work for you?"

"I'm a very busy man."

"Okay. We'll keep trying." The ever-cheerful Natalie looked a bit perplexed. "We'll be having campfires off and on. You're welcome to join us at any time."

"Well, Sunshine, I'll keep that in mind."

Studying him, she stepped back. "Okay. Have a good day." Off she marched with her pesky kids in tow, and there she went again directly through the poison ivy.

"Hey, hey, hey!" he called before he thought to stop himself. "Do you see what you're walking through?"

She glanced toward the ground and pointed out the offending plant to the children. Then she lifted the littlest girl onto her back and waved at him. "Thanks!" she called, as if they were now the best of friends.

Dammit. "Snickers, come." The moment the dog made it inside Jamis shut the door and leaned his forehead against the cold hard wood. Life, in the form of a beautiful young woman, was literally knocking on his door, and God help him but a very big part of Jamis was ready to invite her inside.

"Oh, no, you don't," he said loudly, clearly, hoping to get through that thick skull of his. *You gave up the right to a life four years ago, you son of a bitch.* "Don't even think about it."

Enough was enough.

CHAPTER SIX

RUNNING A FINGERTIP along her lips, Natalie stared out of the porch windows contemplating Jamis's house the next day and wondering what he was doing at this exact moment. No matter what she did or didn't do, she couldn't seem to get the man out of her mind. Somehow, someway, she had to find a way to break through his sturdy armor. A tug on her arm pulled her away from her thoughts and she glanced down.

Toni was standing next to her. "I'm sorry, honey, did you need something?"

"Do they need to be all the same size?"

Without a word, Ryan looked up, the same question burning in his young, oh-so-sincere eyes.

"I don't think so," Natalie said. "They should be kind of small, though. Think about what size you'd want to put in your pocket, and then make some slightly bigger for adults."

It was after lunch and everyone was working on projects to sell at the gift shop in town. She'd gotten a lot of questions about this part of her baby boot camp curriculum until she'd explained the kids would keep every cent earned from the sale of their respective crafts and would be allowed to save or spend as each saw fit, thereby teaching them the beginnings of fiscal responsibility.

Natalie had turned the front porch into a craft room.

Two long, narrow tables with comfortable chairs had been set on either side of the room. Shelving lined the walls and housed various storage baskets, buckets and drawer filled with supplies—glue, beads, ribbons, feathers, paints, frames, envelopes, card stock. If the kids needed something for a particular project chances were Natalie would have it. She'd been ordering and accumulating supplies for months.

The youngest of her kids, Ryan and Toni, were making pocket stones, flat coins of clay stamped with various inspirational words. Although Natalie had over twenty stamps made for them, they got to pick which words to use.

Her four middle-schoolers, Arianna, Ella, Chase and Blake, were making bookmarks with ribbons and beads and choosing their own color combinations from a selection Natalie had ordered in preparation for this camp. She was surprised by how calming these craft afternoons seemed to be for both Chase and Blake.

"Is that a necklace or a bracelet, Sam?" Natalie smiled at the young woman who was busy concentrating on her latest creation. She'd used a Chinese coin, this one with a hole in the middle, wrapped one end in leather bands, strung beads along the leather and was now tying off the ends with some kind of closure.

"Either one." Sam focused on tying a knot. "It'll bring confidence to the person who wears it."

"Why is that?"

"Missy told me that this coin is supposed to attract good fortune. In everything."

Galen grunted with disbelief from where he sat staring out the window at the next table.

"And what are you going to make, Galen?" Natalie turned her attention toward him.

He didn't respond, merely sat back and kicked his feet up on the nearest bookcase.

"I'll tell you what," she said. "You don't want to make any extra bucks this summer, that's your business, but don't complain when everyone else gets the money they've earned from sales at Missy's shop."

The sound of pounding drew her attention to the woods between her Victorian and the log cabin. She caught glimpses of a black T-shirt amidst the green trees. Jamis was out there doing something, and her curiosity was piqued. "Galen, your turn to help the kids," she said, heading for the door.

"Whatever."

"I'll be right back." She went outside, down the path between the two houses, and found Jamis, hammer in one hand and several red and white no-trespassing signs in the other. The implications didn't immediately register, but once she understood his intentions she couldn't help but feel slightly offended. "Where did you get those?"

"Went in to town yesterday afternoon."

"I suppose they're for us."

"You'd be supposing correctly."

"Why?"

He glared at her. "You really don't know?"

"Well…"

"Cake, ice cream, bay leaves, scavenger hunts. Sound familiar?"

Apparently her plan had backfired. "I'm sorry. I didn't mean—"

"Explain to me why you're doing this." He spun around and faced her.

"Pardon me?"

"This camp?"

She thought for a minute. "Because I can."

"No." He shook his head. "There's more to it than that."

"My grandmother left me this big house here and another one in Minneapolis and a lot of money. What else would I do with it?"

"I can think of all kinds of uses for that house. Sell it. Use it as a vacation home. Rent it out. Let it rot." He walked toward her. "For some reason, a camp for kids is the last thing that comes to my mind." He stared at her, waiting.

"I do this because…I've been where these kids are. I know what it's like to feel as if there's no one in the world who cares whether you live or die. I know what it's like to live without hope."

He said nothing for a moment, only studied her, but she had the distinct feeling he knew exactly what she was talking about. "Go on. There's more, I'm sure."

She'd never talked to anyone about this. Her family had known her story, so there'd been no point in sharing it with others. Truthfully, she didn't like rehashing the past.

"I'm waiting," he said, his gaze piercing.

"Let's just say my early childhood experiences were less than ideal. In fact, the only pictures I have of my mother are police mug shots." She glanced at him, expecting to hear some sarcastic response. Instead, he was still waiting, listening, an unreadable expression plastered on his face. "Until I was adopted at ten, I didn't have much hope for my future. But hope is what changed my life. These kids all need hope that things can be better in their lives. I think they'll find it here on Mirabelle."

"What's the point? You've got eight kids here. There are millions out there in the same if not worse shape. You're not going to change anything."

"One child at a time." She took a deep breath. "If this

summer experience gives one of these children hope where there was none before, then I've succeeded. Every child needs hope to be able to dream, and they need to dream to believe anything is possible."

"And when they all return to the same old same old at the end of the summer, then what?"

"They'll go knowing their lives can be different. Better."

"You're setting them up for disappointment."

"I've worked in social services for a long time." She shook her head. "There have been so few true successes along the way. My grandmother gave me the chance to do things my way, to try to make a difference in the lives of these kids." She studied his face, decided it was time for a question of her own. "Do you believe in wishes coming true?"

His eyes turned dark and he clenched his jaw. She'd hit a nerve.

"Well, I do," she said, taking his reaction for skepticism. "These kids need to believe they can make changes in their lives. They need to feel empowered. I want them to know that dreaming is okay, dreaming is important. But we can't just sit back and let things happen to us. *We* have to make things happen in our lives. Wish it, see it, make it happen."

He looked as if she'd punched him in the gut. "Unbelievable." He shook his head.

"I've seen it happen. Dreams and wishes, changing lives."

"You're such a Pollyanna."

Oddly enough that hurt. If he only knew how hard she'd worked to turn her life around. "Wishes do come true, you know," she whispered.

"Yeah. I know," he growled, spinning away from her. "That's why you'd better make sure you tell every single one of your charges to be very, very careful what they wish for."

Talk about hitting nerves. "What did you wish for,

Jamis, that went bad?" She reached out and touched his arm. "Tell me."

"Our little heart-to-heart is over." He shrugged her off and picked up another sign.

She didn't like leaving things like this, but she knew from the look on his face he was all done sharing. "Can you just skip the signs? Please?"

"I have a September deadline and because of the constant interruptions haven't been able to even start the book."

"What if I promise to leave you alone?"

He raised an eyebrow at her. "You expect me to believe you can control yourself?"

"All right, I'll make a deal with you," she said. "One week. If I can go that long without bothering you, will you forget the signs?"

He studied her face, seeming to weigh his options. "Why should I?"

"Simple neighborly courtesy."

"I have absolutely no interest in being neighborly."

She grinned. "Maybe you'll get lucky and get the satisfaction of saying I told you so."

His dark eyes flickered with interest. "Throw your kids into the bargain and it's a deal."

"Deal." She put out a hand.

He glanced at her for a moment, and when he finally reached out, his touch was surprisingly soft, warm and strong. "Deal."

"Wonderful."

He turned around, placed one of the signs against the nearest tree and pounded it in at eye level. Then he turned around and smirked at her.

"But I thought…"

"Sunshine, you won't last three days."

EVERY SPARE MOMENT SHE had the next day, Natalie found herself glancing out her windows toward the log cabin, wondering, imagining, obsessing over that man. What was it about him? Then again, it wasn't entirely his fault. Natalie had never been one to take no for an answer. Tell her she couldn't have something, and that something was all she'd want. In this case, something was Jamis Quinn.

He'd lost his entire family, Natalie reminded herself. The guy was bound to have issues. Trying to put him firmly out of her mind, Natalie went back to the craft room with the rest of the kids after breakfast and helped them with their projects. Galen, once again, chose to not involve himself in a craft.

Natalie glanced at the clock. "Galen, why don't you come help me with lunch." She started toward the door. When he didn't move, she turned around. "Work on a project or help me with our meal. It's your choice."

With a sullen look, he stood, noisily pushed in his chair and followed her out the door.

"You set the table and I'll get out the lunch meat."

He leaned against the counter, crossed his arms and made no attempt at complying.

"You know, Galen, some people make the mistake of assuming that I'm a pushover," Natalie said, needing to clear the air. "This camp is important to me, and I don't want you to ruin it for everyone else."

"You gonna make me go home?"

She opened the refrigerator and set lunch meat, condiments, milk and cheese on the counter. "Not if you don't break the rules."

He glanced over at her. At close to six feet with broad shoulders and shaggy stubble, this fifteen-year-old could pass for a man. If only he'd lose the attitude.

"Galen, there are some choices you need to make this

summer." She shut the fridge door, turned around and faced him head-on. "You have an opportunity to make some changes in your life, but those changes aren't going to happen on their own."

"What difference does it make?"

"It's your choice. Your life."

"What do you know about my life?"

More than he realized.

"What's your story, anyway?" He pushed away from the counter and paced along the other side of the big, oak table, as if to put some distance between them. "Why are you doing this camp, anyway? Why do you care?"

She hesitated. "My childhood wasn't all that different from yours."

"Bullshit." He crossed his arms. "You come from a rich family. Your grandmother even gave you this house."

"I didn't always live with this family."

"So what? You still don't know anything about me or my life."

She set the deli slices of meat and cheese on the table and washed bunches of red and green grapes in the sink. "Some things are different."

"See?"

"For one thing, I didn't live with my mother." She brought the grapes to the table and studied him. "She gave me up when I was two and I never saw her again. She was murdered a couple years later."

He looked away.

"Actually, my story's more like Toni's. Moving from one foster home to another."

She hated dwelling, let alone thinking, about the first ten years of her life. What was the point? What was done was done. So what if she'd never stayed in any of her foster homes more than a year? None of those people who'd sent her packing as if she'd been no more than an outgrown pair of jeans had really cared about her, even if she had come to care for them.

"I was adopted, Galen," she added. They were the only family that mattered now. If not for the Steegers loving her as if she was their own flesh and blood, there was no telling where Natalie would've ended up. "My grandmother knew I wanted to do something like this, that's why she gave me the house."

The kitchen was silent as she took some plates out of the cupboard and held them out to Galen. He only glared at her.

"I know you feel as if you have to be tough," she said softly. "That you have to shield yourself from the world." Though Natalie tended to overcompensate and open herself up to the world, she still struggled with this issue. "But there's no one here in this house who wants to hurt you."

He made no movement to take the plates.

"This summer is going to be what you make of it. Do you want to stay?" She waited and waited.

Eventually, he nodded.

"Then all I ask is that you try."

Finally, he took the plates from her and set them out on the table.

She took out the silverware and handed it to him. "Maybe it would be best if you don't think about the end of the summer."

"Easy for you to say." He threw the forks onto the table. "When this camp is done, you go back to your regular happy life. Me? I go to that place I'm supposed to call home. Square one. As if I was never here to begin with."

"Only if you let it."

"If *I* let it?" Angrily, he pushed one of the chairs away

from the table. "I'm only fifteen. I don't have a choice. My life's not my own."

Suddenly, she wasn't sure how to refute that. Every response she formulated in her mind seemed pat and idealistic.

"My mom was right." He pushed over a chair. "You do-gooders are all alike. The only reason you're having this camp is so that you can pat yourself on the back and tell yourself, tell the world, that you tried to do something good for someone else. You don't care about any of the kids here. You don't really care about me."

All sorts of challenges to his comment were at the tip of her tongue, but as he stalked out the door Natalie couldn't help but accept that a part of what he was saying was true. At the end of summer, she *would be* returning to her nice cozy life, and these kids would be going back to what they'd left behind.

Chase, Blake, Arianna and Ella had homes waiting for them. They weren't perfect family situations, but there was someone home in Minneapolis who truly seemed to love each of them. Chase and Blake's dad would be getting out of jail at the end of summer. Arianna and Ella's grandmother would be out of treatment. In fact, those four kids would be going home a week earlier than the rest of them, their caretakers wanting to prepare them for school starting.

Toni, Ryan, Sam and Galen would be returning to the Twin Cities with Natalie. They had no one in their lives who truly cared. Was this camp fair to them? Jamis's accusations came back to her. Was she setting them all up for disappointment?

Wish it, see it, make it happen.

Somehow, she had to make it happen.

Drumming his fingers on his desktop, Jamis stared at the blinking cursor on his blank computer screen. Had he really called Natalie a Pollyanna yesterday when they'd argued over the no-trespassing signs? God, he could be such an asshole. So what if she got some kind of crazy thrill out of doing good? As long as she didn't mess with him, her issues were none of his business. But, then, that was exactly what he was worried about. Her turning him into one of her pet projects.

A noise on his front porch that sounded distinctly human distracted him. "I knew it. She didn't even make it twenty-four hours." Dreading the prospect of having to look and not touch the slightest inch of skin on that gorgeous woman, Jamis took off down the stairs, wanting to get his dose of daily torture over and done with.

"What now?" he said, yanking open the door.

Instead of Natalie, the teenage boy stood there shuffling his feet. "Hey," he said, his bangs, far too long, hanging in his eyes.

"What do you want?" Jamis glared at the gangly kid, not wanting to remember his name. Galen. It popped up anyway. *Dammit.*

"Um. I was just… I was wondering." The kid looked away. "Do you think I could watch some TV? Here at your house?"

He couldn't be serious, could he?

But then Jamis understood. All those kids. The noise. The constant activity. What normal person wouldn't go positively insane living in that Victorian? Still, there was no way this boy was stepping foot in this house.

"I mean," the kid said, "if it's not too much trouble… I just… Oh, forget it." He turned to leave. Hanging his head, the boy stepped off the porch and absently kicked a rock into the woods. There was something about how his feet seemed too big for his body that reminded Jamis of how awkward his own teenage years had been.

Hell, here I come.

"Hey, kid," Jamis said. Someone else's spirit, a much more kindhearted and compassionate one, must have taken over Jamis's body. "I was just leaving to go into town. You can watch TV while I'm gone." He'd have to give Natalie a pass on their deal for this one.

"You sure?"

"Do you want to, or not?"

"Totally." The relief in Galen's eyes was almost tangible. "I can't tell you how sick I am of watching stupid cartoons and girl shows. They don't have video games. Or even a DVD player over there."

Yeah, life was tough all over. Jamis showed him how to use the remotes. "Do they know where you are?"

He looked away. "Not really."

"How old are you?"

"Fifteen."

Old enough to be gone for a while without Natalie calling Garrett Taylor.

"I kinda had a fight with Natalie," the kid explained.

No way was Jamis getting drawn into this discussion. "Yeah? That sucks."

"She just drives me crazy, sometimes," Galen said, the frustration almost palpable. "You know? All that cheery ass positive thinking bullshit."

"Yeah, I know." Okay. So it wasn't another human that had taken over his body. It was aliens.

"What does she think is going to happen?" He shook his head.

Jamis might have been wrong, but he could've sworn he saw tears gathering in the boy's eyes, and the kid wasn't too happy about it, either. "Okay." He cleared his throat. "Well, this is where I cut out." He gathered up his grocery list, backpack and a package he should've mailed out yesterday and headed for the door. "Come on, Snick. Let's go."

The dog hesitated, glancing from the boy to Jamis and back again before running outside.

"And, hey," Jamis said, pausing on the porch, "this is a one-time deal, dude. And don't you dare tell Natalie or any of those other kids you've been here."

"I won't. Thanks, man."

Jamis shut the front door behind him, closed his eyes and took a deep breath. It was debatable whether or not he'd managed to dodge that bullet, but he certainly stepped directly in front of the next one. When he got to Main Street, the town was crawling with tourists. He glanced at the package in his hand. There was nothing for it. His editor needed this paperwork by tomorrow, and he was not going home to hang out with that kid.

"Come on, Snick. Gotta do it." Avoiding Main, he took a side street to the post office. Breathing a sigh of relief, he stepped inside the cool, quiet building and went to the counter.

A young man appeared. "Can I help you?"

For four years he'd been coming to this post office on a regular basis and for four years there had been only one person who'd ever assisted him. "Where's the regular postal clerk?"

"She's on medical leave."

"Sally? For what?"

"I don't know." The guy squinted at him. "But even if I did, I couldn't tell you that. It's private."

"When will she be back?"

"Don't know."

"Is she okay?"

"Don't know."

"Do you know anything?"

"Look, buddy. They told me to fill in, so that's all I'm doing. Filling in."

"You're not from Mirabelle, are you?" If he'd been an islander, he'd know what was going on with Sally.

"No. Like I said. Just filling in."

He shouldn't care. Really, he shouldn't. Jamis mailed his package and left the post office only to have bright sunlight hit him square in the face. He flipped his sunglasses on, untied Snickers and stood there, debating. Sally McGregor, as gruff as she'd been, had been the only human contact Jamis had had through the years. It seemed strange and unlikely, but he already missed her.

With Snickers by his side, he walked down the street, feeling at a loss. He stopped at Newman's, filled his grocery list and was standing in line behind several people when a store employee, an older man with glasses that Jamis had seen nearly every time he'd been in the store, walked by him.

"Excuse me," Jamis said out of the blue.

"Yes, sir, what can I do for you?"

"Do you know Sally McGregor?"

"I do." His expression turned instantly somber.

"Can you tell me what's wrong with her?"

The man studied him. "I don't know—"

"I'm Jamis Quinn."

"I recognize you, but…"

"I live on the other side of the island. Quinn Roberts?

The writer?" At that several strangers spun around, stared at him and whispered amongst themselves.

"Oh, yeah. Quinn Roberts. I'm Dan Newman."

Absently, he shook the other man's hand. "I'm sorry we haven't met before now…"

A small crowd gathered around them.

"Mr. Quinn," someone said, "could you autograph this receipt?"

Jamis glanced at the woman. There were others looking for pens and paper.

"Why don't you come to my office?" Dan took him by the arm and drew him into an office near the front of the store and quickly closed the door.

"Thank you," Jamis said awkwardly. "The man at the post office said Sally was on medical leave. Do you know if she's all right?"

He studied Jamis. "Well, I suppose there's no harm in telling you. The way the gossip circuit works around this island, all you'd have to do is ask any islander and they'd likely be able to tell you." He sighed. "She was diagnosed with cancer."

"What kind?"

"Pancreatic."

"What's the prognosis?"

"From what I hear, not very good."

"Is she still in the hospital?"

"As far as I know."

"Thank you." Jamis turned to go, feeling oddly disoriented. When he opened the door, a small group had gathered, each person holding pen and paper.

"There he is."

"It is Quinn Roberts!"

They asked him to sign books, papers, T-shirts, hands. Resigned, he quietly went from one person to the next.

A short while later, the storeowner came to him with his groceries bagged. "You better take off."

He reached for his wallet.

"Don't worry about it." Dan waved his hand. "This bag's on me."

CHAPTER SEVEN

ONE DAY DOWN IN HER deal to stay away from Jamis Quinn. Only six more to go. The nighttime hours, especially those after the kids had gone to bed, would be the worst, so Natalie decided it was time to take Missy up on a girls' night out.

Having left Sam and Galen in charge of the rest of the kids for the first night since they'd all arrived on Mirabelle, she now sat at a table in Duffy's Pub with Missy and a couple of her friends, Sarah Marshik, the flower shop owner and wedding planner, and Hannah Johnson, one of the island's elementary school teachers.

Over wine and pecan-crusted fish fingers and stuffed mushrooms, she laughed until her stomach ached at the story Missy was telling about doing tarot card readings for a group of hard-core FBI trainees when she'd lived near the training base in Quantico.

"So I'm flipping over the cards and knives and sword are showing up everywhere," Missy said, pausing. "And I said to the guy, 'I hate to say this, but there's blood in your future.' He looked up at me with this deer in the headlights look and said, 'From what?' I looked at him and said, 'Dude, you're an FBI agent. What did you expect?'"

"He wasn't serious, was he?" Natalie chuckled.

"Totally," Missy said. "Turned out he was an accountant. He was working computer fraud cases and hated guns."

Natalie had so needed this night, needed to get away from the kids and the house, and a wonderful meal cooked up by Garrett Taylor's new wife, Erica, had been an unexpected bonus.

"I can't believe you take care of eight kids all day every day." Sarah shook her head. "One child is enough for me."

"Hey, what about me?" Hannah said. "I have more than ten kids in my classes. All day long."

"Yeah, but you have the summer off. And during the school year you get to go home every night. Alone."

"Don't remind me." Hannah downed the last of her chardonnay and then thrust her hand out across the table, palm up. "Missy, read my love line."

Missy chuckled. "Why?"

"I want you to tell me if I'm ever going to get married."

"It's not like that, honey."

"Then what good is it having your palm read?"

"Not much. All I can tell you is pretty much what you already know about yourself." She grabbed Natalie's hand, flipped it over and studied her palm. "Take Natalie for example. See her very strong, deep line," she murmured.

"What is it?"

"Your heart line." Missy ran her index finger along the line running mostly horizontally below Natalie's fingers.

"What does that mean?"

"The ability for strong and deep devotion." She glanced up at them. "Anyone surprised by that?"

"About a woman running a summer camp for disadvantaged kids?" Sarah chuckled. "No."

"Then again." Missy pointed to a spot in the middle of her palm. "That could be him."

"Who?"

"The love of your life." She grinned conspiratorially at Natalie.

Natalie grabbed Missy's hand and studied her palm. "What does yours say?"

"One true love for my entire life. And I already met him."

"You did?" Sarah said.

Hannah's jaw dropped. "You've never told us."

"What happened?" Natalie whispered.

"Didn't go so well." Missy's expression turned somber as she twirled the straw in her Black Russian. "He died. In an FBI training operation. A helicopter crash."

"I'm so sorry," Natalie murmured.

"Don't be."

"But you said he was the love of your life."

"He was. That doesn't mean we were right for each other." Missy chugged the last of her drink. "I loved him. He loved his job. No getting around that one."

"So that's it? You're done?"

"With anything serious. Most likely." She pointed at each of the other three. "But you guys aren't."

"The only problem is that there aren't any eligible men on Mirabelle," Hannah grumbled.

"You got that right. And the last one was snapped up so fast by Erica, everyone's heads were spinning." Sarah glanced up and noticed Garrett Taylor sitting in the booth next to them with Herman Stotz, his deputy, and Jim Bennett, the ex-police chief. "Hey, Garrett," she called.

He glanced up.

"You got any brothers?"

He grinned and held up three fingers.

"Yeah, but are they single?"

His smile broadened and he continued holding up two fingers.

"So when are they coming to visit?" Missy said, laughing.

"I'm not sure either one of them is Mirabelle material," Garrett said, shaking his head.

All four women returned to their drinks, decidedly more serious than before. Natalie took a big gulp of her Cabernet. "I know an eligible bachelor on the island. And he's very attractive."

"Who?"

"Jamis Quinn."

Sarah put down her martini and leaned forward. "He's come into my flower shop a couple of times. Sent flowers to funeral homes. An office once for someone's birthday. I'll tell ya, he's an odd one."

"Well, if he showed even an iota's worth of interest in me," Hannah said, "I'd be all over him."

Natalie couldn't imagine this woman all over any man. She looked every inch the elementary schoolteacher. Too sweet for Jamis, that was for sure.

Where did that leave Natalie?

"Turquoise and blue," Missy said.

"What's that?" Sarah asked.

"Our auras," Natalie explained.

"Perfectly matched." Missy grinned. "Only Natalie, here, has sworn off all men forever."

"Uh-uh," Natalie objected. "Only until my luck changes."

"Bad luck with relationship, huh?" Sarah asked.

"Don't get me started." Natalie shook her head.

Hannah chuckled. "Must be contagious."

"Like a virus," Missy added.

WELL, I HATE TO TELL you this, Jamis," Chuck Romney's voice came quietly over the phone, "but Natalie Steeger has done a very thorough job in preparing for this camp. She obtained approval from the Mirabelle Island council and has complied with all the state licensing requirements for this type of facility."

Jamis still hadn't started a new book. Even a realistic idea for a story hadn't revealed itself, preoccupied as his thoughts were with the bustling activity on the other side of the trees bordering his property.

"You're sure?" he asked. "You didn't find anything?"

"I took it apart. Piece by piece. You have no grounds to shut her down."

He paced in his kitchen. "What about trespassing?"

"Jamis, give it a rest. Is she truly that bad?"

"You have no idea."

"Do you have no-trespassing signs up identifying your property line?"

"I put them up the other day."

"All right. Well, there's a process to these things. Eventually, you'll have to file a complaint with the police." He sighed. "You sure you want to go that route?"

No. He wasn't sure, but he was getting desperate. "What about buying her out?"

"You have enough money for that?"

"I'll figure it out."

"You go that route and you can forget about getting rid of her before the end of summer."

He sighed, resigning himself to that fact. "Not having to worry about her returning next summer is better than nothing."

"Do you want me to make her an offer?"

"Yes."

"I'll talk to her attorney again, but I'm not expecting to make any headway. That man's made it very clear that she doesn't want to sell, and from the information I've gathered about her she doesn't have to. Along with the house on Mirabelle, she also inherited another house in Minneapolis and a big chunk of change from her grandmother. She's soliciting donations and grants for the future, but with or without outside funding, she can keep this summer camp running for several more years."

"You need to talk to her directly, Chuck." This was for her own good. "Tell her I'll buy her something in town or on one of the other islands. I could give her a donation for her camp on the condition she moves. Do whatever it takes to get her off this island."

"Whatever it takes. All right, I'll give it a shot."

Jamis hung up the phone and immediately became aware of a presence outside in his yard, and it wasn't as innocuous as a squirrel. He glanced out the kitchen window and there climbing around on his rocks was that little girl with the curly dark hair. *No, Jamis. You are not going out there. No way. No how.* That teenage boy was one thing. This little bundle of wide-eyed innocence was an entirely different matter. The kid could putz out there all day long for all he cared, and Natalie was not going to get a pass for this one. Their deal was over, fair and square.

The kid picked up a stone and threw it into the woods. Then she wandered a few feet away, bent down and studied, presumably, an insect crawling through the dirt. Next, she picked a wood violet and another and another, starting a tiny bouquet in her little fingers.

He couldn't keep his eyes off her. Every step. Every movement. She did exactly what Caitlin would've done. His heart twisted inside out as memories of a different little girl in a different, happier time popped into his mind one after another. Caitlin's first steps, her first words, the way her fingers felt on his arm as he read her to sleep, the way her arms felt around his neck as she hugged him with all her might. Little girls. Were they all exactly the same?

Oh, God. He sucked in a quick breath and pushed the memories back where they could cause no further pain. Then she set her bouquet down, reached for the lowest branch of a small pine, and hoisted herself up. She was a good little climber, but every time she reached higher, Jamis cringed. One branch led to another and in no time, she was halfway up the tree, a good fifteen feet off the ground. If she fell—

He caught himself holding his breath. That was it. Yanking open the front door, he stepped out onto the porch and crossed his arms. "Hey, kid. Get down from there. Now."

She glanced over at him with a face as innocent as a bunny rabbit's. "Why? I'm not going to fa—"

"I said get down!"

She frowned, but did as he'd asked, scrambling quickly down the tree trunk. "I've climbed lots of—"

"What are you doing over here?"

She glanced up. "Nothing."

"Then go do nothing in your own yard."

She didn't move. Instead, she whispered, "I thought you reminded me of my daddy, but I guess not."

"Definitely not."

"He died."

Shit. Shit, shit, shit. Jamis swallowed as if the words stuck in his throat. "I'm sorry, but I'm not your dad."

Bending down, she picked up her violets and gathered them back into a bouquet. "Why do you try to be mean?" she asked without looking at him.

"Try? *Try* to be mean?"

She nodded.

And he couldn't do it. Just couldn't. Another pass for

Natalie. Taking a deep breath, he stepped out onto the porch and sat on the top step. "What's your name?"

"Toni."

He felt the name poke at his heart like the tip of a dull knife. "Well, Toni, you remind me of my daughter. And it hurts."

"Did she die, too?"

He nodded. "And my son."

"That's sad."

"Toni!" The call came from next door. "Dinner's ready!"

"Coming!" She glanced up at Jamis. "Here." Tentatively, she offered him the flowers. "I picked these for you."

Unable, unwilling to move, Jamis stared at the little hand.

Before he could step out of her reach, she thrust the flowers into his hand. "I gotta go!" she said, running away. "Want me to come back later?"

"No!" Jamis called, flicking the flowers into the woods. "Please," he whispered after she disappeared into the old Victorian.

If only he could put a no-trespassing sign on his heart.

NATALIE AWOKE AT HER usual early hour, but the kids got to sleep in late this morning. Weeks ago, she'd established the routine for the summer weekends. Saturdays were cleaning days. Saturday nights were pizza and a movie in town. And Sundays were play days all day long. She padded into the kitchen, made herself a pot of coffee and would've given anything at that moment to have an adult conversation. Unfortunately, the only adult within a five-mile radius was a certain grizzly bear of a man who'd made it very clear with or without his no-trespassing signs that he didn't want anything to do with her.

The clear call of a cardinal pierced the quiet of the morning, and she cracked open the window to listen. At that moment, the sound of Snickers's bark joined that of the bird's call, and she noticed motion on Jamis's deck. Curiosity getting the better of her, she snuck outside and into the woods for a better look. She hunkered down and peered through the branches to see Snickers chase through the trees after a squirrel, and grizzly bear Jamis standing near his deck rail. He was holding what appeared to be a steaming cup of hot coffee as he searched the branches, presumably for the bright red feathers of the male bird that was singing his solitary, melancholy tune.

Natalie was dying to stand up and walk over there with her first cup of coffee and talk. "No can do," she whispered. Thanks to that silly bet. *Two days down, five to go. Five? Whose idea was this, anyway? Oh, yeah. Mine.*

All she could do was watch as he sipped from his mug, closed his eyes and put his face to the sky. His longish hair was rumpled as if he'd just rolled out of bed. He was wearing flannel pajama pants and a fleece pullover, as if chilled, but he was barefoot.

What a paradox, that man. There was something so elementally virile about him, but it didn't make any sense. A writer? Virile and sexy? An attractive, intelligent man all alone in the woods? He shouldn't be alone. That man needed a woman. Not just any woman. He needed someone strong and compassionate, someone who could take him in stride.

Someone like her.

She imagined waking up naked in his arms, sliding over his tall, tense frame, and desire sung through her swiftly, cleanly, undeniably. Where was this coming from? Normally, she liked reserved and patient men. Jamis was neither. He was about as tentative as a bullet. He wouldn't ask for what he wanted. He'd take it.

Almost intuitively, his gaze traveled from the water

toward Natalie's house and back out to the trees as if he could sense her there. She squatted farther down and out of sight. *Stop it, Nat. Even if you hadn't sworn off men, you're too busy this summer for a relationship.*

Snickers started sniffing the edge of the woods in front of her and she held her breath. If he came running toward her, she'd die. Die.

"Snickers, come," Jamis called, and the dog quickly ran back to the cabin.

Natalie breathed a sigh of relief. Jamis and the dog headed back inside and then, resolutely, she put the slightly damaged but very sexy Jamis out of her mind, slinked back to her kitchen and focused on her plans for the day. Grabbing the whiteboard, she mapped out cleaning duties and started a load of laundry.

Gradually, over the course of the next couple of hours, one by one, the children wandered into the kitchen looking for something to eat. It was no surprise that Galen was the last one to the breakfast table. The previous night, he and Sam had gotten home only a few minutes past eleven, but she'd heard Galen up and about for some time before she'd drifted off to sleep.

She'd let them all watch some TV while she cleaned up from breakfast and then went into the living room and shut off the TV. "Time to get moving, guys."

Groans all around.

"Cleaning day. Remember? Top to bottom."

Major groans.

"Then tomorrow we're heading to the beach for sailing and kayaking. And today, the sooner we get done, the sooner we can head into town for pizza and a movie!"

That announcement was met with a resounding round of approval, and Natalie assigned chores. Another glance out the open kitchen window gave her an idea, and she grinned. After opening several more windows throughout the house as wide as they would go, she dropped a disk in the CD player and cranked the volume as high as it would go. She might not be able to go over to Jamis's, but their agreement didn't preclude him from coming over here.

JAMIS DRUMMED HIS FINGERTIPS on top of his desk as the sax solo for Ricky Martin's "Livin' La Vida Loca" pounded through the previously quiet forest. He'd already closed all of his windows, but Miss Not-So-Innocent-After-All had the volume so loud he swore the leaves on the trees were vibrating.

"The little vixen." He caught himself smiling.

This wouldn't be such an untenable situation, except for the fact that he was actually, almost, starting to like the woman.

With Snickers taking the lead, he strode to her house and pounded on the back door. When no one answered, he let himself into the kitchen and several heads turned toward him. One kid was scrubbing out the sink. Another was sweeping. Another washing the cabinets. One was vac-uuming the living room. Another one dusting.

He had to give the woman credit. This was nothing like the posh camps he'd attended as a kid. He'd more likely have gotten breakfast in bed than be assigned chores. In any case, he walked past them all, found the CD player and flicked it off.

"Hey!" Natalie, holding a toilet brush in her hand, came out into the hallway from what must've been the bathroom. Goddamn, she looked gorgeous. In jeans shorts and a tank top with her hair up in a messy ponytail. Her skin glowing with a honey-gold tan. "Who shut off the music?"

"It's only considered music when listened to at reasonable decibels," Jamis said. "Otherwise it's nothing more than noise."

She spun toward him, put her hands on her hips, nice, curvy, luscious-looking hips, and raised her eyebrows. "Oh, so you can come over here, but I can't come over to your house?"

He laughed. She'd done this on purpose. Well, two could play that game. "Deal's off." He strode outside.

"Wait a minute!" She ran after him. "I'm sorry. I am."

"No, you're not."

"I am. Honestly."

Refusing to stop and discuss this with her, he stalked through the woods. She, predictably, followed. Within seconds he was standing in front of his house and she was close behind him. He spun around. "See? I was right."

"About what?"

"You couldn't even make it three days." He grinned. "This is where I get to gloat and tell you I told you so."

"What?"

"You, Sunshine, are trespassing."

Her mouth gaped open, showcasing pretty pink lips and a delectable tongue. "You did that on purpose!"

"So what if I did?"

"Of all the—"

That was it. He couldn't take it anymore. Striding toward her, he grabbed her around the waist, pulled her flush against him and kissed her. He'd only intended— Who was he kidding? He hadn't intended on touching her at all, but once he'd started he didn't want to stop. Neither did she. A harmless peck on the lips turned into open mouths, tongues clashing and hands groping. Her hands were on his chest, his neck, diving through his hair. Before he knew what he was doing, his fingers had found their way under her shirt and were making their way up her side toward her breasts.

Then a rap song suddenly sounded from Natalie's house, piercing the air and snapping Jamis back to reality. He stepped back and swallowed, feeling slightly stunned.

Natalie's eyes drifted open. "What…what was that for?" she whispered.

"I've been wondering what you'd taste like." She was a minty orange flavor he had a feeling he'd end up craving for a very long time.

"And?"

He might try to tell himself he didn't enjoy her company, her conversation, her presence, but the truth was he enjoyed her far too much. And he sure as hell didn't deserve to be enjoying much of anything.

"Now I really don't want you on my side of the trees." He stalked into the house, grabbed a few more no-trespassing signs and nailed them up between their two houses on every single tree he could find sturdy enough to hold them. By the time he was done, Natalie was nowhere to be found and the northwest corner of Mirabelle had fallen eerily silent.

CHAPTER EIGHT

SILENCE. A FULL SUNDAY'S worth of it and Jamis had managed to eek out only a chapter. As if a dam or a maze had been constructed in his brain, words were piling up inside him, making it impossible to release them in any coherent form. If they didn't come pouring out fairly soon, he might just explode. But at least he'd started the damned book. Sort of. He had no clue where this story was going. All he knew was that it was finally going somewhere.

Around suppertime, he called it a day. The scene wasn't turning out exactly as he wanted, so he'd have to hammer it into shape another time. As he was checking e-mails, a note came in from his agent. "I'm out next week. Forgot to tell you. How's the book coming?"

He typed back, "It's not."

"What's the problem?"

A woman. And her kids. "Writer's block." He had a block all right. He couldn't seem to think of much outside of Natalie and her lips, the way her skin had felt, like the petals of a wild trillium.

"It's the kids' camp, isn't it?"

"Yes." As he typed, he heard Natalie and her crew returning from wherever they'd spent the day. Snickers barked to go out and rather than argue Jamis left his agent's e-mails and went downstairs to open the door. The dog ran through the trees and up to each child. "Snickers!" they each called, in turn.

They were carrying beach towels, coolers and picnic baskets. A day at the beach—with people, laughter and games, hot sun, cool drinks. Surprisingly, it sounded like a nice way to pass a summer day.

Not gonna happen. Not in your lifetime.

He went to his office to turn off his computer and found another e-mail from his agent. "You going to meet the deadline?"

"No," he typed.

A few moments later, the phone rang. Jamis picked it up and walked across the room. "Yes, Stephen."

"You've never missed a deadline before."

"You think I don't know that?" He glanced out the window.

From this high up, the second floor of his house, he could see Natalie and the kids fishing at her dock. She had her hair up in a ponytail and was wearing a baseball cap. In jeans shorts and a red shirt, he wasn't sure he'd ever seen her look sexier. What would she look like in a bikini?

He closed his eyes and imagined her skin bared, soft and supple. Warm, the way her hand had felt on his neck yesterday, her fingers in his hair. She'd wanted him as much as he'd wanted her. A man didn't have to be a rocket scientist to figure out what might've happened between the two of them if those kids hadn't been next door. His thoughts quickly tracked in that direction. He imagined himself over her, moving with her, making love with her.

"Jamis? Jamis!"

He'd completely forgotten his agent was on the phone. "What?"

"You've started the book, though, right?" Stephen asked, not quite pulling Jamis back to their conversation.

"I have one chapter of a story. Not quite sure what it is yet." He went out to the porch for a better view of Natalie.

"What's going on?"

"I don't know." She bent over, picked up something from the dock and laughed as she threw it into the water. "Too distracting around here, I guess."

Stephen held silent for a moment. "She's pretty, isn't she?"

"Uh-huh."

"Are you looking at her now?"

"Mmm-hmm."

Stephen laughed. "How long since you've been with a woman?"

"None of your business."

"Since Katherine, right?"

Jamis refused to answer that.

"You need to get laid."

"Oh, that'd solve a lot of problems." But there was no doubt that all these years without sex, without human touch, was taking its toll on Jamis.

"You'd be surprised."

No, he wouldn't. He was quite sure that a quick, non-committal romp under the sheets with Natalie would do more than free his mind.

"You miss this deadline, Jamis, and this last publisher will not only close the door in your face, they'll drop all the publicity they've planned for the book you just turned in."

"You think I don't know that?"

"I'll call them. See what I can do."

As Jamis disconnected the call, the sight of Toni sitting with her feet dangling off the end of the dock caught his eye. She reminded him so much of Caitlin. The color of her hair. The curls. That sweet voice. He missed his children. And suddenly he realized the memory of their faces was beginning to fade.

Before he could think better of it, Jamis went to his office and pulled out the bottom drawer of his credenza, a drawer he hadn't opened since a box had been placed inside the day he'd moved into this cabin. He flipped open the flaps and there on top staring at him was the last picture he'd ever taken of his daughter and son. God, it was good to see them again. He picked up the frame and studied their smiles, their bright eyes. Finally, he could look at their beautiful faces without breaking down.

Jamis had taken them to a carnival by himself because it was the type of thing Katherine had hated. He'd loved doing things with the kids. On the merry-go-round, he'd put Justin in front of Caitlin and snapped off a picture.

Justin's dimples brought a smile to Jamis's face. With eyebrows heavier than most babies and a distinctive jawline, people had always commented on how much Justin had looked like Jamis. Caitlin, too, with her dark hair and big brown eyes. Katherine, as much as their marriage had been a sham from her standpoint, had given him two beautiful children.

Katherine.

He should've known better when she'd seemed attracted to him. An ex-model, Katherine had the body of a goddess and, on top of that, an electric personality. It hadn't made sense that such a woman would've been interested in him. Too bad he hadn't listened to his instincts all those years ago. He could've saved himself a helluva lot of heartache.

Well, Jamis was listening this time. He set the picture of his children back down into the box and closed the drawer. Natalie Steeger, a children's camp director and all around do-gooder, could only be interested in him for one thing. She wanted to fix him.

Boy, was she in for a big surprise.

AFTER THAT KISS, NATALIE vowed to give Jamis some breathing room.

For the first day or two that wasn't all that difficult. She and the kids stayed busy. But as the week wore on, Jamis and his kiss seemed to be all she could think about. The unexpected softness of his beard, the strength of his arms, the solid breadth of his chest—he'd taken her completely by surprise and kissed her as if he wasn't sure the sun would rise in the morning. The fact that he'd stated very succinctly that he still didn't want her on his side of the trees confused and confounded her. Maybe it was the way he called her Sunshine. She wasn't silly enough to think the nickname was meant in a kind way, but when he said the word there was a distinctly endearing quality to his voice.

Somehow, someway, she was determined to break through to that man. But how?

Already, it was Friday night and after dinner Galen whipped through his chores as if Arlo Duffy, the town carriage driver, was cracking a horsewhip on the boy's behind. Natalie chuckled to herself as he came speeding downstairs, smelling heavily of cologne.

"Can I go now?"

"Just a minute." Natalie took a box out of the pantry, wanting to catch all the kids before they all wandered away. "I have something for everyone!"

The kids all glanced at her expectantly as she set the box on the table. "What is it?" someone asked.

"Candy?"

"Ice cream."

"Journals!" She beamed, pulling out various shapes and sizes of decorated books filled with nothing except blank pages. She'd hoped this would help them with the dreams and wishes side of this camp. "You don't have to write in them if you don't want, but I'd like each of you to take one and think about it."

"Diaries are for chicks," Blake said.

"These aren't diaries," Sam said, picking up a red silk-covered book heavily decorated with beads. "They're journals."

"This—" Chase picked up a lavender book with tiny pink ribbons glued to the front and held it out "—is a diary."

"Maybe, dude." Galen held out a leather-bound book. "But this is a guy's book. You could use this to draw comics."

"Exactly!" Natalie said, smiling at Galen. Since their talk several weeks ago, he'd been making a marginally better effort to engage in activities and in helping with the kids and household responsibilities. Slowly, but surely, he'd been coming around. "I'd like you to write all your dreams and wishes in here, but they're your journals, so you can use them for anything. Jokes, stories, pictures."

Chase shrugged and took the book out of Galen's hands. Blake grabbed one of the other leather-bound books while Ryan found one covered with sports pictures. Arianna and Ella each picked out books covered in bright, fuzzy fur, but chose different colors. Toni took the lavender book Chase had discarded. "I like this one," she whispered.

"It's yours," Natalie said.

Each child thanked her as he or she wandered into the living room. Sam, though, hung back, glanced at Natalie and raised her eyebrows.

"I know. I know," Natalie said, pulling out another box

from the pantry that had been delivered that afternoon. "I have something else for you, Galen."

"What is it?" he asked.

Sam grinned. "Open it up and find out."

Natalie watched him tear back the cardboard flaps, feeling amazingly unsure for the first time around a kid. "If you don't like it, it's all returnable. I found what looked like a trendy online site and Sam helped me from there."

Sam shrugged. "I tried, anyway."

His face turned serious as he pulled out three sweatshirts and several T-shirts. He glanced up at Sam and a slight blush washed her cheeks.

"I'll let you know how much you can spend and you can order some jeans or shoes, but…" Natalie trailed off. "Is this stuff okay?"

"Okay?" He glanced up at her, and his sullen and disgruntled demeanor disappeared. "Um. Yeah, this stuff is way okay. Thanks."

He hugged Natalie, and by the time she pulled away Sam had disappeared into the living room. "Cool. I'm glad you like it, but Sam is the one who picked everything out."

He got a funny smile on his face. "So she doesn't really hate my guts?"

"No. I'm sure she doesn't."

He shrugged out of his old sweatshirt and into one of the new ones. "See you later." He ran toward the door.

"Isn't Sam going with you?"

"She didn't want to tonight. Can I still go?"

"Sure."

"Thanks again, Natalie. For everything." He paused at the door. "And I'm sorry for being such a jerk. I'll try to do better." Then he rushed outside and disappeared.

Her work with Galen wasn't finished, but they were

making headway. She wandered into the living room to find out what was up with Sam. She'd gone into town with Galen every Friday since they'd arrived on the island and seemed to have a good time. The younger kids were lying on the floor or lounging on the couch. Sam was sitting off by herself in a corner chair, looking bored. "Hey." Natalie nudged her on the shoulder. "You didn't want to go into town with Galen?"

"No, those guys are tr—" She stopped and looked quickly away. "I don't feel like going out. Kinda tired. In fact, I'm going upstairs to my room to read." Taking her journal with her, she disappeared up the steps.

Natalie watched her and wondered what those islander teenagers were getting into, but she couldn't ask Sam to snitch on Galen. *Galen, let's hope you have your head on straight.* She did not want to have to send him home.

"Anyone for a game?" she asked.

"Yeah!" came the resounding response followed by every kid calling out his or her favorite board game.

Several hours later, after a night of playing board games and having stuffed their stomachs with popcorn and soda, the kids all went to their respective rooms and promptly went to sleep. Natalie cracked open Sam's door to see if she wanted to watch a movie and found her sound asleep, her new journal open in front of her. Natalie hadn't planned on spying, but the one line Sam had written was as clear as a bell.

I wish I could stay here forever.

Oh, Sam. Natalie wanted to brush back the long strands of hair that had fallen over the girl's face. *I hope this summer is everything you need it to be.*

Natalie switched off the bedroom light, snuck quietly downstairs, and wandered into the kitchen. She paced in front of the sink, feeling a bit like a caged animal. After debating all of thirty seconds, she scribbled out a note for any one of the kids who might come looking for her.

"Kiss or no kiss, it's time we cleared the air." She grabbed a bottle of wine from the top shelf in the pantry and two glasses and took off through the woods. On reaching Jamis's yard, she noticed him on his deck, Snickers asleep near his chair.

Wearing a black fleece jacket, his feet propped up, his long, jeans-clad legs stretched out in front of him, he glanced up from the book he was reading the moment she came into the clearing. "You're trespassing," he said, frowning.

She held up the bottle. "But I come bearing a gift." Snickers hopped up and ran to greet her and she patted his head.

Jamis snapped the book closed and folded his arms across his chest. "What is it going to take to get you to leave me alone?"

"Come on, Jamis. Our houses are the only ones on this end of the island. Can't we be friends?"

CHAPTER NINE

"FRIENDS?" JAMIS SAID, a note of disbelief tingeing the sound of his voice. "Not possible."

"Sure it is."

"You don't give up, do you?"

"Nope." Natalie opened the bottle, poured him a glass and held it out.

He glanced first at her, then the wine and then back again. As clear as the full moon glowing high in the sky, she could see the memory of their kiss skittering through his mind, but then he seemed to lock it up and put it away. He shook his head and reached for the glass. "All right, Sunshine, but if we're going to do this, I want some honesty. And none of this 'the world is a perfect rainbow of happiness' bullshit, either."

"Okay." She leaned against the deck rail. "Honesty. Why do you—"

"Oh, no. We're going to talk about you." He pulled his feet off the chair and stood. Holding the glass of wine, he studied her. "Starting with what do you want from me?"

She shrugged. "I told you. To be friends."

"See, that's not good enough." Studying her, he slowly moved toward her. "I think this camp isn't enough for you. I think you want to turn me into another one of your projects. I think you'd like nothing more than to be my savior."

"I'm not trying to be anyone's savior."

"Sure you are. You'd save the entire world if you could manage it." He shook his head and chuckled. "I'll bet anything that you've spent your vacations building, painting or repairing houses, haven't you?"

"A couple."

"Ever work in a food bank?"

"Several times a year."

"Give blood?"

"Just got my five gallon pin."

"Women's shelters?"

"I used to answer the phones once a week."

"Figures." Scoffing, he shook his head.

"What does?"

"Neck deep in one crusade after another."

"When you put it that way, it sounds rather pathetic." She set her wineglass on a nearby deck table. She didn't mind standing up for her camp. She'd been doing that for months while getting approvals and licenses, but this personal attack was something altogether different. "You think all I am is a Goody Two-shoes, don't you?"

He said nothing.

"Well, I got news for you, there's more here than meets the eye."

"That I'd like to see." His gaze turned smoky and disconcerting.

"What's so wrong about helping other people?"

"Nothing. As long as you're not using all those activities to avoid your own issues."

"Which are?" She straightened her shoulders.

"I don't know. You tell me."

"I don't have any issues."

"Sunshine, we all have issues."

"Maybe I've dealt with mine."

"Right." He looked her up and down. "Fresh out of college? I don't think so."

"As a matter of fact, I just turned thirty. Thank you very much."

He looked surprised and possibly relieved. "Survived a big one, eh? So why aren't you married?"

She took a fortifying gulp of wine. "Who says I'm not?"

"No man in his right mind would let you out of his sight for three months." He paused and gazed at her. "Smart. Caring. Sexy." His eyes were dark and getting darker. For a moment, she thought he might reach for her. "What's the catch, Natalie?"

Cocking her head, she whispered, "Can't cook."

He chuckled, and it was one of the most fascinating sounds she'd ever heard, full of nuance and suggestion. She tilted her head upward and though she hadn't moved, the distance between them seemed to close. "It so happens I haven't met the right man."

"I don't believe you." He was going to kiss her. Almost sure of it, she quickly turned away, breaking whatever spell had overtaken him. "So that gets us right back to where we started. What do you want from me?"

"I told you. I could use a friend."

"You haven't dated many men, have you?" he asked.

"Plenty. Trust me."

"That many, huh? What's the longest you've been with one guy?"

She didn't like feeling cornered. "That's not relevant."

"Bet it wasn't very long—"

"What is this, an inquisition?" She crossed her arms.

"You're the one who wanted to be friends."

"You going to take down the no-trespassing signs?"

"Maybe."

She considered him for a moment and realized she had nothing to hide. "I've had a streak of bad luck with men. That's all."

"Bad luck. Right." He stared her down.

"All right. Fine. The longest I've ever dated a guy was three months."

"That's not very long. Who was he and why did you break up?"

"He was a coworker's brother," she said, picking up her wine and turning away. "Owned an excavating company. Came from a family of ten kids, but didn't want any of his own."

"And it took you that long to figure that out?"

"He *claimed* he'd made that clear right up front, but I don't remember him divulging that key piece of information." She felt herself getting slightly miffed at Jamis for bringing it all back up. When she'd broken up with Chad, he'd literally fallen apart and blamed it all on her. "How could anyone not want children, anyway?"

"Fatal flaw, huh?" He stepped in front of her, forcing her to look at him. "The one before that?"

"Teacher. Liked kids so much, he wanted—"

"Let me guess. Six."

"Eight." And was so convinced she was destined to be the mother of his big brood that he wouldn't accept the breakup. He'd turned stalkerlike within a week.

"I'll bet you even dated one who was too much like a child himself."

Carl. Now she was getting angry, angrier than she'd been in a very long time.

"I'm sure there were more. Keep going."

"No."

"So now you're pouting."

She glared at him. "There was a personal trainer who couldn't stop looking in the mirror. The perpetual student who never wanted to get a full-time job. The DJ who so much liked the sound of his own voice—"

"—he couldn't stop talking long enough to listen to you." He shook his head. "Why are you always picking men with these glaring flaws?"

"Well, I certainly don't know they have them right away."

"Sure you do. I'm guessing you've known instantly about every flaw of every man you've ever dated."

"That's just…" She stopped.

"Not bad luck, that's for sure. You knew nothing would come of any of those relationships. They were all doomed before they'd even begun."

She backed away from him. "And you're such an expert on relationships?"

"Not even close. But I was married for four years, and filing for a divorce wasn't my idea. At least that tells you I'm not afraid of commitment."

What an infuriating ass of a man. "I'm not afraid of commitment!"

"No. You're afraid of being abandoned. That's why you always pick men with no possible future with you."

Furious now, she didn't—couldn't—say anything.

"You like to fix things, don't you?"

"What does that have to do with anything?" she threw back at him.

"Because all the men you choose are fixer-uppers." He studied her, as if he was working something out. "It gives you an easy out."

She felt tilted off center. Leave them before they could leave her. Dammit, but he could be right.

"What about me?" he whispered. "Am I just another man you want to fix?"

"No. It's not that, it's—"

"What do you want from me, Natalie?"

"Nothing, I—"

He tucked a strand of her hair behind her ear. It seemed an innocent enough gesture, except for the fact that his hand lingered near her neck. "You don't get it, do you?"

"What?" she whispered.

"I don't want you here."

"I think you've made that perfectly clear." He'd been nothing short of attacking her. Maybe it was time to return fire. "Why don't you give me a little honesty? Tell me why you don't want me here and I'll leave you alone."

"Because you came over here tonight thinking if you share a glass of wine, some conversation, then wave your magic wand over me all would be well. You want to fix me just like you've tried to fix all those other men."

"No, I—"

"Only I don't need fixing, Natalie."

"You're wrong. You do. You lost your wife, your children—"

His gaze swung toward her. "Be very careful what you say."

"I wanted to understand why you were here, so I looked up some old online articles. But it doesn't make any sense. It was an accident."

He clenched his jaw and looked away.

"Why do you hate yourself so much?" She put her hand softly on his arm. "It wasn't your fault."

He glanced down at her hand and his mouth parted. "I haven't been with a woman in five years, Natalie. The next time you touch me, you'd better be ready to be touched back."

Five years. That was a long, long time for a man. For some crazy reason his admission felt more to her like a challenge than a warning. She trailed her hand up his arm, over his shoulder and through the locks of soft, curly hair on his neck. His face was only inches from hers.

"I'm warning you," he whispered. "Unlike the rest of your fatally flawed men, I happen to like myself the way I am."

"No, you don't. You just think you do."

Like a wild animal sniffing out its territory, he leaned closer, smelling her neck, then her hair. "You willing to take that risk?"

She closed her eyes and kissed him.

He stood still, ramrod straight as she peppered his mouth with the lightest of touches. But when she lingered a moment, her lips opened and felt his tongue with the tip of her own, his breath left his body. "Okay, Sunshine. You want it, you got it." He dragged her close and held her against him.

As his tongue brushed against hers, something fired to life inside her. This. This is what she wanted from him. *To feel him.* She ran her hands up and along his side. *To touch him.* His back muscles were tight and tense. She'd never kissed a man built so perfectly. He was so strong and demanding.

As if to prove it, his hands dipped under her shirt, traveled up her bare back and flicked the clasp on her bra. He cupped her breast and she shivered. He pulsed his hips toward her and his erection pressed against her, feeling at once wrong and right, startling and bone melting. She wanted her clothes off. She wanted to feel his naked skin next to hers. She wanted—

He pulled back and dropped his hands to his side. "That's what you want from me, isn't it?"

She swallowed.

"Well, I'm not available."

"You are, without a doubt, the most infuriating man I know."

"Well, you know what you can do about that."

"Of all the…" Clenching her teeth, she spun around and ran down the steps and across the yard.

"Don't bother coming back," he called after her. "I am not the broken man you think I am!"

DON'T COME BACK HERE. Don't ever come back.

Jamis watched her stalk away, feeling intense sensations of both relief and regret.

A part of him hadn't wanted to be so damned right about her. A part of him had wanted to be no more than a simple, uncomplicated summer diversion for her. So what? Who could blame either one of them? Neither of them was wet behind the ears. They both understood the consequences to that kind of impulsive behavior. There was nothing wrong with no-strings-attached sex.

But he had been right. Jamis was no more than a summer project for her, like her camp. She planned to fix him and move on, get what she needed from him—the satisfaction she took from helping another human being, or whatever else she got out of it—and then disappear from his life. Just like Katherine.

Jamis closed his eyes. He could taste Natalie, the wine on her tongue, the heat of her mouth. On his lips. He could feel her. On his hands. This was one raging hard-on he wouldn't be willing away all that easily.

Gulping down what was left of the wine in his glass, he immediately filled it again. *You're an idiot.* He'd thought he'd scare her away, make her keep her distance and all he'd accomplished was heightening the tension between them.

She was angry at him? Thought *he* was out of line? He shook his head and laughed. Before the summer was over he had a sick feeling that woman was going to bring him to his knees.

At the sound of the knock, Bradley opened his hotel-room door and in sauntered that woman from the bar. Her lusty gaze settled on his groin.

"Don't do it, Bradley," Natalie whispered into the quiet stillness of her bedroom. "You don't have to do it."

As if he were no more than a piece of meat to be chopped up and fried, she licked her lips. Thought she was hot shit, didn't she? Most of them did. She had no clue what she was getting herself into.

Natalie glanced at the clock. Three o'clock in the morning. She'd started reading Jamis's book after all the kids had gone to sleep more than three hours ago and couldn't seem to put it down. Quickly, she turned the page and kept reading.

He waved her forward with a flick of his fingers. She came to him, knelt before him, and unzipped his fly without a moment's hesitation. When he came in her mouth she didn't even pause to swallow, simply let his fluid drip from her lips.

Scanning to the end of the chapter, Natalie cringed as the man brutally murdered the woman.

She was nothing. Nothing. He watched her eyes dim, reveled in her mounting fear. Too scared to scream.

Natalie slapped the book closed and set it on her bedside table. How could he write about a man ruthlessly killing one person after another? Where did it come from? Even more amazing was how he'd brought her almost to the point of empathizing with the murderer. Worse were the eerie parallels between the killer and the cop chasing him. No wonder they'd made a movie from this story. Jamis was an incredibly skilled and gifted writer, and it was the kind of over-the-top story of conflicted, damaged characters that Hollywood loved.

Not a broken man? Like hell.

The urge to do something for him coursed through her like a river through a wide-open dam and she grew frustrated with herself. Was he just another mission for her? Was she afraid of abandonment? Could he be right on every single count?

She couldn't deny that there was some measure of truth in what he'd said. From the time she'd been adopted, she'd felt the need to pay back what she'd been given. It seemed she had to always be doing for others in order to feel right about herself. That couldn't be good, even if good was being done.

As for men, she'd broken off almost every single one of her past relationships. But that was in the past. There was something different about Jamis. He was strong, despite the fact that he was hurting inside. He made her laugh, sometimes want to cry, and always, always made her want him. And that was, perhaps, the sexiest thing of all about Jamis. He didn't need her. He wanted her.

CHAPTER TEN

"NATALIE! TELEPHONE!"

When someone called from the living room, Natalie was throwing another load into the washing machine from the seemingly endless pile of dirty clothes eight active kids seemed to generate. "Coming!" She threw in some detergent, started the wash cycle, and then took the phone from Chase. "This is Natalie."

"Miss Steeger, my name is Charles Romney. I'm an attorney in Minneapolis."

"Hello, Mr. Romney. What can I do for you?"

"You're a very difficult woman to get ahold of."

"I am, huh?"

"Has your attorney relayed my offers?"

"Nope."

"That's unfortunate. I believe you're missing an opportunity."

At that her warning flags were raised and she kept her mouth shut.

"You recently inherited a home on Mirabelle Island and I represent a party interested in acquiring that property."

Confused, his comment didn't immediately register. "It's not for sale."

"Well, before you immediately discount the possibility

I think you should be aware that money is of little importance in this situation."

She waited.

"My client is prepared to pay you three, four times the current market value of your property. You name the price. It's yours."

Jamis.

Most of her life she'd taken criticism for trying to stay positive in dismal circumstances. She thought she was used to it, immune to its inherent negativity, but this hurt in an unexpected, but no less devastating, way. "He's that desperate to have us gone?"

"I beg your pardon?"

"You can tell Jamis Quinn that I have no intention of selling my grandmother's house. He's stuck with us, Mr. Romney. Goodbye."

"Wait! Natalie!"

She held the phone.

"You want to help kids. I get it, I do." Regret filled his voice. "But eventually your inheritance and your personal savings are going to run out. You may find it extremely difficult to raise funding for your project."

"I already have several donors interested."

"Things can change."

Had she heard correctly? "Are you threatening me?"

"No. Not at all. But I think you should consider that Wisconsin is full of lakes and lake homes that would suit your purposes. You should think about how many more children you could help with that additional funding."

He was right, but so wrong. "Mr. Romney, you probably think you know a lot about me, don't you?"

"Well, I—"

"I'm going to guess you know I was adopted." She took

a deep breath. "So to say that my ancestors built this home generations ago would be a lie. You probably also know that I came to live here when I was ten." She paused, stuffed her shaking hand into her jeans pocket. "What you can't find in any court documents or social services records and the reason why my attorneys refused to bring your offer directly to me is because they understand that Mirabelle Island was a dream come true for me."

Now it was his time for silence.

"I will get funding to continue this program in my grandmother's house if it's the last thing I do. This home is going to continue being a dream come true for a lot more kids. For years and years to come. I will never sell this house."

"You're sure about that?"

"As sure as I am of anything."

"I'll relay your answer to my client."

"Don't bother. I'll tell him myself." She slammed down the phone.

Angry as she could ever remember being, she marched out the door. The sharp sound of Jamis chopping wood filled the air as she charged through the woods to his house. The moment she rounded the corner and found him, his back to her as he worked his way through a pile of wood, she stopped.

Oh, crap, he isn't wearing a shirt.

Mesmerized by the sight of the flexing muscles of his bare back, she could only watch. His biceps pumped with every swing. His leg muscles worked to stabilize his body with every thrust. Her mouth grew dry, her cheeks turned flush. Air didn't seem to be making it past the lump in her throat. She wanted that body, naked and next to her. She wanted to touch and taste and feel. This ache for Jamis seemed to be destroying her from the inside out.

Wait a minute. She was angry with him. Wasn't she?

JAMIS SET THE LOG ON the chopping block, heaved the ax behind him and swung, splitting the wood in two. Keeping half on the block, he swung again, quartering the original piece. Another piece of wood. Another swing and a chop. Again. Again. Hard. Harder. As hard and fast as he could.

After having spent several ineffective hours at his computer, he'd finally given up and come outside to let off some steam. He was letting off steam all right, but his head wasn't any clearer than when he'd begun. He set another log on the block and grabbed his ax handle.

The softwoods, birch, cottonwood and ash weren't cutting it. Today, he needed hardwoods, oak and maple, to work off his demons. He had a damned book due by the end of the summer and he'd barely gotten past the first chapter. He could blame it on the kids distracting him, but that was nowhere near the truth.

It was Natalie. If it wasn't her smile and lighthearted laughter washing away the built-up grime on his soul, it was the look of her long legs in short shorts stirring things up inside him. It was the way she looked in the moonlight pulling him toward her. It was those lips beckoning to be kissed.

The woman was killing him. Even now, it was as if he could smell her on the slight breeze. He stopped swinging his ax in midair, closed his eyes and took a deep breath. She was here. He spun around to find her motionless and staring at him. Sunlight streamed through the trees and lit the soft glints of gold in her hair, but it was the want he saw mirrored in her eyes that sent a jolt to his groin, giving him an instantaneous hard-on.

After a moment, with only the sound of a chickadee piercing the silence, he whispered, "You shouldn't be here."

"I…" She blinked, as if coming to her senses. "I need to talk to you."

"Not now." He turned away from her and set another piece of wood on the chopping block.

"Yes. Now," she said, sounding distinctly irritated.

This time when he glanced back at her, her hands were on her hips and a scowl covered her face. She looked as worked up as he'd ever seen her, and, by God, still all he wanted to do was kiss her.

"I'm not selling my house."

"Good for you."

She didn't seem to know what to say about that. "Are you going to try to tell me that Charles Romney isn't your attorney?"

"No."

"So he is?"

"Yep."

"You are the most infuriating man." She looked perplexed, and he couldn't blame her. She had that exact effect on him. "Do we drive you that crazy that you can't coexist with us?" she asked.

He dropped his ax and walked toward her. "Day and night, I hear children laughing, talking, fighting. Playing." He ran his hands through his hair. "And when I don't hear them, I'm expecting them. To knock on my door. To bring me cookies. Invite me to the fire. Ask if they can watch—" He stopped and spun away. Dammit, he wasn't supposed to say anything about that.

"Watch TV?" she asked. "Is that what you were going to say? Someone came to your house and asked to watch TV?"

He kept his mouth shut.

"Galen?" She shook her head. "I'm sorry. I didn't—"

"No. You didn't." He glared at her and felt something

inside him give way. "But it's not only the kids. It's *you.* You have no clue what you do to me." *You drive me crazy. Thinking about you. Wanting you. I can't get you out of my mind.*

Her mouth parted and she seemed to lean toward him, as if the exact thoughts were running through her mind.

"I came to Mirabelle for peace and quiet, Natalie. You and your kids disrupt my world. I want to be alone."

"And you'll do whatever it takes to get me off this island?"

"Something like that."

"Even if it means blocking the possibility of obtaining future funding for my camp?"

"I don't know what you're talking about."

"At least I'm trying to make a difference, which is more than I can say for the people who hole themselves up in their homes, or their minds, or their islands, all alone insulating themselves from the rest of the world so they don't have to face reality."

"Is that what you think I'm doing?"

"You sit here day in and day out feeling sorry for yourself because you've lost your family. You went through a big trauma. I'll grant you that. But we all have heartache. We've all lost things. The difference between you and the rest of the world is that you're stuck in the past, and the rest of us have moved on."

"You finished?"

"Not even close." She stalked toward him. "You think you're the only one who has bad days? Nasty, depressing thoughts? Well, I've got news for you." She jabbed her finger into his chest. "You're not so special or unique. I have plenty of bad days. Some nights I cry myself to sleep. There are even times when I think maybe life would be easier if I shut myself off from the world and go hide on an *island* somewhere."

He clenched his jaw and waited.

"But I don't do that. You know why? Because I'm not going to give up. I refuse to go down waving a white flag. I'd rather be a Pollyanna any day than a coward."

Her words hung for a moment in the still air between them.

"That's what you think I am?" he whispered. "A coward?"

"Yes." As if someone had tossed water on her angry fire, she seemed to sputter out. Her shoulders drooped and her brow furrowed. "I thought you were a decent person, Jamis. Inside. I thought…we'd made a bit of a connection. I was wrong. So, so wrong. I can't believe you'd stoop so low as to try cutting me off at the knees."

He wanted to object, defend himself, but he kept silent. It would be better for them both for her to continue thinking so little of him.

"We'll leave you alone, Jamis." She turned and stalked away. "From now on, you can go ahead and rot in your own personal hell!"

Jamis watched her march off into the woods. "It's about time," he said aloud. "Good riddance to you. And your kids."

She'd no sooner gone into her house, letting the porch door slam behind her, than she was stalking back outside carrying a hammer.

Now what was she up to?

A moment later, he had his answer. She ripped every one of his no-trespassing signs off his trees and pounded them into her trees, facing his property. Angrily, he swung his ax, splitting the log in two with one strike. Who did she think she was? And had she really called him a coward? Went to show what she knew and understood about him. There was nothing wrong with wanting to be left alone.

But he hadn't wanted it to be at her expense.

Son of a bitch. He stalked into his house and dialed a number on his phone.

"Romney, here."

"What did you say to her, Chuck?"

"Hello to you, too, Jamis." He sighed. "I told her to name her price and it was hers."

"And?" Jamis paced by his kitchen counter.

"She turned it down."

"So you countered with?"

"I told her it might be difficult for her to raise funding for next year."

"And what exactly did you mean by that statement?"

"You told me to do whatever it takes."

Jamis ran a hand over her face. "Did I say that?"

"Yes. You did."

He could've. He *would've.*

"So I did some digging to find out how she's funding this," Chuck went on. "Her inheritance and personal savings will last a year or two. After that, she'll have to finance this deal with donations and grants. I've got a list of the people and organizations she's soliciting."

"You haven't done anything yet to sabotage her obtaining that funding, have you?"

"No. I was just throwing it out there to see if we could get her to take an offer. You say the word and—"

"No." Jamis closed his eyes. "Drop it. Right now. If anything, put in a plug for her *and* her camp."

"Jamis, what's going on?"

"I was wrong. Simple as that. Make an anonymous donation to her camp from my account." He looked around his cabin, a stronghold and prison all rolled into one. "And find me a private island for sale. Anyplace but here!"

"JUST IN TIME!" MISSY exclaimed the moment Natalie and her kids entered the gift shop. "Everything your kids are making is flying off the shelves. I hope you've brought more inventory."

"We certainly did," Natalie said.

Almost a week had passed since Jamis's attorney had called and their resulting argument outside when he'd been chopping wood. Since then, she'd vigilantly kept the kids on their side of the tree line. The result had been some very productive crafting sessions. Galen set a box full of their wares on Missy's counter, and Natalie handed her an itemized list of what they'd brought this time.

"Looks good," Missy said, handing Natalie a check and a statement. "And here's the payment for everything I've sold so far."

Natalie scanned the list of what Missy had sold and the amount due each child. "Woo-hoo, Sam! You topped out at a hundred and twenty-five bucks."

Sam grinned. "That's how much I made?"

"Yep."

"What about me?"

"And me!"

"Me, too."

One by one, she relayed how much each child had made from the sale of their crafts. Galen was the only disappointed one in the crew, but that was to be expected since he'd dragged his feet up until the past week or so. "You'll do better next time," Natalie offered.

"I know," Galen said. "It's my own fault." He'd begun making key chains and wristbands using leather products and had cut and burned his own designs into the smooth tanned surface.

As the kids filed out of Missy's store, Missy held Natalie back. "You okay? You look tired."

"We've been busy."

"You need a break."

"No, I can't—"

"One entire night alone."

"I don't like to be al—"

"I'm not taking no for an answer." Missy stuck her head outside and called out to the kids, "Who wants to go camping tonight with me?"

"You mean sleep in a tent?"

"Yep." Missy nodded.

"Yeah!"

"Cool!"

"I'm in!"

Every single one of the children was excited, even Galen.

"There. Done." Missy turned back to Natalie. "Relax tonight. Glass of wine and a movie. A full night's sleep. Tomorrow, you'll be a new woman."

Knowing Missy wasn't going to budge, Natalie accepted the fact that she needed a break. After they left Missy, Natalie cashed the check at Mirabelle's little corner bank and doled out cash to each one of the kids.

"Let's go to the candy store!" Chase exclaimed.

"Totally!" agreed Blake.

"Are you sure that's what you want to do with your money?" Natalie asked.

The kids glanced at each other.

"You can save or spend, it's completely up to you, but it might be wise to decide on how much you want to spend before you go to the store. That way you won't eat into the amount you want to save."

There were nods all around, and she took them to Mrs. Miller's candy store. They'd all agreed to spend no more than five dollars each, except for Sam and Galen. They both swore they were saving every penny of their earnings.

"How are you doing today, Mrs. Miller?" Natalie said, going to the front counter.

"I'm good, Natalie." Mrs. Miller was watching all the kids as they wandered around the store, suspicion clouding her eyes as her gaze settled on Galen.

"Is it bothering you that I bring the kids here?" Natalie asked.

"It's nothing against you, dear," the woman whispered. "But I did hear a rumor about your older boy causing some trouble."

Natalie tried to stay calm, but this prejudice against her kids was bothering her more than she'd expected. "Are you referring to Galen?"

Mrs. Miller nodded.

At the mention of his name, Galen moved a little closer to Natalie and seemed to tune into their conversation.

"Can't be too careful these days," Mrs. Miller went on. "Honestly, I'm not sure Mirabelle is the right place for your camp."

"Kids!" Natalie called. "Pick out what you want and come on over here and pay for it. It's time to go." She leaned toward Mrs. Miller and said softly, "After today, we'll take our business to the other candy store." It would be a bit longer of a walk toward the other end of town, but they might be more welcoming.

As soon as they got outside, Natalie turned to Galen and whispered, "Do you know what Mrs. Miller was talking about?"

"No." Galen shook his head. "I swear I haven't done anything wrong."

Natalie watched him walking away with the rest of the kids and kept her fingers crossed he was telling the truth.

CHAPTER ELEVEN

"TEN THOUSAND DOLLARS?" Standing in the kitchen later that night, Natalie almost dropped the phone. Missy had no sooner collected all the kids for their campout at the state park on the island than her attorney had called to give her the good news. "Someone donated that much to my summer program?"

"No strings attached," her attorney said.

"Who is it?"

"That particular one was anonymous, but there are several others who've promised some fairly substantial amounts."

"Why all of a sudden?"

"Someone, somewhere put in a good word for you."

Jamis. He had to be behind this.

"I thought you'd be more excited."

"Oh, I am. This is great. Thanks." She hung up the phone and glanced out the window toward Jamis's cabin. Oddly enough, she missed the sound of his voice, his sardonic looks and even his sarcastic comments, and this big house seemed awfully quiet without the children.

No, you are absolutely not going over there!

She ran a bath and threw in some scented salt. Next, she lit a candle, turned on some soft music and got ready for a night of blissful peace and quiet.

JAMIS LAY ON HIS SOFA with Snickers stretched out along-side him. He stared up at the knotty pine ceiling absently petting the dog's head. Jazz played softly. The only light in the room came from a dim lamp in the corner and a small blaze burning in the stone fireplace. It was exactly the kind of idyllic, quiet night Natalie might intrude upon and ruin. Not that he wanted her to. It just made sense to brace for a possible attack.

Then again, he hadn't seen her since that day she'd called him a coward and told him to rot in hell. He still couldn't believe she'd had that in her. He deserved everything she'd said, but that didn't make it any easier to swallow.

A tap sounded on the patio door. Snickers perked up and raced across the room. Then the door slid open. "Hey, Snick."

He glanced over to see Natalie patting the dog's head. She was in a sweatshirt and sweatpants and her hair was wet as if she'd just stepped out of the shower. She smiled uncertainly. "Want some company?"

"Do I have a choice?"

At first she didn't say anything. "I've been thinking." She stayed where she was, the door cracked open behind her. "We started off on the wrong footing."

"You think?"

"Can we back up?"

"Why? What's the point?"

"I'll leave if you really want me to."

He hesitated. God help him, but he wanted her to stay. "There's a bottle of wine up on the counter. Help yourself."

She slid the patio door closed, kicked off her flip-flops and went barefoot into the kitchen. He heard her moving from cupboard to cupboard. He would've told her where to look for a glass, but there was something comforting about the sounds of someone, another body, a real live person rummaging around in his house.

A moment later, she came back into the great room, set the bottle of wine on the coffee table and sat on the other half of the oversize sectional sofa. Snickers jumped up next to her and rested his head in her lap. For an instant Jamis imagined her fingers on *his* head, smoothing back his hair.

"I'm sorry," she whispered. "For all those harsh things I said to you the other day when I was angry. About you being on this island. And being a coward."

"Everyone has a right to their opinions."

"Having them is different than voicing them."

"I deserved it, didn't I?" He shrugged, sloughing it off, though for some reason, her opinion of him was beginning to matter. "If not for that, surely for something else."

"I started reading *Lock and Load* the other night."

He said nothing.

"You're an amazing writer." She took a sip of wine. "I couldn't put the book down for hours, but it was a little like a train wreck."

"That's life, isn't it?"

"Don't you ever write anything…nice?"

He just stared at her.

"Isn't there enough pain in the world already?"

"When people read my books, their own pain seems less significant."

"So is that why you write?" Disbelief tainted the sound of her voice. "To help people?"

He sat up, took a sip of wine and cocked his head at her. "I think you know the answer to that question."

"Then why *do* you write?"

"Because I have to." He was quiet for a moment. "These stories hit me, take over my mind and it seems the only way to get rid of them is to write them down. I can't… I don't know what I'd do if I couldn't write."

"That sounds as if you don't enjoy writing."

"Most of the time, I do. It can feel good to lose myself for a while. Building worlds and immersing myself in them." His gaze turned intense. "I like stepping into other people's lives and knowing what's going to happen. I like the sense of control. I can stop things from happening. Or make things happen. What I say goes."

"Your characters don't do anything you're not expecting?"

"Never."

"What about if—"

"Why did you come over here?"

"The kids are gone. Camping with Missy Charms for the night."

"And you were bored."

She looked away. "I don't like to be alone."

"Why does that not surprise me?"

She shrugged. "I ate dinner, then primped and pampered myself until I couldn't stand it anymore. Now here I am."

All primped and pampered. Her face glowed as if she'd scrubbed it with some mask. If the fresh coat of pink polish was any indication, she'd given herself a manicure and a pedicure. She'd probably even shaved her legs. He closed his eyes against the images of lots of bare skin flashing through his mind.

Oblivious to his thoughts, she stood and walked around. "I can't believe you did all the work on this house yourself."

"The winters here are quiet. And last a while."

"How long did it take?"

"Two years."

She raised her eyebrows.

"It's not such a big deal." He swung his feet down off the couch and watched her. "I had a lot of time on my hands, and I needed the physical and mental outlet."

"Interesting."

"What?"

"Other than these landscapes." She pointed to a set of four pictures he'd taken of the seasons on Mirabelle. "You have no photographs. Anywhere."

"So?"

"Your children?"

"It's…still painful to look at pictures of Caitlin and Justin."

Her expression softened. "Nice names."

He looked away and gulped down some wine.

"What about the rest of your family? Your parents?"

"We're not very close." That was putting it mildly.

"Where do they live?"

"In Minneapolis." He refilled his wineglass. There probably wasn't enough left in the bottle for this turn in the discussion.

"And they never visit?"

"Good God, no."

"Don't you keep in touch with them at all? Even with phone calls?"

"I haven't talked to my dad in…at least six years. He was in China, arranging some buyout or something and didn't bother coming to the funeral for his own grandchildren. That's the last time I saw my mother. She phones occasionally, but all she does is drone on and on about a particular charity drive she'd organized or some society event she and my dad had attended. She's a cliché."

"That's cruel."

Silently, he studied her for a moment. "She was a cruel mother. I have a memory or two of her being relatively attentive when I very young, but for most of my life, she was absent, apathetic or in one way or another disinterested."

"I'm sorry."

"Why? My poor little rich boy childhood can't possibly be worse than yours."

"Strangely enough, sometimes bad attention is better than none. You have no siblings to commiserate with?"

He shook his head. "I don't think my mother and father ever intended on being parents, and they had no clue what to do with their strange, introverted and grossly shy son who didn't fit their lifestyle." He took a sip of wine. "My father couldn't relate to me, so he didn't bother, and my mother, quite simply, rejected what she couldn't understand."

"How did you do at school?"

"Teased, ridiculed. As a nerdy teenager, I disappeared into my stories."

"Did you always write?"

He chuckled. "I wrote my first book when I was eight. It was a short story, only about twenty pages, but by the time I was sixteen, I'd written five complete novels. They weren't half-bad, either. Sold a couple of them later with a few rewrites. College was actually a relatively peaceful time in my life. Had my first date when I was a junior. That was interesting."

"So you were twenty before you had your first date?"

"You're too good-hearted to see the truth, but people don't like me, Natalie. Especially women. At best, I'm strange. At worst an outright asshole. Either way, I'm not a nice person."

"That's not true." She shook her head, releasing the minty smell of her shampoo. "You've just been telling yourself that for so long, you don't see the Jamis you've matured into. The Jamis I'm coming to know is an articulate, confident, fascinating and…handsome man."

He wanted to believe her, but the last time he trusted a woman who was attracted to him he not only had his heart broken, Katherine might as well have run it through a shredder, poured gasoline over the remains and tossed a match. "I'm no different today than I was all those years ago."

"Then maybe your perception of who you were then is shaded, as well."

A truce was one thing, but he didn't like this turn in the conversation. Or his thoughts. He spun away from her, went into the kitchen and poured himself a glass of water, hoping to clear his head.

She studied the landscape photos he'd framed. "Did you take these?"

He nodded. "Here on Mirabelle."

She pointed. "I like the winter picture."

He remembered the morning he'd taken that shot. A heavy, wet snow had settled on the trees and rocks. It was difficult to tell the cloudy sky from the ice-covered lake, the lake from the rocks. The world was white.

She pointed to the storm, lightning and rain, hovering over the water some five miles away while the sun beamed down on Mirabelle. "Is this in the summer?"

"August three years ago." Back when he'd still marveled at Mirabelle's beauty. He walked toward her.

"I can't tell spring from fall."

"Spring." He pointed to the one with tall waves crashing against the shore.

"Is that ice?" she asked, leaning in for a better look.

"There and there." He reached over her shoulder, pointed at the waves, and the scent of her skin, clean soap and warmth, distracted him for a moment. "Those chunks are huge, but you can barely see them." He closed his eyes and breathed her in.

"So that's fall, then," she said, indicating the photo of the ferry loaded down with tourists leaving the island. "Why?"

He looked down at her profile, curious and beautiful. "I look at that when I need to remind myself that the madness of summer tourist season will eventually end."

She chuckled. "Oh, Jamis."

"You think I'm kidding?" And that was when he knew that he would feel differently about this fall because this time around she'd be leaving with all those annoying tourists.

She looked up at him with that wondrously warm smile on her face and stared into his eyes. When she reached out to trail her fingers down his cheek, he froze. Her smile slowly dimmed as heat filled her eyes.

"Natalie, don't—"

She wrapped her hands around his neck, reached up and kissed him. Backing him against the wall, she pressed into him. "I've been wanting to do that all night," she murmured.

He held completely still for a heartbeat, two at most, and then as if a cord finally snapped inside him he drew her into his arms. His answering kiss came hard and fast. There was nothing tentative in his touch. He'd crawled through a four-year desert and she was a cool spring rain waiting for him on the other side.

Lifting her onto the countertop, he stepped between her legs and bracketed her head with his hands, holding her there, devouring her. Then he trailed his hand along her neck, over her breast and dipped his fingers under her shirt.

"It's not enough," she whispered. "More."

He flicked the clasp on her bra and cupped her breast.

She shuddered and groaned beneath his hand. "More, more, more." She dragged his shirt up and over his head, than splayed her hands over his chest. "This is crazy," she whispered. "I want you so badly."

When he dragged his hand along her stomach, she pulsed toward him and he inched beneath her waistband. She groaned and shifted, putting his fingertips only inches from her sweet warmth.

"Touch me." She pressed his hand lower, and lower still.

He shuddered at the first feel of her, swollen and wet and wanting him to take her, right then and there. "You feel like…" He sucked in a ragged breath and stopped. Clenching his jaw, he pushed away from her. "I don't have a right to this," he whispered. "I don't have a right to you."

She opened her eyes, looked dazed from his touch. She wanted him. He wanted her.

"Jamis—"

"Son of a bitch!" He raked his hands through his hair. "All these years alone." He closed his eyes and turned away. "You make me want to live again."

"Is that so bad?" She reached out to caress him.

"Damn right, it's bad!" He spun away. "Before you came here, I was fine. Resigned, if not entirely content. You're here a month or so and you and your kids are messing with me. Making me feel things I haven't felt in years. Making me hope. Making me dream. Making me… want." *You.*

"Jamis, I'm not asking for forever. I'm not even expecting tomorrow. I just want tonight."

She made it sound so harmless, so perfect. And with everything in him he wanted to believe it was okay. One night. Hadn't he suffered enough? She moved toward him, and from there it all happened so fast, he wasn't sure if it was real or a dream. One minute they were in each other's arms again and they were kissing and the next Natalie was naked on the floor and he was driving himself into her as if a demon was chasing him.

He looked into her eyes and felt a connection with her that he'd never felt with anyone. Then she groaned and shifted her hips to meet him. One more thrust and he felt her orgasm pulsing around him. And that was all she wrote. Like Lake Superior waves crashing against the rocky shore, they collided, came together in one violent upheaval.

A few moments later, as residual tremors faded and sanity returned, he rolled off her. "Holy hell," he whispered. He hadn't even paused long enough to take off his pants. Confused and even slightly disoriented, he zipped back up. "That wasn't supposed to happen."

"Not that fast, at least." She sat up.

"Not ever." He sucked in a shaky breath. *Dammit all. Damn Natalie. Damn this island. Damn this life.* He'd fucked up everything. His marriage. His children. Why him? Why, why, why?

"Jamis, are you—"

"You need to leave." He stood.

"Why?"

Keeping his eyes averted, he gathered up her sweats and held them out to her. If he saw her naked beauty again, there was no telling what might happen.

She took her clothes and he could hear her dressing. "Can we talk about what just happened?"

"A mistake happened." He couldn't look at her face, couldn't bear to see the hurt he heard in her voice. "Nothing more, nothing less."

"It didn't feel like a mistake to me."

"Natalie, leave. Before we make this night any worse."

"Why are you closing yourself off from the world? Protecting yourself so fiercely?"

He looked at her then, and he'd never seen a more tragic sight. Her hair mussed. Her lips slightly swollen from his kisses. Her neck reddened by his beard. Her eyes clearly showing her vulnerability. She'd been marked by him and he damn sure didn't have a right to claim anyone. "It's not me I'm protecting."

"Then who?"

"You."

"From what?"

"Me." He gritted his teeth, knowing he had to shut her down. "Tonight was about one thing and one thing only. Sex. Don't read anything more into it than it deserves."

"You're wrong," she whispered.

"Am I?"

Suddenly, she didn't look so sure.

"You're a woman," Jamis said. "And you were here. That's all there is to it."

"This isn't over," she said, slowly backing toward the door.

"Yes. It is." Fighting the urge to withdraw everything he'd said, Jamis turned his back on her. As the patio door slammed shut behind him, he smelled her sweetness on his hands. "For your sake." Then he reached for a bottle of wine, hoping to wipe the memory of her naked and beneath him completely from his mind.

NATALIE'S CHEEKS BURNED with humiliation as she ran through the woods. The possible physical complications of no protection didn't bother her overly much, given it was the wrong time of the month by at least a few days. She was safe and healthy, and Jamis having had no sex since he'd come to Mirabelle meant he was most likely safe as well. But how could she have let tonight happen? How could she have gotten carried away by a man's touch to the point of losing all sense of reason?

Because Jamis's touch *had* carried her away. Their encounter may have been a record quickie for her, but it was the most satisfying orgasm she'd ever experienced.

And what had it all meant to Jamis? Had it been simply a mistake? Spontaneous, earth-shattering and over far too quickly, yes, but a mistake? If not a mistake, had it truly been just about sex? Then why ask her to leave?

Feeling confused and raw to the bone, she stopped and glanced behind her, panting for air. Dim light spilled out through Jamis's windows into the night. He was in his kitchen, pacing and drinking wine straight from the bottle. Suddenly, he stopped, slammed the wine down on the counter and covered his face with his hands.

No. Tonight was not a mistake. And he knew it.

JAMIS AWOKE THE NEXT morning to the shrill sound of his phone ringing. He held his head as a raging pounding shot through his skull. A hangover. Damn, it'd been a long time since he'd had one of those. In an effort to stop the noise, he grabbed the phone. "What?"

"Good morning to you, too." It was Stephen. "Worked things out with your publisher. They're giving you another six weeks. That's the best I could do. The book is now due November fifteen. You gotta get it done before Thanksgiving. Can you do it?"

Did he have a choice? "Sure."

"Jamis—"

"I said no problem."

"My, but you're crankier than normal this morning. Hangover?"

"Screw you, Stephen." He hung up and tossed the phone onto the bed.

After dragging himself to the bathroom, he puked all but his guts out. On standing up, he caught his reflection in the mirror and stared. Who was that man with his scraggly beard and too-long hair? He looked nothing like the image in his mirror for most of his life, nothing like the clean-cut man on the back cover of his books. *I look like a freaking wild man.* How had that happened?

"Well, I've had enough of you." He grabbed a pair of scissors and a razor and chopped, trimmed and shaved. By the time he was finished, aside from a few more wrinkles and severely bloodshot eyes, his reflection looked damned close to the old Jamis. Then he crawled back to bed, covered his head with a pillow and passed out again.

CHAPTER TWELVE

AMIDST THE CHATTER OF eight children finishing break-fast, Natalie stood at the counter making a last batch of waffles, lost in thought. More than a week had passed since that fateful night at Jamis's house, and she still couldn't get the feel of him, or the way he'd made her feel, out of her mind. Being with him had felt so perfect, so right, it was hard to feel any degree of shame over what had happened. What would an entire night with Jamis be like?

But that wasn't likely to happen. Even if she managed another night alone this summer, Jamis would never let it happen. Why did he feel the need to protect her from him? What had he done? And why was she so bound and deter-mined to break through to him?

The waffle iron started steaming. "Okay, who wanted more?"

"Me," Chase said.

"And me." Blake raised his hand.

She split the waffle between Chase and Blake. As she headed back to the counter, she glanced up through the kitchen window hoping to catch a glimpse of Jamis through the trees. No such luck. Either he'd barricaded himself in his cabin or he was doing an awfully good job avoiding her.

The sound of a golf cart drew her gaze to the path through the woods only a moment before the island's chief of police, Garrett Taylor, drove into her yard. "I'll be right back." She set the waffle iron down and went outside. "Hello there, Chief Taylor. It's good to see you again."

He stepped from the cart and shook her hand. "Natalie, you gotta start calling me Garrett."

"Hard to do with you looking so official in your police uniform, but I'll try to remember." When Natalie had discussed the minor renovation work she'd wanted him to do on the house, he'd been wearing jeans and a faded work shirt. "By the way, congratulations on your marriage."

He grinned and ducked his head. "Thank you." For such a big tough guy, he certainly looked whooped.

"But you didn't come all the way out here for small talk, though, did you?"

"I'm sorry, no." His smile disappeared. "Last night there was a break-in at the Hendersons'. A bunch of movies and CDs were stolen along with several hundred dollars from a bank deposit bag."

Natalie's brain started buzzing. "And?"

"One of your camp kids, Galen, was seen heading through the woods not far from the store about the time of the theft."

"What time?"

"Around midnight."

"But he was home. In bed."

"You know that for sure? You saw him?"

She thought back. As usual, she went to bed around eleven after checking on the younger kids. But she'd passed on Sam and Galen, thinking they had a right to some privacy. Had he snuck out sometime during the night? "No, I didn't see him here at midnight." She had to be honest, no matter how protective she felt toward her kids. "You need to talk to him? See if he was there and saw anything?"

"Please."

"Do you want to come in?"

"I think it'd be better if he came out here."

That didn't sound good. "You don't think he did it, do you?"

"Just have him come out, Natalie, please."

"I'll get him." But when she turned around Galen was already stepping out onto the porch. Sam stood in the doorway with the younger ones filling in behind her.

"What's up?" Galen asked, glancing warily at Garrett.

"Could you come out here, please?" Natalie watched Sam's reaction. The teenager shook her head and rolled her eyes as if she'd expected this outcome. "Sam, can you take the kids inside and start cleaning up from breakfast?"

"Come on, guys." Sam closed the door.

Natalie shifted her attention back to Galen. "Chief Taylor would like to talk with you."

He came toward her, but his gaze turned guarded. "Yeah? What about?"

As Garrett glanced at Galen, his demeanor changed from pleasant handyman to suspicious cop in seconds flat. "Were you hanging out downtown last night?"

Galen glanced at Natalie.

"Tell him the truth," she said.

Galen hesitated. "Yeah. I was."

So he had snuck out of the house. Disappointment washed over Natalie, but she struggled to stay objective. This didn't mean he'd committed a robbery.

"Who were you with?"

Galen crossed his arms over his chest and that old, sullen look passed over his face.

"Galen," she said, "you snuck out of the house, so you know you're in trouble, but don't make this worse. If you don't have anything to hide, then there's no reason to not cooperate with Chief Taylor."

"I was with Dustin and Chad," he said. "And a couple of girls."

"What were you doing?"

"We played some foosball and pool and then we hung out in the woods for a while. Built a fire. Talked."

"Were you drinking?"

Galen didn't say anything.

"The truth," Natalie urged. "Lying will only make your situation worse."

"No," Galen bit out. He glanced at Natalie. It was clear her opinion was more important to him than Garrett's. "I was not drinking."

Garrett studied him. "Then why did we find empty beer cans and liquor bottles at your fire pit?"

"First off, it's not *my* fire pit, okay?"

"Relax." Natalie touched Galen's arm, but he shrugged her off.

"And the empty cans and bottles weren't mine."

"You telling me the others were drinking, but you weren't?"

"I got nothing else to say to you." He turned to go into the house.

"Friends don't give up friends, huh?" Garrett said. "Were you aware the Hendersons' store was broken into last night?"

Galen stopped, kept silent.

"There was a theft."

"Great. Just great." Galen shook his head and paced. "You think I did it, don't you?" He glared at Garrett, but when he turned his gaze to Natalie, a look of intense betrayal and hurt filled his eyes. "You can't do this to me," he yelled. "This isn't fair."

"Galen, settle down—"

"No, Natalie! I snuck out of the house, that's it. I didn't do anything else wrong."

"Garrett, have you talked to Dustin and Chad?" Natalie asked.

"Yep." Garrett kept his eyes on Galen. "They're both claiming that it was Galen's idea. That he's the one who broke the rear window and snuck inside." He paused, waiting for a reaction. "What do you think of your friends now?"

Galen looked away.

"If you didn't do it, then who did?" Garrett asked. "Did you see anyone else?"

At first, Galen didn't answer. Finally, through clenched teeth he said, "No. I didn't see anything."

"You're sure?"

"Positive."

Natalie took it one step further. "Do you know anything about the robbery? Anything at all that might help Chief Taylor?"

"No!" he yelled at Natalie. "Can I go now?"

She glanced back at Garrett.

"At the moment," he said, "that's all I need."

Without another word, Galen stalked back into the house. Natalie turned to Garrett. She was going to trust there was a wealth of compassion under that hulky, formidable exterior. "I think you should know that if Galen is charged with theft, the rules of my camp require he be sent home to Minneapolis immediately."

Garrett considered her. "That's a good rule."

"I have a zero tolerance policy with regard to breaking the law."

"Does he like it here? At your camp?"

Natalie felt her protective instincts kick into high gear. "He pretends not to, but I think he does."

"What's waiting for him back home?"

She sighed and rubbed a hand across her forehead. "A drug-addicted mother who steals from him and kicks him out of the house."

Garrett nodded. "Do you think he's telling the truth?"

Natalie paused, giving the question fair consideration. "Yes." She nodded. "I do."

"We lifted a couple prints off the scene," he said. "If Galen comes in on his own to get printed, that'll say a lot."

She nodded. "I understand."

"I'll do some more digging."

After Garrett left, Natalie went into the house. Sam had taken all the kids into the craft room and had gotten them all working on their projects. "Where's Galen?"

"Upstairs." Sam came out of the porch and dragged Natalie into the living room. "What happened?" she asked.

Natalie explained the situation.

"Those losers!" Sam crossed her arms. "I knew something like this was going to happen."

"Is that why you wouldn't go with them the other night?"

She nodded. "They're bad news."

"Sam, I need to talk to Galen. You got things under control down here?"

"Sure."

Natalie went upstairs and knocked on Galen's door. "Can I come in?"

"No."

"For sneaking out last night without permission, you're

grounded next Friday night." She waited for a protest, but nothing came. "I have something more important to say, and I don't want to say it from the hallway."

The door cracked open to show a defiant young man standing with his arms folded across his chest. "I might as well just pack my bags now, huh? Is that it?"

"No." She glanced into his face and her heart ached for all the pain, frustration and insecurities she saw there. "I wanted to tell you that I be—"

"Screw it!" He turned his back on her. "I'm just going to pack—" He stopped, spun around and stared at her. "You do? You believe me?"

She nodded.

"Why?"

She shrugged. "It's not that I don't think you're capable of stealing. In fact, I'm sure you are. Most people are. And I'll tell you something I've never told anyone else. I stole something from the Hendersons' store when I was about thirteen."

He was listening, studying her.

"A tube of mascara that I really, really wanted." She walked into his room and was happy that he didn't try to stop her. "My mother found out and made me go back and apologize. I felt ashamed about it for years."

"You still went to work at that store anyway?"

She nodded. "Bob and Marsha are good people. Working for them helped me get over a lot of guilty feelings." She tilted her head at him. "Kids steal for a lot of reasons. Attention. Sense of entitlement. For the fun or adventure. Every once in a while, they steal because they have to."

"Maybe I just wanted to impress someone," Galen said, trying to stay tough.

"No." She shook her head. He was testing her and she

understood. "I know, in my heart, that you didn't steal anything from the Hendersons. Because I know, in my heart, you wouldn't risk having to leave this island."

The sullen tough guy disappeared as he hung his head and looked away.

"Chief Taylor said they found some prints at the scene of the robbery. He said that if you go in to get fingerprinted that would send a strong message that you were innocent."

"I am innocent! I shouldn't have to prove it. It's supposed to be the other way around."

"Galen—"

"No, Natalie! If Chad and Dustin go in to get printed, then I will, too."

How could she argue with that? "The only problem is that if Chief Taylor believes there's enough evidence to charge you with this crime, then regardless of what I believe you'll have to go home."

"I get that," he said, pushing past her and down the hall. "I'll figure it out."

"Galen," she said, "you don't need to figure this out all alone."

"Yes. I do."

Much to Natalie's dismay, Galen refused any further discussions on the matter. The next time they went into town rumors of Galen having been involved in the robbery at Hendersons' had spread like wildfire. Missy had told her there'd even been a special town council board meeting to discuss whether or not her camp license would be renewed for next summer. By the time they were finished with their errands, Natalie had had enough.

"I'm sorry, Natalie," Galen said as they left the gift shop. "But I didn't do it. If they close down your camp, that'd be so unfair."

"Galen, you and I need to stop at the Hendersons'."

"You sure that's a good idea?"

"Bob's on the town council. I need to know what he's thinking." Natalie turned to the group.

"I'll get everyone home," Sam said.

"Thanks." Natalie sent her an appreciative smile. "We'll catch up in a few minutes."

"Come on, guys." Sam led the way to where they'd parked their bikes.

Natalie went into the Hendersons' store first and noticed Galen hanging back. She spun toward him. "Do you have anything to apologize for?"

"No."

"Then we need to explain that to these people and clear the air." She was glad to find Bob and Marsha together restocking one of the aisles. "Hey there, you two."

"Natalie!" Marsha hugged her. "It's so good to see you again." But her smile turned down when she noticed Galen's sullen expression. "Marsha and Bob, this is Galen." Natalie tugged him forward. "He has something to say to you."

Neither of the Hendersons said a word.

Slowly, Galen looked up from his study of his tennis shoes. "I didn't… I think you should know…I wasn't the one who broke into your store."

"There are a couple of witnesses who say otherwise," Bob said.

"They're lying," Galen said, his eyes turning angry.

"Do you know who did it, then?" Marsha asked.

Galen looked away.

"Whoever broke down the back door, stole a bunch of stuff and made quite a mess of things in here."

"I'm sorry, but it wasn't me," Galen said, crossing his arms.

"Why should we believe you?"

"You don't have to." He turned and headed toward the door. "Doesn't make any difference to me."

Bob sighed and glanced at Natalie. "There goes one stubborn young man."

"Do you believe him?" Marsha asked Natalie.

"I do." She nodded. "I don't know these other Mirabelle kids that are involved, but I know enough about Galen to know he's telling the truth."

"Those other boys got into some minor trouble last summer," Bob said. "Honestly, though, we don't know who to believe."

"You trusting him is enough for us, dear," Marsha said.

"Well, I don't think it's enough for the rest of the town." Natalie sighed. "I've heard there's a town council board meeting scheduled to talk about not renewing my camp application for next year." She glanced at Bob. "Is that true?"

Bob nodded.

"Are you still on the board?"

He nodded again. "The council will hold off on any final decisions until the police get to the bottom of this. I'll talk to Garrett and see if he can speed things up."

"I don't think anyone was too keen on having us on the island even before the robbery."

"You're not going to let that stop you, now, are you?" Bob asked with a smile.

As she caught up with Galen and the rest of the group, she noticed a somber mood had settled over every single kid. By now they'd all heard about what was happening with Galen, and were very likely aware of how some of the islanders were shunning their business.

She couldn't shake the feeling that Mirabelle may not have been the best place for this camp after all. Even worse, maybe camp alone wasn't enough to make a difference in the lives of these kids. Every single one of them needed a safe home and loving care all year-round. How could she ever trust another person to care for these children? How was she ever going to say goodbye? But what else could she do?

Her thoughts flashed on the house she'd inherited from her grandmother back in Minneapolis. It was big enough for four, maybe even six kids. She'd been planning on selling it to provide more funding for her summer camp, but maybe that wasn't the answer. Maybe the answer was a year-round group foster home.

Her stomach fluttered at the thought. She'd already gotten cleared as a foster parent during the licensing process for this camp, so that wouldn't be an issue. But what about the job she'd taken a leave of absence from for this summer? What about all her other commitments? What about her future plans for this camp?

How far would she go to make her dream happen?

By the time Jamis became fully aware of what he was doing, he'd not only made a huge batch of chicken noodle soup, he'd also cooked up two small pans of lasagna and a batch of tuna casserole. For some reason cooking had seemed like a reasonable outlet for all the pent-up frustration he was carrying around.

Almost two weeks had passed since he and Natalie had been intimate—the term *sex* seemed too cut-and-dried and the phrase *making love* inaccurate—and while he'd actually gotten some writing done, he'd been distracted. Five years without sex and he'd managed okay. One night, or should he say five minutes, with Natalie and he couldn't get the woman out of his mind.

Normally, he'd freeze all this food, but a better use

suddenly came to mind. By the time he'd split the food into individual serving containers and set off for town, it was after four o'clock. With Snickers on a leash by his side, he queried the first islander he recognized, Jan Setterberg. "Excuse me," he said.

She stopped and glanced at him, surprise mixed with wariness registering on her face. "Yes?"

"Can you tell me where Sally McGregor lives?"

"Why?" she asked, understandably suspicious of him.

"Because…I wanted to take her some meals."

"Seriously?"

He nodded.

She studied him another moment. "You are a very strange man."

"I'm aware of that."

"Big yard behind the church—1215 Maple."

"Thank you." He walked past the church and found Sally's house, a redbrick French Colonial with white trim and a green shingled roof, and headed up the sidewalk, carrying his pack filled with food. He knocked on the door and waited. Through an open upstairs window, he could hear movement, someone coming down the stairs.

She opened the door. "What the—?" She stopped, blinked, took a moment to recognize him, clean shaven as he now was. "What are you doing here?" she asked, self-consciously running a hand over her bald head.

"I…heard you were sick."

"So?"

"So I made you some meals. Just in case you're too tired to cook for yourself."

Staring at him as if a bug-eyed green alien had just burst out of his chest, she tightened her pale blue robe.

"Look, I know it seems odd, but we all know I'm

an…odd kind of guy. So here." He unzipped his pack and held out several of the containers. "Take these."

She glanced at the offering, then up at him and backed away from the door. "Why don't you come in, Jamis?"

Surprised, he stood there, unsure.

"Have you eaten dinner?" she asked.

"No."

"Then why don't we share something you brought?"

"That wasn't… I didn't mean…"

"Please." She paused. "More than the food, I could use the company."

Funny, so could Jamis. He stepped inside and closed the door behind him.

"So what did you make?" She walked toward the back of the house. "I hope it isn't stew. After the mediocre batch Lynn Duffy brought over the other day, I don't care if I ever eat stew again as long as I live."

He followed her into the kitchen. "Chicken noodle soup. Lasagna. Tuna casserole."

"Well, I've never been much for tuna. You can take the casserole home with you." She turned around and then awkwardly said, "I'm sorry. I didn't mean—"

"You don't need to be sorry."

"I offend people. Seems I've gotten worse since my husband died some years ago."

"You don't offend me. I like the way you talk. I feel comfortable around you."

"Then we're a couple of sorry excuses for humans, aren't we?"

He nodded. "Sit. You look like you might fall down." He heated up one serving each of chicken noodle soup and tuna casserole in the microwave, dumped the contents into a couple of bowls and joined her at the table. This was the first time Jamis had shared a meal with a live human being in four years. For him, it felt strange and awkward.

They sat eating in silence for a short while. Finally, Sally said, "I see you've shaved and cut your hair."

"Yeah." He ran his hand along his smooth cheek. "Guess it was time."

"How's that kids' camp going?"

"Noisy."

She grunted. "If it's any consolation, I didn't want her on the island, either."

He glanced up. "Either?"

"There was quite a heated debate at the town council meeting when she first applied for that camp."

He'd probably gotten notice in the mail and had, as he did most things, tossed it out without reading. "They're good kids."

"Got you hoodwinked, anyway. She must be pretty."

He cocked his head at her.

"She is, isn't she?" Sally chuckled. "Do you like her?"

"She's…different."

"Well, that isn't saying a whole helluva lot, now, is it?"

Natalie's scolding that afternoon when he'd been chopping wood about him being stuck in the past, about him being a coward, hit him again, and again he found himself curiously offended. Why should he care what the woman thought of him?

"I'm planning on leaving Mirabelle," he said.

She glanced at him.

"As soon as I finish this next book and can find another place."

"Because of the camp?"

Because of her. "It's best I'm left alone."

"I hear the council's already considering not renewing her license for next year. You complain and—"

"No." He shook his head.

"It wouldn't take much. Not with people thinking that oldest boy of hers robbed the Hendersons."

"What? Galen?"

She filled him in on all the details.

"I can't believe he'd do that." He shook his head when she'd finished.

"This island's no place for that camp."

Jamis frowned and looked away.

"You disagree?" Sally asked.

He glanced up at her. "I don't know what I think."

She considered him for a moment. "Hmm. Interesting."

They finished the rest of their meal in silence. She never commented on the food, but he could tell the soup had met with approval. After they'd finished, he suggested she relax in the living room while he picked up the kitchen, put away the clean dishes in her dishwasher and loaded it with the dirty dishes in the sink.

After he'd finished, he found her sitting in an old and frayed easy chair in her den off the rear of the house. Her eyes were closed and her breathing even. Unsure what to do, he glanced around. Much to his surprise, bookcases lined every wall in the room, and it appeared she read everything from classic literature to genre fiction, including mysteries and romance. The books appeared alphabetized by author—popular, big names and more than a few surprises. There was even a row and then some of Quinn Roberts's books. He looked through the titles and it appeared she had every single book he'd ever published.

"I think I liked your last one the best."

He spun around to find Sally awake and watching him. "Why?"

She grunted. "The ending. Kinda left a reader guessing."

"Ha! My editor hated that ending, but I refused to change it." He'd gotten a lot of disgruntled reader letters over that one. "What did you think of *Harry Stone?*"

"Eh." She shook her hand in a so-so motion. "Not your best work."

He laughed.

"Not sure I'll be around to read your next one."

He fell quiet, considering her. He hadn't wanted to bother her with questions about her prognosis. What was the point? Pancreatic cancer seldom had hopeful outcomes. "I could print the manuscript off my computer. Would you like to read it now?"

"You know what I'd like even more? For you to read it to me." She paused, a scowl on her face. "My eyes aren't what they used to be."

He nodded. "I can do that."

The doorbell rang, and Sally scowled. "What is this, Grand Central Station?" When she opened the door Doc Welinsky was standing on the steps and holding a plastic container filled with what looked like food. "Willard," she whispered. "What are you doing here?"

"I thought you might be too tired to cook." He looked a little uncomfortable as something almost intimate passed between them.

A slight pink flush rushed to her cheeks. "Well, come on in then."

He stepped inside and pulled up short on seeing Jamis. "Sorry, Sally, I didn't know you had company."

"Doc has been administering my chemo treatments," she explained to Jamis.

He'd been wondering how she was accomplishing that on an island this size.

"You were getting ready to leave, weren't you, Jamis?"

"What?" Jamis was taken aback, until he noticed the look passing between Doc and Sally. "Um, yeah, I was about to leave." He took his cue and went out the front door. *Well, I'll be damned.* Maybe gruff old Sally wasn't as lonely as he'd thought.

CHAPTER THIRTEEN

NATALIE AWOKE AROUND midnight feeling as if she was going to die. Staggering to the bathroom, she barely made it to the toilet before vomiting violently. Even after her gut was empty, dry heaves racked her body. Finally, exhausted, she rinsed out her mouth and glanced in the mirror, expecting to find a rash covering her face. This felt like her allergy to shellfish, but there was no rash. She glanced down at her arms and her stomach. No rash there, either. A new kind of food allergy? Or food poisoning? No, the kids would be sick, as well. Had to be the flu.

As she opened the bathroom door the knob fell off in her hand. Great. If it wasn't one thing it was another. Then she heard the steps creaking. She walked down the hall but stopped when she noticed movement on the stairs, a figure sneaking up the steps.

"Galen?" she whispered. "What's going on?"

He spun around. "I was…outside…going for a walk."

"After midnight?" She took a deep breath, steadying her stomach. "Are you lying to me?"

He clenched his jaw. "I went to talk to Dustin and Chad."

"Why?"

"Because they lied to Chief Taylor."

"You don't need to do that. Garrett will get to the bottom of this." Although he hadn't sounded too positive when

Natalie had called to inform him that Galen refused to be fingerprinted unless the other two boys came in, as well.

"And what if he doesn't? Then what?"

She held her stomach.

"You look sick," he said. "Are you okay?"

"There must've been something we ate at dinner that I'm allergic to. Either that or I've caught a flu bug."

"Do you need anything?"

"Yeah. To be able to trust you. To not have to worry about you sneaking out at night anymore." She held her stomach as another wave of nausea rolled over her. "To not have to worry about whether or not you're doing your job of taking care of the younger kids while I'm sick in bed tomorrow." And she was going to be sick, very likely for a couple of days.

"I'm sorry, Natalie," Galen whispered. "I'll let Sam know what's going on. We'll take care of everything. I promise."

She wobbled to her room and collapsed onto the bed.

AFTER A RESTLESS NIGHT's sleep, Jamis had gotten up and gone straight to his computer to write a scene that had come to him in a dream. He'd made breakfast and, on a roll of sorts, returned to his office. He sat in front of his computer now, frustrated that he couldn't get this scene perfected. Something wasn't playing out properly and he couldn't figure out the problem. Deciding to break for a while, he went to the kitchen and made himself a roast beef sandwich.

It'd been close to three weeks since he'd seen Natalie, giving him a glimpse of what it would be like around here come September. Quiet. Peaceful. Back to normal. And incredibly lonely. The house seemed, somehow, too quiet, so he went outside onto the deck. A fragrant summer breeze met him the moment he stepped through the patio door, but there were no sounds of children playing, laughing or fighting. In fact, now that he thought about it, he'd heard nothing from Natalie and the kids all day. Everything was too quiet, and it wasn't even Sunday.

He took a few uneasy bites of his sandwich. Something wasn't right. "Come on, Snick. Let's check it out." Within minutes, he was knocking at the back door of the Victorian. "Natalie?" He could hear the TV blaring inside the house, but it seemed to take forever for someone to answer the door.

"Hi," Sam said, holding a dishrag in her hand. "What's up?"

"I haven't seen anyone out and about today." He stepped inside the house to find Galen ineffectively cleaning a kitchen in a state of total disarray. "What's going on?" Stacks of dirty dishes filled the sink and counter, and sticky pots and pans covered the stove. A kitchen chair was pushed up against the counter as if someone short had needed to reach a high shelf.

He stalked into the living room to find couch cushions dislodged, every table littered with dirty cups, cans and bowls, and the younger kids watching TV. "What's going on here?"

The kids shot out of their respective seats, as if caught in some wayward act. Someone reached for the remote and lowered the sound on the TV. "Umm. Nothing," Ella said.

"We were just watching some TV," Arianna added.

He glanced from one face to the next.

"I'm hungry," Blake said.

"Me, too," his brother, Chase, agreed.

"You guys just ate," Sam said, disgusted.

"Where's Natalie?" Jamis asked.

"Sick," Galen answered from where he was filling up the dishwasher.

"With what?" Jamis walked into the kitchen.

"Some kind of food allergy or the flu."

"Since when?"

"Last night."

"Where is she?"

"Sleeping in her bedroom."

"Which is?"

Sam pointed. "Down the hall."

Getting oddly angrier by the minute by their obvious lack of concern, Jamis walked toward Natalie's room. He passed a bathroom and another room that appeared to be a laundry room and knocked on the only closed door at the end of the hall. "Nat, are you in there?"

A low groan was the only response. On opening the door, he found the shades drawn and the room dark and cool and a figure balled up under the covers. He sat on the edge of the bed and brushed the hair from Natalie's face. Her skin pale, she lay on her side. "Jamis, is that you?" she whispered, reaching up to touch his cleanly shaven cheek. "You shaved and cut your hair."

"Yeah."

"Why?"

Because he was sick of himself, only cleaning himself up hadn't changed much of anything. "Needed a change."

"I'm sick."

"I can see that." He felt her forehead. She didn't have a fever. *But, dammit, why wasn't anyone taking care of her?* He searched the room, found a heavy blanket in the closet and folded it over her prone form. "Have you eaten anything today?"

"No, my stomach is too queasy. There must've been some type of shellfish in something I ate," she whispered. "Maybe it's the flu."

"Do you need me to get Doc Welinsky?"

"No, it's all out of me by now." Her smile was weak. "And I used an emergency shot of antihistamine to be on the safe side. I'll be better tomorrow."

Tomorrow. And in the meantime?

"Are the kids okay?"

"They're fine." But they needed supervision and he wasn't going to be able to walk away from this one with a clear conscience. "I'll keep an eye on them until you're better."

"You don't have to do that. Sam and Galen will take care of things." She closed her eyes and fell back asleep.

He pulled the blanket up to her chin and brushed a lock of hair from her face. The indomitably positive force of Natalie Steeger felled by a little shellfish. "Amazing." He quietly closed the door on his way out of her room.

On reaching the living room, he grabbed the remote and flicked off the TV.

"Hey!"

"Turn it back on."

"Who did that?"

"I did," Jamis said. "And if you ever want to see this remote again, you're going to have to get your butts in gear." He glanced at Sam and Galen as they came in from the kitchen. "Natalie put you two in charge, correct?"

They nodded.

"Then what are these guys supposed to be doing?"

"Helping us clean the kitchen," Sam said, glaring at all of the younger kids.

"But they kept ignoring us," Galen added.

"Well, the party's over, little ones," Jamis announced. "Get up and get moving."

His order was met with sighs and groans, but Sam and Galen did indeed take charge. Jamis supervised as dishes were washed, counters were wiped down, beds were made and laundry was done. He marveled at the bulletin board Natalie had prepared for the week, outlining not only a daily menu, but everyone's duties and responsibilities.

"Does this thing actually work?" Jamis asked Sam as she came into the room for cleaning supplies.

"Surprisingly, yes."

Today they were supposed to be having macaroni and cheese for lunch. He found the supplies in the cabinets, and an hour later the kids had been fed, the kitchen cleaned and the whole gang, per the chart, was outside for their daily dose of fresh air before craft time.

Jamis retrieved some chicken noodle soup from his freezer, heated it up and carried it in to Natalie along with a stack of soda crackers.

She cracked open her eyes. "What is that?"

"Chicken soup. Can you eat?"

"Probably not. Even the smell is making me nauseous."

He set the bowl on the bedside table, reached under her arms and lifted her up. His palms brushed the edges of her breasts, and the only thing stopping him from letting his hands linger for a while was the fact that she was as limp as one of the noodles in the soup.

"Try one of these first." He handed her a cracker.

She nibbled on an edge and then ate the rest. "That's sitting okay."

"Try some soup." He put a spoonful of broth to her lips.

She swallowed.

"Still okay?"

"So far so good."

He gave her another few sips and waited.

"Thank you," she whispered.

"This is a one-time deal," he grumbled. "Don't get used to it."

"THERE. THAT SHOULD DO it," Jamis said to Galen as the teenager tightened the washer on the new heavy-duty garbage disposal they'd installed under Natalie's kitchen sink. "What do you think?"

"Thanks for showing me how to do that." Galen slid out from under the sink.

"No problem."

Refusing to get involved in all that crafty business happening out on the porch, Jamis had figured he'd work on a few things around Natalie's house. Galen had chosen to help him. While Sam kept an eye on the younger kids, Galen and Jamis had spent the day fixing the doorknob on the main-floor bathroom, replacing a warped shelf in the pantry, unclogging both bathtub drains, fixing the basement stairs railing and installing a metal hose on the washing machine. The old rubber one had been cracked, the sure sign of a flooded floor waiting to happen. While there was a host of other projects to be done, one day wasn't enough for him to take care of anything more than the most pressing.

As they were putting tools away, steps sounded on the porch. "Hello in there," Garrett Taylor said through the screen door.

"Hey." Jamis opened the door for the police chief. "What can I do for you?"

Taylor eyed Galen as he stepped into the house. "Natalie here?"

"She's sick. A food allergy. Can't get out of bed."

"So you're helping with the kids?" He looked surprised.

For some unknown reason that irked Jamis more than it should have. He shrugged. "Neighbors helping neighbors, you know?"

"In that case, can I talk to Galen?"

"What do you need him for?" Jamis asked, feeling oddly protective of the kid after what Sally had told him.

"It's personal, Jamis. Galen, can you come outside?"

"No," Jamis said, stepping in front of Galen. "Either you tell me what you want, or you can come back another day when Natalie can be present."

Taylor glanced at the teenager. "You okay with me telling him what happened?"

The boy shrugged. "Whatever."

Jamis wanted to hear Taylor's side of the story, so he kept silent as the man relayed the details of a robbery of cash and hundreds of dollars worth of CDs and DVDs at Hendersons' and the allegations thrown at Galen.

Jamis glanced at the boy. "Did you have anything to do with the robbery?"

He shook his head. "No."

"Dustin and Chad said you threatened them the other night," Taylor said. "They claim you promised to kill them if they didn't lie for you."

"I never said that!" Galen's face turned red. "I told them to tell you the truth or I would."

"Galen," Taylor said. "What is the truth? You don't tell me, and all I've got to go on is their word."

Jamis put his hand on the boy's shoulder and held his gaze. "These guys aren't your friends, man. Your friends are here in this house. Tell Taylor the truth."

Galen hesitated. "I don't know for sure who robbed the Hendersons' store, but while we were around the campfire, Dustin and Chad started talking about raising some hell. The girls got up to leave, not wanting anything to do with their bullshit, and I left with them. And came home. That's all I know."

Taylor shook his head. "That's more than I had before."

"It's enough," Jamis said.

"Anything else you can remember?"

He shook his head. "No."

"There's one more thing to think about," Jamis said to Taylor. "Why would Galen steal a bunch of movies when they don't have a DVD player here?"

NATALIE CRACKED OPEN HER eyes to find her room pitch-black. She'd slept all afternoon and night had fallen. Before getting up, she munched on a couple of crackers Jamis had left on her bedside table. Feeling rather disoriented, but physically much better, she swung her feet down to the floor and stood. Most of the nausea had passed. Feeling a bit wobbly, she walked into the hallway. Except for soft light coming from the living room, the house was dark.

Only a few steps down the hall, she heard the steady sound of a deep, resonant voice. She paused and listened. Jamis was reading aloud from a popular young adult novel. The inflection in his voice was perfect for the dialogue, and his narrative intriguing and entertaining. Sneaking quietly toward the living room, she peeked around the corner.

Galen was lying on the floor with his eyes closed, but awake and quite likely listening. Snickers was snuggled up alongside Galen, sound asleep. Sam was sitting with her chair pulled up to an end table and using the bright lamp-light to illuminate the necklace she was making. Chase and Blake were lying on the floor on their stomachs, their chins in their hands, staring at Jamis. Arianna and Ella were curled up next to each other in one of the oversize chairs. What surprised Natalie more than anything were Ryan and Toni. They sat on either side of Jamis on the couch, snuggled into him as if he were a cuddly teddy bear.

They'd never even done that with her. Of course, she

may very well have discouraged it, not wanting them to get too attached. But look at him. Big, gruff Jamis, connecting effortlessly with all eight of her camp kids. If she hadn't seen it with her own eyes, she may never have believed it. And he seemed to be enjoying himself.

She watched his face, his smile, his eyes twinkling as he read to her kids. She wouldn't have thought it was possible, but he was even more handsome without the beard. Despite her weakened condition, arousal stirred low and deep. She wanted him again, fixer-upper or not.

Jamis glanced up, caught her gaze and suddenly looked a bit self-conscious. "Hey. You're alive."

All the heads in the living room turned toward her.

"How are you feeling?" Sam asked.

"Good." She stepped into the room. "I'm actually hungry."

"I can get you something." Galen stood, his hands stuffed in his pockets. "Jamis made tacos for dinner and there were some leftovers."

"Too spicy." She glanced at Jamis. "Is there any of that chicken noodle soup you gave me at lunchtime?"

"It's in the fridge, Galen. That blue container I brought over from my house earlier today."

"I'll heat some up for you." Galen disappeared into the kitchen. He was probably sucking up in the hopes he wouldn't get into too much trouble for sneaking out, but it still felt nice to be waited upon.

"I should probably go." Jamis shut the book.

"No!"

"Just one more chapter!"

"Please, Jamis?" Toni held his arm.

"Don't leave on my account." She plopped into one of the chairs so she could watch Jamis as she listened to him. "You have a very soothing voice."

"All right. One more chapter. And then from the looks of Natalie's chart, it'll be time for bed, but let's wait for Galen."

Galen brought in her bowl of soup and Natalie quietly sipped away as Jamis read another chapter. Like the kids, she felt as if she could've listened all night to him. By the time he'd finished, all of the kids looked sleepy.

"Bedtime." He closed the book.

This time without any grumbling, they all stood and started toward the stairs, even Galen and Sam.

Ryan straggled behind the rest. He turned on the first step. "Jamis, will you read again tomorrow night?"

Natalie felt her eyes grow wide. Ryan had actually spoken when he hadn't been spoken to.

"I'm not sure, Ryan. We'll see."

After the kids had gone upstairs, Jamis headed for the door. "I need to get home."

"Thanks for holding down the fort," she said. "You must have made quite an impression on Ryan. I've never heard him say more than one or two words at a time."

He opened the door and hesitated.

She didn't know what to say, how to be, at least not after everything that had happened between them this crazy summer.

His gaze skittered self-consciously away from hers as if he knew what she was thinking. "Snick, come on."

The dog had roused from his sleep, but sat in the living room staring at Jamis as if to say, "Do I have to?"

"Come, Snickers." He whistled.

The sight of the dog walking toward the back door was nothing short of comical. Head hanging low, he walked as slowly as he thought Jamis would tolerate.

"He liked being with the kids today," Jamis explained.

"Looked like you did, too."

"Me?" He shook his head. "I can't wait until September when you'll all be gone."

SEPTEMBER. IT WAS ABOUT a month away. Not long ago, Jamis had thought the end of summer couldn't come soon enough, but now he knew it would come too soon. Natalie—and the kids—would be leaving before the end of August.

Yellow light glowed from the windows of that big, old Victorian, beckoning him. In the shadows of the woods, he stopped and glanced back to see the lights on in the kids' bedrooms. He imagined them smiling, joking, talking, interacting with one another. Jamis had no more wanted to leave that house or the comfort of Natalie's presence than had Snickers. He wanted to be in that big, old house, with all those noisy kids, with her. Somehow, someway, the thought of leaving Mirabelle once Chuck found him a private island for sale didn't bother him nearly as much as the thought of being without Natalie.

CHAPTER FOURTEEN

SUNLIGHT HIT HER FULL in the face. That was strange. Natalie rolled over and glanced at her clock. Nine? In the morning? How in the world had she slept so late and why hadn't anyone woken her?

She sat up and nausea swept through her. Again. She'd been battling this flu for a couple of days. Running to the bathroom, she slammed the door behind her and vomited. For a moment, she felt better and then another wave of whatever the heck it was went through her. Brushing her teeth and rinsing out her mouth, she looked for the emergence of any kind of rash. Still nothing. She was positive she'd eaten nothing that normally caused her an allergic reaction. And as for the flu, it was odd that none of the kids had gotten sick—

"Oh, my God," she whispered to her suddenly pale reflection in the mirror. "I…can't be." How could she not have been paying attention? Because she'd thought she'd been safe. Her last period was—she counted back on the calendar. If she ovulated earlier than most women by several days, she could be. "Pregnant."

You don't know that. She put her hands on either side of the sink and waited out another wobble in her stomach. *Get through this morning. Get to the drugstore in town as soon as possible. And then everything will be fine.* She put on a pair of sweats and a T-shirt and found the kids in the kitchen cleaning up after breakfast.

"Ryan and Toni, it's your turn to wash and dry dishes," Galen said as he wiped off the countertops.

"I get to dry," Toni said.

"All right," Ryan murmured.

"I'll sweep," Sam said.

"And I'm taking out the garbage," Galen offered.

"Well, look at this," Natalie said. "Running like a smoothly oiled machine."

They all turned to look at her leaning against the door frame.

"Are you okay?" Galen asked.

"I couldn't get you to wake up," Sam said.

"You look sick," Toni said.

"Yeah, I'm not feeling very well this morning."

"More food allergies?"

"No. It's the flu. I'm going to run into town quick and get some medicine."

"I can go," Galen offered.

"Thanks." She smiled weakly. "But the fresh air might do me some good." She headed for the door and turned. "And thanks, Sam and Galen, for taking care of things. All of you, thanks."

As she glanced into each and every kid's eyes, a sense of overwhelming pride filled her. The summer was winding down, and they'd done okay. Every single one of them had grown these past couple of months. She felt herself getting emotional and quickly grabbed a baseball cap and headed out the door. "I'll be back in half an hour."

She glanced at Jamis's house as she pulled the cap low on her brow and kept her fingers crossed that she wouldn't run into him until she could reconcile herself one way or another to what would be. Not up to biking, she grabbed a golf cart and headed into town.

Breathing a sigh of relief that a college kid she didn't know and, more important, didn't know her, was manning the front cash register, she bought a pregnancy test and snuck out of town. The kids were busy on the porch with their respective projects when she made it home. She ran to the bathroom, followed the directions on the packaging and waited for the results.

She paced in the little room. When the designated amount of time had passed, she glanced at the finished test stick and a dizzy spell hit her. Sitting on the toilet seat, she put her head between her knees. *Pregnant.* She had a baby growing inside her. She touched her belly. Could she—should she—be a mother? The very limited options ran through her mind and she quickly eliminated all but one.

But can I do this?

Yes. This summer, with these kids, had taught her at least that. She was capable of having and supporting this child, and that's exactly what she was going to do. She was going to be a mother. She was going to have Jamis's baby.

LOST IN THE MIDST OF writing another chapter—apparently sex had done wonders to unblock him—Jamis was completely unaware of his surroundings. Until Snickers came and pawed his leg, he'd had no idea someone was outside. A moment later, a quiet knock sounded on the front door. Jamis crossed through the great room, opened the door and stepped back the moment he saw Natalie. Her expression was serious and determined. There was no point in fighting her. If she wanted in, she'd get in, one way or another.

Without a word, she came inside and glanced around. "Are you alone?"

He raised his eyebrows. "You seriously need to ask that?"

"I need to talk to you."

Something was wrong. "Okay." He shut the door.

She walked around the house, paced was more like it, from the great room into the kitchen, then out onto the porch, back into the great room. Jamis stayed where he was and waited. When she didn't seem to be able to start the conversation, he said, "Natal—"

"I'm pregnant." She stopped moving and stared at him.

He stared back at her, her words not completely registering. "With a baby? You're going to have a baby?"

"Yes."

Holy hell. Relax. Get the facts. He took a deep breath. "Don't take this the wrong way. I'm making absolutely no judgment, but could you have been pregnant when you came to the island?"

"No."

"Has there been any other man other than me?"

She shook her head. "No."

"So you think…" Could she be lying to him? Could another man be responsible? The way Katherine had used and manipulated him ran through his mind.

"Jamis, I know," she whispered. "You're the father."

He glanced into her face, her eyes, and knew she wouldn't lie to him. This was Natalie not Katherine, so it had to be true. He'd fathered a child. A child. *Good God.* The room around him seemed to almost tilt as if on an axis.

He imagined Natalie pregnant, her belly growing round and beautiful. He imagined her giving birth, him holding a tiny bundle. He'd love everything about being a father. The baby-soft skin. The gurgles and gummy smiles. The bedtime rituals. Those wide, dark eyes looking into his soul as if in that moment nothing, no one else on earth, mattered. Even the diapers.

And he'd miss it all. He just couldn't be a father again, not after messing it up so horribly the first time. "I can't be. Natalie…I can't be."

A sad, melancholy sound escaped from her throat. "We had unprotected sex several weeks ago. You are this baby's father."

"That's not what I meant. I believe you." Jabbing his hands through his hair, he paced as panic set in. "I… I…can't be a father."

Silent, she studied him.

"Don't you get it? I had two children, and I lost them. I don't deserve a second chance."

"Jamis, you're wrong. Every person deserves a second chance."

For a moment, he let himself believe what she said was true. He let himself imagine. Was she carrying a boy or a girl? If only he could— *No. No, no, no. Don't you dare think for one damned minute that you can have anything to do with this.* "Not me." He turned away from her. "Not after what I've done."

She quickly grabbed his arm, made him look at her. "What did you do, Jamis? What?"

She needed to know. She deserved to know. He shrugged away from her. "Years ago, I met a woman, Katherine, at a nightclub."

"Your wife."

He nodded. "My career was skyrocketing. I'd just signed the biggest contract I could imagine and was celebrating with a group of friends." He stepped away from her. "Katherine, I thought, was the icing on my cake. Sexy, sultry, mysterious. My limited experience with women made me, I guess, an easy mark. We were married six months later. A month after the wedding, despite all our talk about spending a few years alone before starting a family, she got pregnant. I remember being upset. All our plans would change. This would curtail our travel, our fun."

Afraid if she uttered one sound he might stop, Natalie bit her tongue.

"But when Caitlin was born, I took one look at my daughter's beautiful face and everything changed for me. I know it sounds corny, but she became the light of my life." He smiled. The curve of his lips was so tender, yet so filled with agony, it was all Natalie could do not to reach out and hold him. "So when Katherine got pregnant again within the year, I was happy. A boy. Justin. Those chubby cheeks and legs. Those blue eyes. I was so delighted, I was blind to what was going on."

"What was happening?"

"Katherine filed for a divorce a day after Justin's first birthday."

She sucked in a breath. That had to have crushed him. "Why?"

"She'd never loved me." He shook his head and paced. "Even admitted it privately. She was too old to model, so she'd married me and had two children merely to secure her financial future. It was as simple as that. She smeared me in court, using my books as evidence that I was an abusive husband and an even sicker human being."

How could anyone be so cruel? Her heart ached to comfort him, but she held back, waiting, knowing there was more.

"Like an idealistic idiot," he went on, "I fought what was happening. We argued. Incessantly. Then finally, on Caitlin's birthday, in the midst of nasty custody proceedings, I gave in. I went to the house. There was a winter storm that day, and the roads were icy, but I'd promised Caitlin we'd all go out to dinner together, like a real family. Before we left, I took Katherine aside. I offered her every penny I owned, every home, every car, everything in return for full custody of the children." He covered his face with his hands. "Even that wasn't good enough. She said the kids guaranteed her future child support payments. She would never, never give them up." He ran his hands through his hair. "Two minutes later, we got into the car to go to dinner and that's when I made the biggest mistake of my life."

She held her breath.

"I made a wish." He looked away, wouldn't hold Natalie's gaze. "I put every ounce of energy and hope and emotion I had in that one wish. I wished Katherine would just die, then my nightmare would be over. I wanted it so badly for her to simply go away. I even envisioned ways it could happen."

Wish it, see it, make it happen. Natalie cringed inside.

"She could fall in the shower," he continued, "and crack her head open. She could choke on one of her low-cal, high-fiber wrap sandwiches. She could slip down a flight of stairs. An elevator could crash. Lightning. Flood. Earthquake. Aliens. Ghosts. You name it, I pictured it. Including a car accident." He spun away from her. "A minute later, I skidded through an icy intersection and we were broadsided by a truck."

"Oh, my God," she murmured, unable to imagine what he must've gone through. The guilt and shame. The agony.

"Everyone died, except for me."

"And Snickers," she whispered.

He glanced at her and the anguish in his eyes made her chest ache. "He was just a puppy. He was thrown from the car and landed in a pile of fresh snow in the ditch."

"I'm so sorry." She felt tears gathering, tears of sadness and understanding.

"Don't look at me like that." He glared at her. "I don't deserve your empathy. If you'd seen my babies after that accident, you wouldn't be so quick to make excuses for me. Justin. My sweet, chubby son took the brunt of the force. His body was barely recognizable. Caitlin. My beautiful little girl. Looked like she was sleeping. Sleeping. Except that the back of her head was smashed in and caked with blood. Me? I walked away without much more than a scratch."

That wasn't true, but Natalie imagined that for Jamis anything less than his own death was mercy he didn't deserve. She brushed away the tears streaming down her face.

"I never deserved those children."

"Jamis, it was an accident. You didn't mean for that to happ—"

"Doesn't matter! I wished it. I saw it. *I* made it happen."

"But you didn't—"

"You believe. I know you do. That wishes can come true. How many times have you told your kids 'wish it, see it, make it happen'?" He stepped toward her. "Natalie, I was driving. Sure the roads were icy, but I was distracted by my anger, by making that damned wish. I was the one who went through the red light. Not the truck driver. Me. How can you tell me that I didn't make *my* wish happen?"

JAMIS HAD FATHERED another child. Of all the stupid, short-sighted, selfish things he could've done, this was the worst. Not even bothering to try to write, he sat at his desk and stared off into space. At the distinct sound of a child humming outside, Jamis glanced through his open window. Toni was sitting on the bottom branch of his maple, swinging her legs and peering innocently through the windows of his house. Her concentration was focused on his first floor, so she didn't notice him upstairs.

She peeked through the windows and sighed. Swung her legs and hummed a little louder, clearly trying to get his attention. He tried to summon some anger, or at least a little agitation, but all his steam seemed to have blown off when he'd spilled his guts to Natalie. He just didn't have it in him anymore. It wasn't Toni's fault she reminded him of Caitlin. It wasn't her fault he missed his children.

Caitlin and Justin. And an unknown, a boy or girl growing inside Natalie. He desperately wanted to be a part of that baby's life, but somehow it didn't seem fair to go on without Caitlin and Justin as if they'd never existed. It was time he accepted that there was no wish, no magic spell, no fairy dust he could sprinkle to get them back. He swung around, opened the bottom drawer of his credenza, and pulled out that last picture he'd taken of his children. Reverently, he ran his fingers over the smooth glass and then set it on his desk, near the screen, so he could see them as he worked. Then he pulled out everything else he had in the drawer and walked around his house displaying the items.

Clay figures Caitlin had made with him on a lazy Sunday in winter, he set on his desk. Several photos he arranged in his kitchen and great room, his favorite on his bedside table. He'd framed a couple of the pictures they'd drawn, so those he hung on a wall downstairs. He could never forget his children—didn't want to even try—but at least for today he could remember them with a smile in his heart.

As Toni watched him through the window, he walked over to the front door and stepped out onto the porch. She straightened and smiled hopefully. "You again," he said, trying to sound gruff. "You know you shouldn't be in that tree."

"But I'm a good climber."

"Even the best fall. Don't you think Natalie would be sad if you got hurt?"

She grimaced. "Oh, all right." Swinging down from the branch, she jumped the remaining few feet to the ground.

"I've got an idea."

"What?" She glanced up.

"How 'bout I make you and the other kids a simple tree house? In your yard?" It would only take him a few days and give them a fun way to end the summer.

"Really? You could do that?"

Nodding, he smiled. "If it's okay with Natalie."

When Natalie came back to Mirabelle next summer, Jamis would be gone. He had no other option. A tree house wouldn't be much, but it'd be something to remember him by.

SHE SHOULD'VE SAID NO.

Natalie had known she'd made a mistake within a few hours of agreeing to let Jamis build that damned tree house for the kids. For three days, she'd watched him through the kitchen windows, measuring, planning, sawing and hammering the wood. And for three days, she'd been nothing short of tortured, watching the concentration on his face and his strength as his muscles flexed and released. She wanted him even now. But this was her body reacting irrationally, and her body had gotten her in enough trouble already.

How could she reconcile in her mind the cranky man she'd met on move-in day what seemed a lifetime ago to the quiet, peaceful man who'd read aloud to her kids when she'd had her first massive bout with morning sickness? How could a man put up no-trespassing signs one day and a few weeks later build the very same people he'd tried keeping off his property a tree house? If that wasn't enough, the patience he'd showed over and over again with Galen these past three days, who'd adamantly insisted on forgoing craft time to help construct the tree house, had been nothing short of admirable. But how could she put aside his wish about Katherine, without bringing into question and discounting everything she believed? Her conviction that wishes came true was the entire reason for this camp.

Natalie was in the kitchen folding clothes when she glanced outside to gauge progress on the tree house. About eight feet above ground in a mature maple in the backyard, the tree house sat on a large platform that Jamis had first built supported by two large branches. He'd then secured a tall railing around the edges, foregoing solid walls. Natalie's only condition was that she be able to see the kids at all times to be sure they were safe. Jamis and Galen were now putting the finishing touches on the roof when she saw Garrett pulling into the yard on a golf cart.

Immediately, she dropped the clothes and went outside. "Hey, Garrett."

"Hi, Natalie." He stepped off the cart and looked up into the tree. "Sweet tree house. Who's building that?"

"Galen and Jamis."

"Jamis?" Garrett said. "First he was babysitting and now this."

"I know. Strange."

Garrett shrugged. "I came out to give you and Galen some good news."

"Yeah?"

"Dustin and Chad confessed to robbing Hendersons'."

"They did?"

He nodded. "When I found out you guys didn't have a DVD player, I put some more pressure on the girls who were with the boys that night. Turns out their stories pretty much matched Galen. After I told Chad and Dustin's parents what was going on, they decided to search through the boys' rooms and found the DVDs. It's a done deal. They've signed confessions."

"So Galen wasn't involved at all?"

Garrett shook his head. "Not at all."

"Does the town council board know?"

"They will, Natalie. I'll make sure of it."

"Thanks, Garrett. For getting to the bottom of it."

"That's my job." He glanced back up into the tree. "Tell Galen I hope there's no hard feelings."

"Oh, I think he'll just be glad it's over."

Galen glanced over the edge of the tree house railing just as Garrett hopped back onto his golf cart and drove away. "What did he want?" he called down to Natalie.

She smiled at him. "I'll tell you when you get down."

"We're almost finished."

Then as if the word *finished* had echoed all the way into the house, Toni came running outside, followed closely by Arianna and Ella. Ryan, Chase, Blake and Sam weren't far behind the young girls. "Are they done yet? Are they done?" Toni asked excitedly.

"Almost."

"Can we go up and see?"

"Not yet," Natalie said. "They'll let us know when it's ready."

Toni and the kids stood there for a few minutes before Toni called out, "When can we come up?"

"In a minute," Jamis called back. "We're putting the last board on the roof and then it's all yours."

A drill sounded, some pounding, and then a moment later Jamis climbed down the ladder with a load of tools and scrap wood. His feet had no sooner touched the ground, than Toni ran to him, throwing her arms around his waist.

"Thank you, Jamis!" She grinned.

"You're welcome," he said, ruffling her hair and stepping back. "Now up you go!"

One by one, the kids all scrambled up the ladder.

"Galen!" Jamis called up to the tree house.

"Yeah?" The teenager stuck his head out over the rail.

"Show them how to lock the gate, so you all stay safe up there."

"Will do."

Jamis glanced at Natalie and asked quietly, "How are you feeling?"

"All right." She crossed her arms, hugging herself. "I've been keeping soda crackers by my bed and pop a few in my mouth before I get up. Eating more often, smaller meals. It's all helping."

He looked away. "Good."

"Thank you, Jamis. For the tree house. You and Galen did a beautiful job."

He glanced back at her and his eyes were filled with so many emotions Natalie couldn't name them all. Quickly, he looked away. "I hope they like it."

"Are you kidding? I won't be able to get them down from there." All eight kids fit with plenty of room for more. "Next summer, we'll have to put in a swing set and other play equipment."

Jamis was silent.

"Maybe you could help?" she asked, holding her breath. She wanted him to at least see his child so he'd know who he'd be turning his back on.

"Next summer." He nodded at her, but she couldn't read what was going on inside his head. "Right."

She watched him walking slowly away, confusion rattling her thoughts. Who was Jamis Quinn? Really? There was something he wasn't telling her, something she hadn't figured out.

"What did Garrett Taylor want?" Galen had climbed down from the tree house and his shoulders looked tense, his expression worried.

She grinned. "Chad and Dustin confessed." She relayed everything Garrett had told her.

Galen relaxed and smiled. "Sweet."

"I didn't even think about telling him we didn't have a DVD player. How'd he find out?"

"Jamis told him."

"Jamis?"

"That day you were sick."

"He did?"

Galen nodded. "Turns out he's pretty cool."

Yeah, he was. Natalie looked out through the woods and barely made out Jamis heading into his house. They should've never made love without protection. It had been totally irresponsible. Even so, she couldn't help wanting Jamis's baby with all of her heart.

IT WAS A GORGEOUS, LATE summer afternoon. Preoccupied as he was about Natalie and her pregnancy, Jamis had all but given up writing this damned book until September when he figured he'd be able to concentrate. He pulled on his wet suit, hiked down the hill and dragged his kayak to the water's edge.

"Hey." The voice came from behind him, down the shoreline.

He spun around and found Galen sitting on a large flat boulder nestled on the hill.

"Going kayaking?"

Wet suit. Paddle. Kayak. A smart-ass comment came to mind, but Jamis didn't have the heart today. Especially not after having spent three days working side by side with the kid making that tree house. The boy had proven to be not only a hard worker, but also smart and good with tools. "Yeah, I'm going kayaking."

The kid threw a rock into the water. "Can I go with you?"

Spend some guy time with a kid and all of a sudden we're best friends. "Dude, do you see another kayak around anywhere?"

Galen threw a couple more rocks into the water. "I could rent one in town. If you wouldn't mind waiting for me."

Jamis looked away. "Something happen between you and Natalie?"

"No, we're cool." He shrugged. "Chief Taylor got those townie jerks to confess, so I'm in the clear. Thanks to you telling him we didn't have a DVD player."

"That's good. So what's wrong then?"

The kid shrugged again. "Nothing."

"Bullshit."

"Guess I just don't want the summer to be over."

"Don't want to go home?"

The kid didn't say anything.

Jamis took a deep breath and against his better judgment caved. "All right, Galen. Get up and get moving. I'll meet you in town at Setterberg's Rental. If you're not in a wet suit and on the beach waiting by the time I get there, I'm leaving without you." It was an empty threat, but the kid didn't need to know that.

Before Jamis could climb into his kayak, Galen had already set off running through the woods. In truth, Jamis didn't mind spending time with the boy. It made him wonder what Caitlin and Justin would've been like had they lived to become stubborn, know-it-all teenagers. It made him wonder what it would be like to be a father again.

CHAPTER FIFTEEN

A CRACK OF THUNDER, deafening in intensity, jolted Jamis from a sound sleep. Lightning flashed, illuminating the rain pouring into his open bedroom window. He jumped out of bed, cranked the window closed, and noticed the electricity had gone out. He was wiping up the wet sill and dabbing at the carpet when a loud pounding sounded on his front door.

Snickers barked and ran downstairs.

He trailed after the dog and swung the door wide to find Natalie standing on his porch. He hadn't seen her since he'd finished the tree house more than a week earlier and he had to admit pregnancy was looking damned good on her. Dressed in only pajama pants and a very wet, clingy T-shirt, the fact that she wasn't wearing a bra became immediately apparent, and it was all Jamis could do not to stare.

"Can you please come to the house?" she asked, shivering, her wet hair flattened to her cheeks.

He almost went with her, no questions asked, until his sanity returned. "What for?"

"It's Toni. The storm." As if just now becoming aware of the wet state of her dress, she crossed her arms over her chest. "She woke up screaming and keeps calling your name."

"*My* name? You're joking."

"Please, Jamis. I know you and I have issues, but all the kids are scared. Toni's upsetting them even more."

"Why me?"

"I don't know." Natalie shook her wet head. "You must make her feel safe."

Him? The king of horror? He made a child feel safe? What a crock. "I'm not… I don't—"

"She wants you, Jamis. Not me."

He looked away and swallowed the sudden lump in his throat.

She shivered and her shoulders sagged. "Well. If you change your mind, you know where to find us."

"Fine," he said. "I'll come." He grabbed his slicker off the rack and handed it to her along with a flashlight.

"I'm already wet," she said. "You—"

"I'll be all right. Come on, Snick."

After grabbing a couple more flashlights, he followed Natalie as she raced down the path between their two houses. Every window was dark in her house. Candlelight illuminated the shapes of kids looking through the windows. The moment they entered the house, he heard the screaming.

"Is that her?"

Natalie nodded. Either her face was wet from the rain, or she was crying, probably both. She grabbed a bath towel off the top of the dryer and handed it to him. "Go, please. I'll take care of Snickers."

After rubbing the towel through his wet hair, he stepped into the kitchen and found all of the kids loitering around, a couple of them holding their hands to their ears. The only light came from several candles on the table and counters. The littlest boy, Ryan, was crying, but Jamis guessed Natalie could handle him.

"Where is she?" he asked.

"Follow the screaming." Galen pointed upward.

Sam glared at Galen. "I'll show you."

Jamis followed her up the stairs.

"In here." She stopped outside an open door. "Toni? Jamis is here."

The screaming continued unabated.

Jamis entered the bedroom and glanced around. It was a pretty girly-girl room with a fluffy multicolored shag rug, pale pink walls and white furniture, including two sets of bunk beds. A lantern-style flashlight on the bedside table provided the only light in the room.

Another jolt of lightning and a crack of thunder and he saw Toni huddled in the corner on one of the lower bunks. "Toni?" He sat on the bed and reached for her. "Hey, it's okay. Nothing's going to hurt you." He reached out to touch her arm and she jumped.

He waited, rubbing her back in a soothing motion, but when her cries didn't subside he gently picked her up and pulled her onto his lap. Still hysterical, she flailed in his arms, kicked, scratched and swung her head.

"Shh, shh, shh. It's okay." And like that, it all returned to him, what he was supposed to do and say to calm a little child. "Sweetheart, you're okay. Toni, shh, shh, shh."

He rocked her, kissed the top of her head, patted her back and smoothed her curls away from her tear-streaked face. He did everything he could think of, every trick he'd used years ago on his own two children, to calm her. Within a few minutes, her high-pitched screams fell to a loud wail, then her body, tired and stressed, shuddered in relief.

She turned her face into his chest and her little hand gripped his arm, and it was all Jamis could do to keep his own tears at bay. What had happened to this child to frighten her so badly?

"Is…Snickers…here?" Her words came out in a choppy cadence.

"He is. Do you want me to get him?"

"No! Don't leave!"

"I'm not going to leave." Standing, he carried her to the door. "Snickers, come!"

The dog bounded up the stairs and flew into Toni's room.

With Toni on his lap, Jamis sat on the bed, and together they petted the dog's head.

"Can he sleep with me?" she asked.

"Absolutely. Come on, Snick, up."

The dog jumped onto the mattress and licked Toni's tear-salted cheek. She hugged him and kissed him back.

"If you lie down, I'll bet Snickers will cuddle right up with you."

Clearly exhausted, she fell onto her pillow. "I don't want you to go."

"Then I won't." He sat on the floor and held her hand. "I'll be here until morning."

"Promise?"

"Promise."

Jamis leaned back against the mattress, kicked his legs out in front of him, and listened to the sound of her breathing. If Caitlin had lived, she'd have been around Toni's age. He turned his head and glanced at the little girl, her eyes closed, her mouth slack, her small form moving slowly with each breath. He had the strangest feeling Natalie was carrying a girl. A girl. What would she name her daughter? The thought of her giving birth and raising a little one without him twisted his stomach in knots. He was going to miss out on so much.

All at once, the joy and pride Jamis had experienced in the very short time he'd been a father came back to him in a rush. He'd probably spoiled both his kids, but considering how awful his own parents had been at the job,

Jamis had done all right. Until the end. He'd be paying for that one wish the rest of his life.

IT TOOK FOREVER TO GET the kids settled. Eventually, they all fell back into peaceful slumber, the boys and Sam in their respective rooms and Arianna and Ella in Natalie's room downstairs. After changing out of her wet clothes, Natalie silently crept upstairs, poked her head into Toni's room and was relieved to find the girl sound asleep with Snickers snuggled in front of her. What gripped her heart was the sight of Jamis asleep sitting on the floor, one arm resting on the bed and Toni's doll-like hand swallowed up by his big mitt. For all his blubbering to the contrary, Jamis had a heart of gold, coming over here in the pouring rain and helping a child for whom he wasn't the slightest bit responsible.

His eyes cracked open and he spotted her at the door.

"You don't need to stay," she whispered. The worst of the storm had moved southeast of the island, and the rain had slowed to a steady pitter-patter.

He carefully disentangled his hand from Toni's and came out into the hall, pulling the door nearly closed behind him. "I promised her I'd stay until morning," he whispered. "If it's okay with you, I'll sleep on the other bunk, so if she wakes she'll see me there."

"Are you sure?"

He nodded and looked away, uncertain.

"What's the matter?"

"Why?" he asked. "Why was Toni so frightened?"

"Kids get scared in storms—"

"No, she wasn't just scared. She was hysterical."

Natalie wasn't supposed to share private information, but Jamis deserved an explanation. "Let's go downstairs, so we don't wake the kids." Using a flashlight, she went into the kitchen. Thunder rumbling in the distance and steady rain beating against the window over the sink made the room seem cozy.

"Toni's parents were killed about a year ago. She was in the backseat of the car when the vehicle got stuck on a railroad track. There was a bad storm that night. Like tonight, it was raining, lightning and thundering when the train hit the car, killing her parents."

Jamis looked down. "And Toni?"

"She was in the hospital for several weeks with a concussion and a broken leg." Natalie rested her hand on his arm. "She has no relatives that could take her. She's been bouncing from one foster care home to another since she got out of the hospital."

"I suppose every kid here has a similar story."

"Some have it a little tougher than others, but, yeah, not one of them has had an easy life."

"I was wrong, Natalie. What you're doing here is important."

She couldn't have been more shocked by his humble admission. "Thank you." The moment turned awkward, as if neither knew where to go from there. "Your shirt is still wet from the rain," she said. "I think I've got something that might fit you." She went into the laundry room and found a T-shirt she'd bought for Galen that had come a size too big. "Here. This might fit."

"Thanks."

Natalie hadn't intended on watching as he shrugged out of his wet shirt, but from the moment she caught sight of his bare chest and the mat of dark, curly hair, she couldn't peel her eyes away from him. He drew the dry shirt over his head, caught her gaze, and quickly looked away. "Now where's your fuse box? I'll see if I can get the electricity going again."

"In the basement." She cleared her head, grabbed a flashlight and opened a door next to the pantry. "I've never done this before, so can you show me?"

"Sure."

She went down the basement stairs. The old-fashioned fuse box was located toward the far end of the room, so with Jamis following, she walked across the cool and dank room on the uneven cement floor. Aside from the beams from their flashlights and the faint light coming from the top of the stairs, the basement was pitch-black. "Here it is."

She stood beside him while he showed her how to tell which fuses had blown and how to replace them. She'd never noticed before how comforting his voice could sound when he wasn't being sarcastic. No wonder Toni had asked for him. After a few moments, she shivered with the chill in the air. Heat emanated from him, and she found herself inching closer to his tall frame.

"There. That should do it." He turned, bringing them mere inches from each other. He smelled fresh, like the rain that had dried on his skin. "We should go."

"Do we have to?" she whispered.

He was silent for a moment. "Yes. Now." In the darkness with shadows all around, she couldn't see his eyes, but somehow she sensed his arousal.

Her knees turned weak at the thought, and he reached out to grab her. "I'm having a hard time forgetting our night together," she whispered. "You should know that kind of thing has never happened to me before. You know…sex… just like that."

He said nothing. Only the sound of his breathing turning

quick and raspy gave any indication he'd heard and been at all affected by what she'd said.

She closed her eyes and leaned toward him and his mouth slowly descended toward hers. The first touch of his lips was soft and slow, exploring and testing. Tentative. Not at all like the other night when they'd made love, but then she reached for him, felt the muscles of his chest and shoulders, and a whimper of pure, unadulterated appreciation escaped her throat.

Then everything happened almost at once. His kiss went from gentle to insistent with one thrust of his tongue. "You're killing me," he whispered, pressing her against the wall. And then his hands, his touch, seemed everywhere at once, from her neck to her breasts, her stomach to her butt, thrusting under her shirt, dipping just below the waistband of her shorts.

She was no better, gripping, groping and scratching him. She couldn't be sure, but she may have even bit his lip. "What is it with us?" she murmured against his lips.

"Put a man who's only had sex once in five years in close proximity to a beautiful woman and he's going to…"

"Is that all this is?"

"No." He buried his nose in her hair. "I've never… You're the only woman I've ever… Hell, I don't know."

"I know I want you." She leaned into him, pulsed her hips against him.

He groaned as if in pain. Then he stepped back and threw his hands in the air. "No. This is wrong. Haven't we done enough damage already?"

"A baby is not damage. At least not as far as I'm concerned."

"Natalie, we're moths to the flame, you and I. You don't want me. Not really. I may have fathered your child, but that's not going to change anything. As far as you're concerned, I'm just another man that you want to fix. And as soon as things get too messy, you'll find some fatal flaw in me and then move on to your next project."

"You think, huh?" she murmured.

"I know. I'm doing us both a favor."

She held his arm as coherent thought returned. "There was some truth to everything you said about me being afraid of abandonment, but I swear, Jamis, you're different. I'm not sure how, but you are."

"I'm unavailable. That's the difference." He pulled away and stepped back.

"I leave to go back to Minneapolis in a little more than a week. How can you turn your back on this? On your child? You were a good father. I know you were."

"This is your baby, Natalie. I'll provide whatever financial support you want, but it'll be *your* child. Not mine. I can't—won't—be involved in any way other than to pay bills. I lost my family. I don't deserve another one." He grabbed his flashlight and went upstairs to Toni's bedroom.

LYING ON HIS BACK, Jamis slowly opened his eyes. If the wedge of sunlight streaming from the edges of the window blind was any indication, it was already midmorning. He glanced up to find cutouts of magazine pictures plastered overhead. Ella or Arianna must've taped them onto the bottom of the top bunk. Rather than a collage of fanciful pictures, it was more like a photo layout. Most of the cutouts were of models, but whoever had done the cutting had obviously decided she could do better than the original designers.

In paper doll fashion, a scarf and a pair of shoes had been glued over one model. Pants and a jacket onto another.

A dress, made from a mishmash of clippings, had been taped or glued onto a third. A coat and hat onto a fourth. A necklace, earrings and purse onto the last.

"You're sleeping in my bed." The little girl's voice coming from the other bunk was soft and sleepy.

So Toni was the wannabe fashion designer. He glanced over at her. Other than her eyes being slightly puffy from crying, she looked no worse for wear. "It's very comfortable. Why aren't you in it?"

"It's by the window."

The lightning last night during the storm. "Oh." Not wanting to embarrass her, he wasn't sure what else to say.

"Thanks." She stared at him, and without uttering another word, he understood how grateful she was.

"Why me?" he asked, needing to know. "Why did you ask for me last night?"

"'Cause I was right the first time. You do remind me of my daddy."

"You mean I look like him?"

"No. You…feel like him."

He *comforted* her? How was that possible? This was a crazy damned world, and he'd never understand it.

"You hungry?" His stomach felt like a gurgling pot of acid. She nodded.

Chairs scraped and cupboards closed in the kitchen below them, signaling breakfast time. "Then let's go get something to eat. Natalie does feed you, doesn't she?"

Toni made a face. "She tries."

Jamis laughed and smoothed her hair.

Toni swung her feet out from under a pink, green and white quilt. By the time they got to the kitchen, the rest of the kids were dressed and sitting around the table and Natalie was dishing up French toast. "Well, good morning!"

He glanced at her. With the sun streaming through the window behind her, she looked almost angelic. "Morning."

They'd set a place for him at the table and everyone appeared to be waiting for him to sit. A family. What would it feel like to have one again?

"Will you stay for breakfast?" Toni asked.

He was getting in deeper by the minute, but how could he refuse that sweet face? Taking a seat, he forked a piece of French toast as the plate was passed around, squirted on a blob of syrup, took a bite and nearly gagged. "Did you make this?" he asked Natalie. As if there was any doubt.

"Mmm-hmm." She nodded. "It's my grandmother's secret recipe."

Almost as bad as her baking soda cookie, this concoction was so orangey and rich he barely choked it down. "What's in it?"

"Well, if I told you it wouldn't be a secret."

Too bad the recipe hadn't died with the old woman.

And you're such an ass, Jamis.

He glanced at the faces of the children around the table. "Do you kids like this stuff?"

No one said anything.

"I know." Natalie sighed. "Mine never seems to taste quite like Grammy's."

"May I try?" he found himself asking, suddenly remorseful over the nasty thought about her grandmother.

"Go for it."

He went to the counter and threw the rest of her French toast into the sink.

"By the way, thanks for installing that new garbage disposal," Natalie said, coming to stand by him. "We really needed it."

Well, there was a big surprise.

"Can I help?" she asked.

His instinct was to keep her as far away from the stove as possible, but her expression was so earnest it was impossible to not concede. "Crack the eggs." She couldn't screw that up, could she? Apparently, he was wrong. After scooping out a few tiny shells Natalie had missed, Jamis scrambled the eggs, added milk, vanilla and cinnamon. "This your secret ingredient?" He held up the bottle of Grand Marnier liqueur.

She nodded.

"A little of this stuff goes a long way. Like vanilla." He poured a small amount into the egg mixture. Five minutes later, he was piling hot French toast onto a platter. "Dig in, guys."

Natalie took a bite and closed her eyes. "Mmm. Now that's just like Grammy's."

Syrup clung to her lips and Jamis resisted the urge to lick it off. She opened her eyes and caught him staring at her mouth. Instead of looking away, their gazes locked and held. *This was complete craziness.* And he couldn't believe it was all going to be over in a little more than a week. Then he could go back to being completely and miserably alone.

CHAPTER SIXTEEN

ANOTHER FEW LONG, slow days passed during which Natalie had neither seen nor heard from Jamis. Although Snickers made several visits a day to her house, he would merely appear and then disappear without a sound from his master. The summer was almost over and Natalie felt as if her world was unraveling.

Arianna, Ella, Blake and Chase were going home today. Natalie and the other kids would be following a week later. Although Ryan and Toni hadn't yet grasped the ramifications of the four middle kids going home, Galen had barely said a word all morning, and Sam was sniffing back unshed tears. As they left the house and went into town to catch the Mirabelle ferry to the mainland to meet Arianna and Ella's grandmother and Chase and Blake's father, the mood of the group was a jumbled-up mess of excitement, sadness, joy and resignation.

The closer they got to the mainland, the more the home-bound children got excited. Suddenly Arianna screamed, "Grandma! Ella, there she is." She pointed toward the pier and jumped up and down, waving.

"Do you see Dad?" Blake asked Chase.

"Not yet," Chase said.

"He'll be there," Natalie reassured them. "I talked to him on the phone last night, and he's all ready for you guys."

"You sure?" Chase asked.

"Positive."

"There he is!" Blake called as the ferry pulled up to the pier and docked. "Dad!"

"Dad!"

The ferry gate no sooner opened than the four children raced onto the pier. Sam and Galen helped Natalie carry off the luggage and Ryan and Toni followed, suddenly dragging their feet. After the girls were finished hugging their grandmother, Natalie shook hands with the older woman and then hugged each girl tightly. "We're going to miss your girls," she said, standing.

"Not as much as I missed 'em." The woman wiped tears of joy from her cheeks. She looked a bit on the haggard side, but clean and sober.

Blake and Chase's dad turned to Natalie as soon as he extricated himself from the boys' arms around his neck. "Thank you, Natalie." The man looked tired and drawn, but overjoyed to see his boys. "You turned what would've been a horrible summer for these boys into something they'll never forget."

"It was my pleasure." She hugged both boys.

Natalie could barely watch all the kids saying goodbye. By the time the rest of the kids and Natalie returned to the ferry for the return trip to Mirabelle, there wasn't a dry eye on the pier. No one said a word on the windy trip home across the water. She had no clue how she could possibly say goodbye to these last four children. Not these kids. For the first time Natalie could ever remember, three months was feeling to her as if she was just getting started.

Maybe a foster home wasn't such a bad idea. Maybe it was time for her to make a commitment to something even more important than this camp. Maybe she needed to make promises to these kids that went beyond summer care. It was so much more than she'd bargained for when envisioning this camp, but somehow it was starting to feel more right than anything Natalie had ever set out to do. The big question was would they want her?

By the time they got back home, it was late in the afternoon. Knowing their big old house was going to seem mighty quiet without the four middle kids, Natalie had invited Missy, Sarah and Hannah over for dinner and a campfire. Late that night, after the kids had gone upstairs and were settled in bed, she and the other women walked the path to the fire pit.

"So that's where the beast lives," Missy murmured, pointing to Jamis's log cabin.

"Shh," Natalie said. "He'll hear you. Voices travel at night out here in the woods." They all helped build a small fire and then poured out a few glasses of wine and sat back to stare into the flames and talk. Rather than risk possible questions, Natalie simply didn't drink the wine.

"Well, I for one can't believe that jerk tried to close you down."

"But he didn't. That's all that matters."

"You're awfully forgiving," Sarah said.

"He's not as bad as you think."

Natalie threw a stick onto the fire.

"Why are you making excuses for him?"

"I don't know. I like him."

"Why?"

"He's interesting. And funny. And compassionate."

"He's hot," Hannah said. "I'll give him that."

"But have you read anything he's written?" Sarah asked.

"His books aren't anything like him."

"There has to be some screw loose for him to come up with that stuff."

"Can we not talk about Jamis anymore?"

The other three women glanced at Natalie, Missy for a particularly long time.

"So who's met the new doctor helping out Doc Welinski?" Sarah asked.

"I have," Hannah said, smiling. "Dibs!"

JAMIS LAY IN BED WITH his windows wide-open. He was about to drift off when soft voices came to him on the cool night breeze. Feminine sounds, giggles, laughter, conspiratorial whispers. It might have been a comforting way to fall asleep had he not been able to make out so much of their conversation. As it was, though, at least half of what they said was easily decipherable. And they were talking about him.

Surprisingly, most of what they said cut more deeply than he'd expected. He'd always known the world looked upon him as an oddity, but it was different to hear people he knew being so blunt and honest. At least he could easily tell Natalie's voice from the others, could hear her defend him in a way. Maybe that was the most surprising part of it all. Would she go so far as to tell them she was carrying his child? He didn't care what the islanders thought, but he hoped Natalie understood his decision.

"Can we not talk about Jamis anymore?" Natalie said.

Thank God. Now he could fall asleep. They murmured about this and that, most of it mundane chick-speak.

"You okay with this camp coming to an end?" asked one of the women.

Jamis stilled.

"Actually, I'm thinking about being a foster parent for Galen, Sam, Ryan and Toni."

What? His breath hitched in his throat. Emotions, left and right, assaulted him. Concern. Was she ready for that, especially with a baby coming? Regret. Had he spurred her on somehow by claiming she lived in fear of abandonment? But mostly there was envy. She was moving on with her life, a life that would no doubt be rich and full even without him.

ONLY TWO MORE NIGHTS left on the island. After Toni and Ryan had gone to sleep, Natalie stood in the kitchen thinking she'd do more packing. Instead she found herself gazing out at Jamis's house. Every day, since the four middle-schoolers had left, Natalie had felt a sense of almost panic rising higher and higher inside her. By now, she'd hoped to have come to some resolution regarding Jamis, but there seemed to be no clear direction.

Although questions had plagued her for days about Jamis's true character, she was finally content with the belief that no matter what Jamis wanted the world to think, he was an inherently good man. He was a good man who'd not only been betrayed by the woman he loved, he'd lost his children. Natalie refused to believe that was the price he'd paid for a terrible wish. The world couldn't possibly work that way.

Somehow, someway, she had to convince Jamis to be a part of her life and their child's life. Leaving Mirabelle without him was going to be the hardest thing she'd ever done.

Sam came into the room, went to the refrigerator and poured herself a glass of milk, then grabbed a couple cookies. She leaned against the counter. "You okay?"

"I'm fine. Just thinking."

"About what?"

Natalie glanced at Sam's earnest, innocent face, thought about how much this young woman had grown through the summer. Not long and she'd be an adult. "Do you believe wishes can come true?" Natalie asked.

"With all your talk about *wish it, see it, make it happen,*" Sam said, smiling, "you expect me to answer that?"

Natalie chuckled. "Not fair of me, I know, but I'd appreciate your honesty."

Sam took a bite of cookie and washed it down with a gulp of milk. "Well, *honestly,* I don't know if I believe in wishes coming true. But I can tell you that no matter what happens when I go back to Minneapolis in a couple days, I don't think my life will ever be the same."

Natalie desperately wanted to tell the kids about her idea for a foster home, but she couldn't. Although she'd made the necessary calls to check into fostering all four kids and faxed in all the appropriate forms, final approval hadn't been given. "So you don't think your life will be the same. How so?"

"Well, I may not be able to change what my foster family believes or what they do or how they act, but I can feel a change inside myself. I believe I can make a difference in my own life."

"Yes!" Natalie closed the distance between them, hugged the young woman and then stepped back. "That's it! That's what I'd hoped you come to understand before the end of summer. It's that make-it-happen part that brings it all together. I'm so happy for you!"

Sam shrugged, but the brightness of her eyes belied her seemingly nonchalant attitude and Natalie hugged her again. As she stepped back and looked into Sam's eyes, something hit Natalie. There it was. The key. "The make-it-happen part," she whispered. "That's it."

"What's it?" Sam asked.

Natalie looked up, her thoughts racing. "Oh, just something I've been thinking about."

"Well, I'm going to bed," Sam said.

"G'night, Sam." She couldn't let things sit the way they were between her and Jamis. She had to try one more time to convince him to come with her. To ease his fears and change his mind. Before she could second-guess herself, Natalie picked up the phone and dialed. "Missy? I know it's late, but could you do me a really big favor?"

THE NIGHT HAD TURNED CHILLY and Jamis had made a fire inside. The flames, though, had made him think of Natalie, so he'd come outside. With a blanket wrapped around his shoulders he now stood on his deck and stared at the moon in all its full and bright and magical glory. Occasionally, leaves rustled quietly in the woods, signaling a raccoon, perhaps, or a deer on its nighttime search for food. In the distance, an owl hooted his intermittent and mournful song.

Come to me. One last time, come to me.

Weak man that he was, Jamis closed his eyes and put the wish out there. Sick of hating himself. Sick of the self-loathing. Sick of his pathetic, solitary existence, he wanted Natalie. He wanted to taste her. Touch her. Love her.

"No," he whispered to himself. "I take it back." *For her sake.*

Lost in thought, he didn't hear the footfalls until they landed on the steps behind him. He turned. There she stood, her face and hair pale in the moonlight, shadows making her eyes unreadable. Was she nothing more than a figment of his imagination, a dream?

Without a word, she moved toward him, but it wasn't until her hand rested on his chest that he knew she was real. "You came. Why?"

"Because I want you. More than anything in the world, I want you."

"You, of all people, should hate me for what I've done."

"I could never hate you, Jamis. I needed time to think to—"

"Find a way in that great big heart of yours to forgive me?" he said, unable to keep the scorn from his voice.

"No." She held his gaze. "Jamis, there's nothing to forgive."

"I killed my family."

"You didn't. You haven't done anything, thought anything, wished for anything worse that most people in this world. We've all had moments where we've wished ill on someone."

"Not you."

"Trust me. I have. There's a big surprise, huh? I'm human, like you. But unless you took steps to actually make that car accident happen, it wasn't your fault."

"Wish it, see it." He glared at her. "*I* made it happen."

"I hate to break it to you, Jamis, but you're not that powerful."

He looked away. She didn't get it.

"I know what you're thinking, and you're wrong. I do get it." She touched his arm. "Our dreams and wishes breathe inside *us*. Help us to make changes inside us. Wishing something and visualizing alone isn't enough. Nothing happens until we take steps to make it happen. Our wishes don't change the world or other people or their lives. They change *us*. You didn't kill Katherine and your children because you didn't take any purposeful steps to make it happen. You didn't intend for anyone to die."

What she said made sense, but he didn't know how to let go. "Why then? Tell me why they're all dead?"

"I don't know, Jamis." She reached out and caressed his cheek. "But I do know that with or without you and your

wish the accident would've still happened. I do know that
you need to forgive yourself and step out into the world.
Because I know the world will be a better place with you
out there muddling through it like the rest of us." She
wrapped her hand around his neck and kissed him.

He held her away from him. "I can't do this," he said
softly. "Touching you is killing me."

"That's because you want more and so do I. If I have to
leave without you, give me one night. Tonight, let's—"

"No—"

She took his face in her hands and kissed him, deeply,
honestly. It was the sweetest sensation Jamis could
remember, but he pulled back. "You're leaving." It was
a lame excuse, he knew it, but he'd throw out anything
he could to make her keep her distance. "What's the
point?"

"I want to do it right this time. I want to know what
could be."

"You shouldn't do this," he whispered, grasping again.
"Your kids?"

"Missy's staying the night. In my room. I have no place
else to go."

With a frustrated groan, he turned away. He felt her
warmth as she wrapped her arms around him. She
splayed her hands against his chest and he threw his head
back, looking to the stars and refusing to move. "Natalie,
don't."

"A woman throws herself at you and you remain
unmoved."

Oh, he'd been moved all right.

"What are you afraid of?"

Jamis said nothing, just stared.

"Jamis, please."

"Please what?" he groaned. "Nat, what do you want from me?"

"I want tonight. I want to make love with you. That's all." She made it sound so harmless. So safe.

Safe. He almost laughed out loud. What a word. He wasn't safe from her. From this night. From his own devastating wants and needs. From the feelings he had for her. But in two days she was going to be gone. Gone. Out of his life. Forever. He wanted this, too.

"Tonight," he whispered. "That's all I've got to give."

"I'll take it."

He took her hand and drew her into his cabin. The moment the door closed behind them, she unzipped her jacket and shrugged it off. Next came her shirt, then her jeans, her socks. He stood there watching, frozen, just a man wanting a woman. When she reached behind her to unsnap her bra, he came to life. No more fear. Not tonight. Tonight, holding nothing back, he wanted to make love.

"Wait." He stilled her hands. "Let me look at you." He trailed his fingertips along her collarbone, her arm, her waist, then back up to rest on her lips. She looked like an angel, pale and perfect. Even her bra and thong were white, almost virginal. Goose bumps broke out on her skin. "You're cold."

"No."

He entangled his fingers with hers, unsure of how to proceed. Although once upon a time, he'd gained confidence and proficiency in pleasuring women, he'd never been close to a ladies' man. Suddenly, he felt awkward and clumsy as if this was the first time.

"Jamis?"

"I—"

She silenced him with a kiss as soft as it was sweet, as slow as it was warm. A touch of her tongue. Her hands kneading his chest, his shoulders and instinct took hold. He unsnapped her bra, tore off her thong with a quick tug and devoured the sight of her. The curves of her hips, her breasts, even the angle of her shoulders.

Reverently, he touched her, savoring every one of those curves, from breasts to bottom, from waist to face, from neck to back and all over again. Then he couldn't stop himself. He reached lower and touched the wet, swollen spot between her thighs. He groaned and sucked in a breath. "So very, very sweet."

She pulsed against his fingers and let out a shaky sigh, and then she took her turn discovering him. Her hands took over, on his stomach and chest, his arms and his neck. Anxious and needy, she worked the fly on his jeans. She pushed away the knit fabric of his boxers and cupped his erection.

"No," he groaned and jerked away. "You touch me and it'll be over."

She pulled him down to the rug in front of the fire and then pushed him onto his back. That's when the virginal angel turned into every inch the wanton devil. Naked, she straddled his waist. He closed his eyes, hoping to contain himself. Then she kissed him, moved over him and before he understood her plan, she eased down on him with her wet warmth and took him inside.

"Oh, Natalie." He jerked and moaned. "Stop. Don't."

She moved, slowly, purposefully in a primal rhythm, and when he opened his eyes, took in the sight of her, mouth slightly parted, eyelids heavy with lust, breasts moving with her every thrust, he was lost. Pulling her hips down to meet him, he thrust hard inside her one last time, in a pulsing, thorough, complete release.

She ground against him, dragging out the agonizingly sweet intensity until he thought he'd go mad. "Nat, stop," he rasped, putting his hands on her hips and holding her still as he caught his breath.

He opened his eyes and looked into the face of a triumphant woman. "You planned that, didn't you?"

She smiled, a leisurely curve of kiss-reddened lips, before smoothing out his brow. "I wanted to do that for you."

"I've told you over and over," he murmured, "I am not a man who needs to be fixed. I'm not a charity case. Don't get me wrong. That was…amazing, thrilling and damned hot, but not what I wanted for you."

"No?" She grinned at him.

"No."

"Then show me."

He lifted her off him and grabbed a heavy blanket and lay back down with her in front of the fire. Now that his urgent need had been satisfied, he could take his time. He leaned over her and kissed her. He lingered at her mouth, her lips. Trailed his tongue down her neck and stopped at her breasts. "This is what I want from you."

She moaned and arched toward him as he took first one breast then the other, drawing her nipples into his mouth. All the while, he felt tension mounting inside him. By the time he moved past her stomach, he was hard again. Spreading her knees, he lingered between her legs, licking, sucking, dipping his fingers into her heavenly wetness. And loved her. In only a moment or two, she was squirming. Over and over she whispered his name.

"Come," he whispered.

"No. You. Inside me."

The need to own her coursed through him. He fought it and failed. Moving up and over her, he entered her slowly, deliberately, lovingly. He moved with her until she whimpered and moaned as momentum gathered for them both.

She wrapped her legs around him, gripped him and he watched her sweet, beautiful face as she flew apart around him. "Jamis!" she cried.

But he wouldn't let himself go yet. Not yet. He took her again, watched the desire spiraling within her and then, and only then, he came inside her. A moment later, nearly spent, he collapsed over her, his lips at the hollow beneath her ear, his fingers entwined with hers above her head.

"Was that more of what you had in mind?" she whispered, a smile in her voice.

"We're getting there." He kissed her. "But I have one night to make up for five long years, and if I can help it I'm not wasting a minute of it sleeping."

FINALLY, JAMIS HAD FALLEN asleep. Curled next to him, Natalie studied his profile backlit by the red-orange flames in the fireplace. Without a single worry line on his face, he looked almost happy. Surely, he appeared peaceful and satisfied, not at all the tortured soul he was when awake. She barely kept herself from outlining his lips with a fingertip, from running her hands along his soft cheek, from entangling her fingertips in the mat of hair on his chest, a chest that rose and fell in a contented rhythm.

What in the world did you do, Natalie?

Again, she'd miscalculated. She'd come here to make love to Jamis, hoping against hope she might bring him back to life. Instead, he'd turned the tables. He'd made love to her, lifted her up and rocked her world. He'd filled a hole in her heart, a hole she'd never before admitted to herself that she'd had. He'd been right. He didn't need to be fixed, and she could see herself wanting much, much more than three months of Jamis.

As she tucked herself next to him and closed her eyes,

she realized she loved every crazy thing about him. His intensity, his sardonic grin, that look in his eyes that always made her wonder what he was thinking, the curiously easy way he had with her kids. Even his sarcasm. There was no doubt about it. She'd fallen in love with Jamis. Easily. Effortlessly.

So where was the fatal flaw?

Could it be there wasn't one?

CHAPTER SEVENTEEN

NATALIE AWOKE TO A stream of harsh sunlight hitting her in the face. Shielding her eyes, she rolled over to find Jamis gone. As memories of last night returned, she stretched and smiled. "Jamis?" she called. "Where are you?"

Snickers ran down from the loft, came to her side and licked her hand. As she petted the dog's head, she heard a cabinet closing only a moment before Jamis came downstairs. He was dressed in running clothes, and she wanted nothing more than to run into his arms.

"What do you need, Natalie?"

The instant the impassive look on his face registered, her heart sank. Last night's magic was as cold as the ashes in the fireplace. "I wanted to see you." Wrapping the blanket around her naked body, she stood. "To talk about last night."

"There's not much to talk about, is there?"

"I wanted to make sure we were okay."

"We're fine. Why wouldn't we be?" He spun away from her and put his coffee cup in the sink.

"Jamis, don't do this."

Leaning against the counter, he crossed his arms over his chest. "What is it that I'm doing?"

She stomped into the kitchen and glared at him. "You can't pretend that last night didn't happen. That it wasn't completely and wonderfully amazing."

"Last night was last night. And, yes, it was amazing. But you did your thing, Sunshine. You waved your magic wand over me. Voilà. I'm fixed. All better. Now you can go back to Minneapolis tomorrow with a clear conscience. Okay?" He glared at her. "You even got a baby out of the bargain."

"Wha— Oh!" She growled. "You're such an asshole."

"Really? Here I thought I was stating the facts."

"That's not fair. I wasn't trying to get pregnant the first time, and last night wasn't about me trying to fix you."

"Then what do you want? A long-distance affair? Phone sex and e-mails? Happily ever after? I'm confused."

"I want you. For me. And this morning—"

"A lot of things become clear in the light of day."

"I want to keep seeing you. I want you to be a part of our baby's life. Part of *my* life. I want to find out where this goes."

"I can tell you right now where we go without all the hassle of tears and fights and broken hearts. I've made my situation perfectly clear to you. Why is this a problem?"

She closed her eyes. "Because you…you can't just walk away."

"I'm not the one who'll be doing the walking," he said, leveling his gaze on her. "You will be. That's been your plan all summer long. Last night changed nothing. Nothing!"

It had changed everything, but she had a sick feeling in her gut that there wasn't anything she could say that would make him admit to it. "So that's it? You're just going to hide away here on Mirabelle forever?"

"Actually, no." He looked away. "I'll be gone before you return next summer. As soon as I can find my own island, I'll be moving."

Anger built inside her. How could he simply throw away what they might have together? How could he *do* this? "You know if you didn't have any feelings for me," she bit out, "I'd be okay with this, but you're lying, Jamis. To me. To yourself. I know what I saw in your eyes last night when you touched me. When you kissed me. When you came inside me. That look was not the look of a man merely releasing pent-up *sperm*."

That was when it came to her. What this was really all about.

"You're afraid," she whispered. "Afraid you might want me too much. Afraid to feel. Afraid you're going to fall in love with me. Then what? I'll hurt you, right? The way Katherine did? The way Caitlin's and Justin's deaths did? Do you think I'm going to die? Leave you? Use you?"

He spun away, refusing to look at her.

"This isn't one of your books, Jamis. Neither of us knows what's going to happen next. You think I'm not scared? You think this is easy for me?"

"A helluva lot easier for you than for me," he ground out. "I'm just another fixer-upper to you. You'll just screw around with me until you think I'm all better, claim I have some flaw that'll make it impossible for you to commit to me and then toss me out the door."

She was right. He was scared to fall in love again. She walked toward him. "Not this time, Jamis. You're different." She stroked his cheek. "Because I love you."

He groaned as if a jagged knife was cutting him inside out. "Well then, there's your fatal flaw." He stepped back. "I can never love you back." He took off for the door. "Snickers, come!" he called. When the dog didn't budge, Jamis took off running through the woods without him.

AFTER HAVING RUN ALL the way around the island, Jamis stopped on the side of the dirt road by his house and bent to catch his breath. He'd run so fast and so far that his lungs were burning and his legs nearly gave out from under him, but he couldn't run away from the memory of Natalie's expression when he'd told her he could never love her back.

She couldn't have looked more hurt than if he'd sucker punched her. Her skin had turned ashy white and her lips parted as if she might gag. It'd killed him to see her reaction, but he'd had to say it. For her sake. Now she could leave, move on and raise her baby with a clear conscience and without him.

"This is for her," he whispered. "For her."

IT WAS THEIR LAST FULL day on Mirabelle. As Natalie and the kids readied for their departure, cleaning and packing things away, a curious mix of emotions swirled through the house. Sam, Ryan and Toni fell quiet and seemed sadly resigned to the end of summer. Galen, on the other hand, was angry. He didn't show it. He didn't speak about it, but Natalie could feel it like a river's current under layers of ice.

Late in the afternoon, Natalie had gotten a call from the social services department back home, letting her know she'd been approved as a foster parent for Sam, Ryan and Toni. Galen, though, was going to be a problem as his mother had clear custody and she wasn't about to relinquish her rights. On the bright side, he turned sixteen in a month. His age, coupled with the fact that his mother was on probation for dealing drugs, might be enough to convince a judge that Galen would be better off with Natalie. While she was excited about the news, she was also nervous about how her foster home idea would be received.

A somber mood had settled around the less than normally hectic dinnertime and had only grown heavier as the night progressed. "I think we should have one last campfire," Natalie said, putting thoughts of Jamis firmly out of her mind and focusing on the kids. Everything was packed and ready to go. In the morning, they'd have breakfast and head to town to catch a ferry to the mainland. "What do you say?"

"Yeah!" Toni said.

"Okay," Sam and Ryan said in unison.

Galen glanced at her.

"Come on, guys. Let's go." She took off outside and headed for the fire pit.

By this time, they all knew the drill. Once the blaze was going, Natalie poked the fire with a stick. Had she done the right thing? Had this camp accomplished its objective? For Sam, it seemed as if it had, but what about the others? She glanced at each one of the faces illuminated by the flickering firelight and was happy to see Ryan had put on some weight.

No one seemed to want to talk, but, regardless of what their reactions might be, she had to throw her foster home idea out there. "I have a question for you guys," she said. "What did you think of this summer? What did you think of living with me?"

Sam glanced up and frowned. "I had a good summer. I'm glad I came. I'll miss you."

"Same," Toni said, her voice small.

"Same." Ryan threw a handful of leaves on the fire and they crackled and exploded into flames. "But I don't want to go home. I want to stay here. With you. All of you."

Everyone stopped what they were doing and stared at the little boy who'd rarely spoken more than a handful of words all summer long.

"Galen? What about you?"

He picked up a rock and threw it into the woods. "I don't want to go home, either."

Natalie took a deep breath. "What if…none of you had to go back to the places you were living before we started this camp?"

All four heads turned in her direction, but no one said anything for several moments.

"Do you mean stay here?" Sam asked.

"I mean…coming to live with me in the house my grandmother left me in Minneapolis," Natalie said tentatively. "You wouldn't have to if you don't want to. It's just a suggestion. I have enough room. It's a big house."

"Like a foster home?" Sam asked.

"Yes," Natalie said. "If you want, I could be your foster mom."

"All of us," Toni asked.

"Even me?" Ryan said.

Galen looked away. He was old enough and smart enough to understand it wasn't going to be so easy for him.

"Well," Natalie said, careful with her response, "Sam, Toni and Ryan have already been approved. Galen's situation is a little more complicated."

"My mom will never let me go," he said, his anger apparent.

"But if you can prove you're better off without your mom, you may have grounds for what's called emancipation of a minor," Natalie said. "And then you can decide for yourself where you want to live."

For the first time all day, the worry lines on his face cleared, his anger dissipated. "Do you really think that'll work?"

"I do, Galen. And if you want to live with me, I'll fight for you," Natalie said. "So do you guys want me? Or not?"

"I want you." Toni came toward her and hugged her around the neck.

"Same," Ryan said, coming to her other side.

Sam's eyes glistened with unshed tears. "Yeah. You can foster mom me any time you want, Nat."

Everyone turned to Galen.

"Are you kidding?" He shook his head and grinned. "What do you think I've been wishing for *and* visualizing all summer long?"

All five of them fell into a group hug. The news of a baby on the way would wait for another day, but she had a feeling they would all make wonderful foster siblings.

"What's going to happen between you and Jamis?" Sam asked.

"What do you mean?" Natalie said, feigning innocence.

"You know what she means," Galen said.

Boy, am I in for trouble, Natalie thought ruefully. "I don't know yet, but I can tell you there's something I'm wishing for and visualizing on top of fostering you kids. I'd love for Jamis to be a part of our lives." But it was going to have to be up to him. "That okay with you guys?"

"Yeah," Sam said.

"He's cool," Ryan said.

"Totally," Toni said.

Galen nodded, as if he understood better than any of them the possibilities. "You say when, though, and I'll take him out."

YESTERDAY, JAMIS HAD watched the activity taking place next door. From the sounds of the music blaring through the open windows, there'd been cleaning and packing going on all day long. Now this morning, boxes and suitcases were being stacked on the porch. Natalie was sending a message, loud and clear. She and what was left of her crew were leaving today.

He spun away from the sight of the Victorian and

covered his face with his hands. He'd been unable to sleep more than an hour or two last night. All morning, he hadn't been able to eat. His gut was a nauseous mess, his brain a disconnected stream of thoughts. He should go over there. No. He couldn't. He should say goodbye. But how? And with what words? Even Snickers wasn't himself. The way a dog knows something is going on, he'd been running back and forth between their two houses all morning, anxious and watchful.

When a knock sounded on the cabin door both Jamis and Snickers jumped. Snickers whined and glanced up at him.

"Let's get this over with." He opened the door and Galen and Toni stood on the porch.

"We're leaving now," Galen said. "We'll be catching the next ferry."

Jamis nodded.

"We wanted to say goodbye," Toni said, her eyes watering.

"And thanks," Galen added. "For everything you've done for us this summer."

"This is for you." Toni held out an envelope with his name scrawled across the front in childish print.

Jamis nodded and took the card. Still no words.

Awkward silence filled the next long minute.

"Well." Galen held out his hand. "See ya."

Jamis shook the young man's hand and that motion seemed to shake him from his stupor. "Galen, good luck with school." *Good luck in life.*

"Thanks."

"Goodbye, Jamis," Toni whispered, her voice cracking.

"Bye, Toni. You have a good year at school, too, okay?" She nodded.

Galen turned and reached out for the little girl's hand. "Come on. We have to go."

Toni let her hand get swallowed by Galen's, but kept her eyes on Jamis as they walked down the porch steps. When their feet reached the ground, Toni stopped. "Wait." She tugged free, raced back up the steps and launched herself at Jamis. "Goodbye," she said in a choking voice.

Jamis knelt down and wrapped her in his arms and did everything he could to keep from falling apart. "You're going to be all right," he whispered in her ear.

She sniffed. "But I'll miss you. And Mirabelle. And Snickers." She wrapped her arms around the dog's neck. Snickers licked every last salty tear away, and then she spun around and ran to Galen.

Before Jamis knew it, the kids were climbing onto the golf carts. They'd be gone in minutes. Panic nearly immobilized him, but he had to do this. "Come on, Snick." He followed the dog's well-worn path. By the time he reached Natalie's yard, she was stepping off the porch.

She stopped when she saw him. When hope filled her eyes, he regretted this decision, but again this wasn't for him. It was for her. "I came to say goodbye," he said, setting her straight right away.

"Don't. Please." She shook her head, her eyes bright.

"It's for the best."

"No, it's not." She came to him. "You should be coming with us. You still can."

He glanced into her eyes. She loved him. That, he didn't doubt. But as his gaze slipped to her stomach and he imagined that sweet, innocent little life growing inside her, he knew he had no other option. "You're better off without me—"

"I don't want to hear more of that. It's not true."

"It is, Natalie. You'll be a wonderful mother. I know it. You're all that child needs. I'd only mess it up."

"You're wrong. More wrong than you've ever been in your life." She stepped toward him, her face set with determination. "But I want you to know that the love I feel for you isn't going to change. I'll still love you in four months, two years, ten years, until the day I die."

"Good luck with that."

"You're such an asshole." She shook her head and smiled. Smiled. "When you change your mind, I'll be waiting."

"I wouldn't do that if I were you."

"Well, you're not me." Without another word, without a kiss or a touch or a backward glance, she climbed onto a golf cart and left.

As they drove away, Snickers looked from Jamis to the kids and back again and barked his head off. He wagged his tail, barked some more and made it very clear he was all ready to go with Natalie and her crew.

"You want to go, then go." Jamis forced the words from deep in his soul. "Go, Snick, go on. You'd be better off without me, too."

Snickers looked after the quickly disappearing golf carts and whined. Then he quietly lay down, rested his head in his paws and sighed.

Stupid, stupid dog.

Yeah. And Jamis was such a genius.

FROM THE FERRY, NATALIE watched Mirabelle's shoreline grow more and more indistinct. With every cold wave hitting the side of the massive boat, her sense of panic escalated.

No, no, no. She hugged herself, holding herself together. *He's not leaving you. You're leaving him. And oddly enough, this time it's the right thing to do. If—when—if he comes to you, it'll be what he wants. It'll be his choice.*

"Choose me, Jamis," she whispered, closing her eyes and turning her face into the warm, late-summer sun. "Choose me. And our baby."

CHAPTER EIGHTEEN

"THE VICTORIAN IS for sale."

On some level, the words Chuck was speaking over the phone registered in Jamis's brain, but he couldn't seem to make sense of them. "What did you say?" He sat back from his keyboard. For the past two months, the pages of his latest book had been flying off his fingertips and he was close to the halfway point. He'd refused to stop writing. When he did, thoughts of Natalie flooded his every sense.

"Natalie Steeger is selling her grandmother's house."

The possibility that she might not come back had never occurred to Jamis. She swore she'd never sell her grandmother's place. This was what he'd done to her. She was doing this for him. She didn't want him to move.

Jamis glanced at the dust-covered envelope Toni had given him just before they'd all left the island. Unopened, he'd set the card on his desk that morning after they'd gone and hadn't touched it since. He couldn't bring himself to open it. "Is Natalie buying another place on Mirabelle?"

"There's nothing else for sale. Except for your cabin once you decide on the island you want. You did get the realty information I sent, right?"

"Yeah." He'd gotten the listings of private islands for sale in both Minnesota and Wisconsin, but he couldn't seem to make himself look at them.

"What do you want to do?" Chuck asked.

"Buy the Victorian," Jamis said without a moment's hesitation. "Do whatever it takes. I want that house."

"I take it that means you're not moving."

"I don't know what I'll be doing, but there is no way I'm letting anyone else get Natalie's house."

He hung up the phone and stared at the page full of words on his computer screen. The horror story he'd been trying to write all summer long had fallen by the wayside within a few days of Natalie's departure, and he'd started a new book, something different from anything he'd ever written. The entire story had been nearly fully formed in his head. All he had to do was get it down on paper, but just now, that didn't seem important. He yearned for the sound of children's laughter out his window, the sight of Natalie, her voice, her touch. Her. Just her.

Pushing away from his desk, he grabbed his coat and walked with Snickers into town. The fall colors had long since disappeared from the treetops and bare branches swayed in a wind that held the promise of an early snowfall. He walked down the sidewalk and glanced around, needing…something. It was late in the afternoon, almost dinnertime. Main Street was deserted, many of the residents having left for their winter homes. The off-season had once been his favorite time on Mirabelle. Now he couldn't seem to stand the quiet.

As he walked by Duffy's Pub, the sound of laughter and music made him stop and glance through the window. A young woman he'd never seen was serving a nearly crowded bar. Feeling so distant from the world, he sat on the nearest bench, closed his eyes and listened.

"You look like you could use a beer."

He knew that voice. Jamis opened his eyes and found Sally standing in front of him.

"Come on. It's two for one. Happy hour."

"No, I don't think that's a good idea."

Sally sat next to him. "So she's gone, huh?"

He nodded.

"Why didn't you go with her?"

He could find no words. He might have been able to type them on his computer, but nothing that made sense was going to come out of his mouth.

"I'm dying, Jamis," she said.

Startled at her being so blunt, he glanced up at her. Her hair was growing back and she looked at if she had energy again. "But you look good—"

"I stopped the chemo treatments." She took a deep breath and looked down the street.

"Why?"

"Because I knew they weren't going to work."

"You could extend the time you have left. Who knows what could happen in the field of cancer treatments?"

She shook her head. "I'm old. I've done what I've wanted to do. It's my time. I don't have any regrets."

"Postmaster on Mirabelle? That's it? That's all you want out of life?"

"I was born on Mirabelle. Never had any interest in going anyplace else. These people know me. Accept me as I am. It's not glamorous or exciting, but I've been happy."

"So you're just going to quit? It's over."

She nodded. "You should know what that's like. You've done the same thing."

He studied her face.

"At least I have an excuse," she said. "I'm old. You? You're a young man, and you've already given up."

"This isn't about me—"

"Oh, yes, it is. I have terminal cancer. Stepping off the merry-go-round is allowed for me. What you've done is a travesty. A waste of four years of life. Four years you can never get back." She tilted her head at him. "So your wife and kids died. So you feel partly responsible. Get over it, Jamis. Get over yourself. You've wallowed on Mirabelle long enough. A life without pain is a life without joy."

"I know that."

"Then start acting like you believe it." She stood, went to the door to Duffy's and glanced at him. "It's time, Jamis, don't you think?"

Jamis didn't know what it was time for, but a beer or two had never hurt anything. Then again. "I can't leave the dog out here for very long."

"Ah, bring him in. Anyone gives you guff, I'll tell 'em where to go."

Jamis stood, held the door for Sally and then followed her inside. Heads glanced up from the bar and the few faces he recognized looked surprised, but no one said a word about Snickers.

"Sally!"

"How you feeling?"

"Good to see you here again."

"Ah, quit making a fuss," she said, sitting next to Doc Welinsky at the bar. "Well, I owe my friend here a drink. Everyone, this is Jamis Quinn. He's the oddball who's been living in that log cabin at the other end of the island."

Jamis took the open seat on the other side of Sally, next to Garrett Taylor. "Hello, Garrett."

"Jamis." Garrett nodded and proceeded to introduce the residents lining the bar. Jamis had heard most of the names, Setterberg, Henderson, Newman and so forth, but had previously met only a few of them. "And this is my wife." Garrett's eyes softened as he indicated the bartender. "Erica."

"Hey, Jamis." Erica reached out and shook his hand. She was noticeably pregnant and the sight of her, the shape of her, made it hard for Jamis to breathe. "This is our nephew, Jason." She indicated a young boy sitting near the end of the bar drawing pictures with markers.

"Hi." Jason glanced up at him and smiled.

Jamis, unable to find his voice, could only nod in response. He never would've believed how much he could miss the sight and sound of children. He cleared his throat and glanced at Erica. "When is your baby due?"

She locked gazes with Garrett. "February twenty-fourth."

"I'm going to have a cousin," Jason said, grinning.

"Congratulations."

"Thank you," she said.

The love passing between those two was palpable, and immediately Jamis regretted his decision to come to town. There was so much life in this bar he was nearly choking to death. He was about to push back his chair and hightail it out of there when Sally's hand came down on his arm.

"Well, for crying out loud," she said, tightening her grip and holding him there. "What's a person have to do to get a drink around here?"

Erica brought Jamis a mug of beer and Sally a gin and tonic.

"So where the heck are Arlo and Lynn?" Sally asked.

"Went to visit their boys for the holidays," someone said.

"Then they're spending a month in Florida."

"No kidding?" Sally said, glancing at Doc.

He shrugged. "I suppose this is as good a time as any to tell everyone."

"You tell them," Sally said.

Doc cleared his throat. "Sally and I are both retiring, and then we're heading to Arizona."

"Together?" someone asked on a note of incredulity.

"Together," Sally said.

"Well, I'll be damned," someone murmured.

"Good for you two."

"Miracles never cease."

"What are we gonna do for a doctor?"

"He's already here," Doc said. "That young man who's been filling in for me here and there has decided to stay."

Amidst the sound of questions erupting around the bar, a slow, romantic song played on the jukebox. Sally turned to Jamis. "I'm thinking I'd like to dance."

"You asking?"

She grabbed his hand. "It's time for you to start living again, Jamis. Don't you think?"

He'd been dead so long, he wasn't sure he remembered how to live.

"You'll remember how to dance, Jamis. Put one foot in front of the other. It's as easy as that."

CHAPTER NINETEEN

SHE WAS GONE. CALEB couldn't blame her for leaving. Not after what he'd done. "I wish…" He stared into the bitterly cold night sky. "For Susan…to have a happy life."

"That's because you're a sap." Jamis's hands stalled over his keyboard. He took a deep breath and quickly exhaled. "But a nice sap. After what you've been through, you might actually deserve her."

He heard a sound behind him and turned. "Susan."
"There's only one person," she whispered, "who can make that wish come true."
He didn't dare hope, didn't dare dream.
"You, Caleb. There's no happy life for me without you."
The End.

There. Done. Another perfect ending even if it was happily ever after. Once upon a time, Jamis wouldn't have believed he could write such an ending, but now? Now he would've given anything to roll the clock backward and write his own ending to this past summer. It certainly wouldn't have involved Natalie leaving Mirabelle.

He e-mailed the last chapter of this latest book to his agent, turned off the computer and glanced out the window.

Without realizing it, he'd written through the night and finished only a week past his deadline. At least it was done. With an unseasonably cold November wind whipping up the light dusting of snow that had fallen last night, the sun rose over Lake Superior. Through the bare tree branches a brilliant sun dog lit the ice crystals in the air, creating an early winter rainbow of pale oranges and reds.

Snickers whined and Jamis glanced down at him. "Bored, aren't you? Well, don't look at me. You had your chance to escape, dude. You snooze, you lose."

The dog swished his tail.

"All right. Up you go." Jamis patted his lap and Snickers joyfully jumped up and rested his head on Jamis's chest.

Absently, Jamis rubbed the dog's ears and patted his head. It was Thanksgiving weekend. Almost three miserable months had passed with excruciating slowness. There'd been no children's laughter and no outside sounds of running feet. In all that time, Jamis had never once turned on the TV. All he'd done day and night was write. He had nothing to say to anyone, and no one had anything to say that he wanted to hear. Except for that day he'd gone into town and Sally had convinced him to go into Duffy's.

He frowned, remembering the obituary he'd read in the town flyer in his mail the other day. Sally had died, less than a week ago while in Arizona with Doc. He couldn't believe she was gone. Just like that. The way four and a half years had slipped away from him. Some of the last words she'd ever spoken to him thrummed through his memory. *Put one foot in front of the other.* It was time.

"I'm sorry, Katherine," he whispered suddenly. "I wish things had been different. I wish you, Caitlin and Justin were alive. I wish I could've seen my children grow." He paused. None of those wishes were going to come true. "I wish there was peace on earth. I wish for food on every table. I wish…I wish she was here." None of those things was going to happen, either. He could wish and wish and wish, day and night, night and day, and none of them would come to fruition.

Snickers hopped to the floor and lay down at the top of the stairs.

Could we change the course of other people's lives? Yes. No doubt. By things we do or don't do. Natalie had proven that to him. Every one of those kids that had stayed with her for the summer had gone back with a vision of a better life. But she couldn't have made those changes by simply wishing for them. His wish, as fervent as it had been, hadn't killed his family. The semitrailer truck had killed them. And he could finally accept that.

So what was he still doing on Mirabelle?

Apparently, Natalie had called it. He was frightened. Scared to immobility of losing what he loved. And he loved Natalie. But how could he—Jamis Quinn, odd man extraordinaire—have done something as stupid and naive and honest as fallen in love?

Since the first moment he'd laid eyes on her on moving-in day all those months ago, he supposed, these emotions had been struggling to take root inside him. From her terrible cookies to her bright smile, once she'd made a crack in his veneer he hadn't a chance of fighting her. His feelings for her had taken off like a weed, nearly choking him.

The love he'd felt for Katherine paled in comparison to what he felt for Natalie. He knew it. He could feel it. When Katherine had asked him for a divorce, he'd been hurt and angry. His heart had cracked that day there was no doubt, but the truth was he'd rather cease to exist than live without Natalie. He was scared, scared of how much he loved her, scared of how much he was going to love their child, scared of falling in love with Toni, Galen, Ryan and Sam. And, ultimately, frightened beyond even his own comprehension of losing them all.

But if he stayed on Mirabelle wouldn't he lose them anyway?

Reaching for the envelope Toni had given him that last morning, he carefully opened it and extracted a handmade card. On the front, she'd drawn a colorful picture of the tree house with the kids inside, smiling and waving from up high. Two other figures stood next to each other near the base of the tree. The one with the beard was clearly Jamis, and the other with her long and curly yellow hair had to be Natalie. Inside, Toni had written in her childish hand:

My Daddy was a good Daddy. That's why you remind me of him.
Love, Toni
XOXO

Jamis wiped away the lone tear trickling down his cheek. He had been a good father. He'd tried his best as a husband. He deserved another chance. But how could a man put one foot in front of the other when he'd completely forgotten how to walk?

His phone rang, startling him. When the sound of his agent's voice on the answering machine registered, Jamis reached across his desk and picked up the call. "Stephen. Hey."

"Jamis. Holy shit, man. This is the best book you've ever written."

Honestly, he didn't care. It was out of him. That's all that mattered.

"The only problem is that it's nothing like your other books."

"So?"

"They can deal with it being a week late, but your contract with the publisher calls for another horror story. This is a freaking romance."

Jamis laughed. "Weird. I know."

"You don't happen to have a spare horror story lying around the house, do you?"

"Sorry, no."

Stephen sighed. "Well, I'll have to send it to them anyway and we'll take it from there."

"Whatever."

There was a short pause on the line. "Jamis, are you all right?"

"No." He glanced again at the tree house picture Toni had drawn for him and at the sight of the curly-haired stick figure an ache spread through him. "I did a really, really stupid thing, Stephen." He set the card on his desk and looked away. "I fell in love."

Stephen was silent for a moment. "That's good, isn't it, Jamis?"

Jamis walked outside and took a deep breath of cold morning air and knew exactly what he had to do. The only question was whether or not Natalie would have him. After almost three months without so much as a phone call, she'd have every right to slam the door in his face. Then there was the not-so-little matter of her most likely fostering four kids. And a baby. His child. The thought of being a father again scared him witless. But he had to try. He closed his eyes and imagined Natalie saying yes. He imagined himself being a loving husband and father. He imagined himself stepping off the shores of Mirabelle.

"Jamis?" Stephen's voice pulled him back. "I'd like to help."

"Then find me Natalie Steeger's address and the quickest way to Minneapolis."

Stephen chuckled. "How does a helicopter sound?"

"Not fast enough, but it'll have to do." He was about to hang up, but had one more thing to say. "Stephen?"

"Yeah?"

"Thank you. For everything you've done over the years."

"I'm glad you're back amongst the living, my dear friend. It's about damned time."

NATALIE PLUGGED IN THE last string of lights on the Christmas tree. Continuing with her family's tradition of getting a tree on Thanksgiving weekend, she'd taken the kids out that morning. "Okay. It's all yours."

With holiday music playing in the background, Ryan, Toni and Sam dug into the ornaments and began hanging their respective favorites. Galen cocked his head. "I've never seen that many lights."

"The more the merrier. As it is with so many things in life." She grinned, elated that she'd decided to go one step beyond being a foster mom. Social services had just that previous week approved her requests for adopting all four kids. She swung an arm around his shoulder and squeezed, and he surprised her by not pulling away.

"Thanks for taking a chance on me," Galen said. "I promise I won't disappoint you."

As they'd all expected, Galen's mother had put up a stink over the whole fostering thing, but the moment Galen had turned sixteen and filed a petition requesting emancipation, the woman had huffed out of the courtroom swearing that she'd never take him back. Once he'd joined them at the house, the decision to adopt them all had been a no-brainer for Natalie.

"I'm already proud of you, Galen," she said. "Be proud of yourself."

"I'm getting there."

She smiled, but it was hard to completely disguise the deep sadness in her heart. All the kids understood she missed Jamis, and every change her body went through as a result of the pregnancy only made her miss him all the more.

"You know you don't need him," Galen whispered.

"I know." She only wanted Jamis with an ache as deep as Lake Superior. "Go," she said. "I'm okay."

He joined the other three kids hanging ornaments on the tree, and Natalie watched them. There was only one thing that could make this moment more perfect. Her smile slowly disappeared. "Anyone for some cocoa?" she asked, hoping to keep the mood light.

"Yeah!"

"Sounds good."

"Can we help?" Sam asked.

"No, no," Natalie said. "That's one thing I can't screw up." Barely stifling the tears, she went into the kitchen. After putting a kettle of water on the stove, she wrapped her arms around her waist and collected herself. If any of the kids saw her like this, it would ruin their nights, especially Galen's. He'd been so protective of her lately.

The doorbell rang as she was pouring boiling water over cocoa mix into five mugs.

"I got it," Galen called.

There was a moment of silence, and then the sound of a dog barking, the younger kids screeching with excitement, and then muffled voices that got louder and more vehement with every word.

"I like you, man," Galen said. "But you need to go away."

"I get it. I do."

Jamis. Running into the living room, she stopped at the sight of him standing on the front doorstep with Snickers jumping from one child to the next and wiggling ecstatically.

"Snickers remembers us," Toni said, grinning.

"How could he ever forget?" Jamis murmured, his tall frame outlined by Christmas lights strung around the entryway. Big, fluffy snowflakes fell slowly in the darkness behind him. Part of Natalie was elated to see him. The other part felt every second of every day of the past three months like pinpricks to her skin.

Galen was blocking his path into the house. A concerned look on her face, Sam was holding hands with Toni and Ryan. Jamis glanced up and his gaze locked with Natalie's, but his expression was unreadable.

"Galen, it's okay," Natalie said. "You guys keep decorating the tree. I'll go outside." Grabbing a jacket out of the front closet, she went out into the chilly night air, closing the door behind her. She crossed her arms in front of her. It wasn't that cold outside, but it gave her hands something to do when all they wanted was to hold him.

"How are you feeling?" he asked, glancing quickly at the small bulge in her sweater.

"Good. The morning sickness is completely over." She tightened her arms around herself. "How are you?"

"Been better. Only one other time I've been worse." He backed up a step, giving her some space. "I've discovered I can survive without you, but it's not very pretty. I guess I did need fixing. I needed you."

Unable to help herself, she smiled. "Oh, Jamis."

"I'm sorry it's taken me so long to come to you. I guess

I needed some time to clear my head and figure things out. If you don't want to see me, I understand."

"That depends on what you have to say."

"I know why I want you, Natalie. You brought me back to life. Gave me hope. Make me think anything is possible. Make me *feel* like a better man than I am. You truly fill each and every one of my days with sunshine." He paused, reached out but then stopped.

"But?"

"Why in God's name do you want me?"

"I love you," she said.

"Why? What could you possibly love about me?"

"Oh, Jamis." She reached out and caressed his cheek. "I love you because you make me look at the world differently. You made me see myself. You make me laugh and think. You're caring and passionate. You believe in wishes coming true. And you're a good cook." She smiled. "But mostly, your flaws fit remarkably well with mine."

"You sure? Because a three-month stint isn't going to be enough for me. I want a helluva lot more from you."

"I'm sure." She nodded. "A three-month stint wouldn't be enough for me, either."

"Natalie." He fell to his knees in the snow. "Will you marry me?"

"Are *you* sure?" she whispered, unable to catch her breath.

"I am."

"There's something else you need to know, though. You'll be getting quite a handful in this bargain."

"I know. You're fostering Toni, Ryan, Sam and Galen. I think it's a great idea."

"That's not exactly it," she said, shaking her head. "There's more."

"If you love me half as much as I love you, nothing else will matter."

"You can be such an ass." A tear slipped down her cheek. "I love you…more than you could ever imagine. More than you could ever dream. More than you could ever, ever *write*."

"Nat—"

"I'm adopting all four of them."

"Adopting them?" His stunned gaze flew to the window. They were, all four children, looking outside the window. Along with Snickers.

She put a hand low on her sweater and wished she could take it back. She shouldn't have told him. Not yet. Not like this. If the adoptions cost her Jamis, her heart would break all over again. "It's all right if you change your mind. I know…I know it's a lot to take in. You probably didn't plan on being a father of so many so quickly…"

He looked away, clearly overwhelmed. "I don't—"

"Oh, Jamis, don't say it." She cupped his face in her hands. "You'll be a wonderful father. A wonderful husband. This baby deserves you. So do those four kids in there. And me. You're who we want. No one else."

Could he live up to her image of him? Could he be the man she believed in? What would Caitlin and Justin say?

The image of his daughter swam in front of his eyes. His baby son, chubby and perfect. He'd done his best to never fail them. That was what they'd say. He deserved a second chance to get this family thing right. "I will give you everything I have to give." He held her face in his hands. "Marry me, Natalie, and I will do the best I can to become the man you think I am."

"You already are." She kissed him to the sound of hoots, laughter and whistles coming from inside the house. "The man I've been wishing for my entire life."

"I love you." He leaned in and returned her kiss.

Snowflakes fell on their cheeks, their lips. They both looked to the window and found all four kids standing just inside the house watching and smiling. Snickers had his front paws on the sill as he stared at Jamis.

"Come on in and help us decorate the tree," she coaxed. "The only thing this house has been missing is you."

As she drew him inside her home, her life, Jamis realized even he could never have written a better ending to his story. This was perfect. Thanksgiving. A Christmas tree. Big, fluffy snowflakes falling gently in the night.

Then again, there was always making love on a warm, sunny beach with palm trees blowing in a soft breeze. He smiled inside. No. Those things didn't matter. Sunshine, rain, clouds, snow, Mirabelle, Minneapolis. As long as Natalie was with him, every scene in Jamis's life—the good, the bad and the sexy—was going to be absolutely and perfectly…real.

EPILOGUE

"SEAN, EVERETT, Vincent and Gregory!" Natalie pointed to the upstairs boys' bedroom. "You guys are in that room."

"Ashley, Kally, Lindsey and Sarita." Sam spread an arm toward the girls' bedroom. "You, young ladies, are in here."

"And you guys, Erin and Matt—" Galen walked to the end of the hall to show the two teenage summer helpers to their respective rooms "—are down here."

"Cool."

"I get the top bunk."

"No, I do."

"I *want* the bottom."

"Well, good for you."

"I get this dresser."

"Oh, no, you don't."

"I hate pink."

"Don't touch me."

"Don't touch *me*."

"You started it."

"I did not."

It was the first day of summer camp and the previously quiet northwest end of Mirabelle Island was bustling with activity. Apparently, mayhem and unbridled energy were the rules of the day. What could be better? Snickers, of course.

He chose that moment to scamper up the steps, race

from one room to the next and jump from bed to bed. Kids were screeching and laughing, and the dog was ecstatic to be back on the island. No more fenced-in yards or leashes. He could go where he wanted, when he wanted.

This was going to be a great summer. Maybe Natalie's best ever. "Okay, kids," she said to the new campers. "Unpack your stuff. You'll see I left a fun surprise for each and every one of you on your beds." New sweatshirts and more. "And then meet me outside in the yard."

She glanced at Sam and Galen, her oldest daughter and son. She loved thinking of the two teenagers that way. Her son and daughter. "Well," she said, "what do you guys think?"

Sam grinned. "I'm glad to be back on Mirabelle."

"Galen?"

"Ten kids this summer? I think you're nuts." He shook his head and smiled. "But I'm glad to be a part of it. Even more glad to have graduated to the log cabin this time around."

Natalie had hired a head camp counselor who would be staying in the Victorian with the camp kids. Natalie, Jamis, Sam, Galen, Ryan and Toni would be living at Jamis's log cabin. The quarters sometimes felt a little tight, but they were managing.

"Let's go see what the others are up to." Natalie hooked her arms through Sam's and Galen's and tugged them down the stairs and out into the yard.

The sight that greeted her the moment she stepped onto her grandmother's back porch made her heart flutter. Holding a little pink bundle, Jamis sat on one of the swings of the play equipment he'd built when they'd first arrived back on Mirabelle last week. He was busy gazing into the face of their baby, rocking her gently and nuzzling her cheek. Toni and Ryan were hanging out in the tree house tower high above Jamis's head.

Jamis glanced up as they stepped out into the yard. "What's going on up there, World War Three?"

"Isn't it great?" Natalie smiled. "They're settling in well."

"Oh, goodie," he murmured.

Galen laughed and held out his arms for the baby. "Can I have her?"

Reluctantly, Jamis handed her over.

She fussed a bit with all the jostling. "Shh, Anna, shh," Galen whispered in his sister's ear and patted her back.

"I get her next," Sam said.

"Then me!" Toni called.

"And me," Ryan added.

Natalie held back tears of complete and unadulterated joy as Jamis wrapped his arm around her shoulder. They'd been married since early December, and she couldn't imagine a day without him. "I love you," she whispered into his neck.

"I love you, too." He rested his forehead against hers. "But you need to quit avoiding the discussion about how many babies we're going to have."

"Shoulda gotten that firmed up before you said I do." She chuckled. "Coulda used it as the fatal flaw."

"Need I remind you, Sunshine, the log cabin has only three bedrooms?"

"Well, then, it's a good thing you're so handy with tools."

He sighed and glanced at their kids, his family. "Your mother is something, you know that?"

"Yeah," Sam said with a smile. "We know."

Anna started crying and Galen handed her over to Natalie. She brought her daughter up close and kissed her soft cheek. "Shh, Anna." She glanced up and caught her husband watching her, the look in his eyes filled with so much love, Natalie felt as if she might burst. Her husband.

He sighed contentedly. "I gotta get to work."

He was writing so much these days that chances are the words wouldn't fly off his fingertips quickly enough. His last book had placed third on the *New York Times* bestseller list and had hung in the top ten for four months. They were expecting his romance due to be released any day now to do even better.

"What are you writing this time?" she asked.

"Could be a romance. Or a horror story." He grinned, that sardonic twist of his lips that had captured her heart. "I'm not sure yet."

The new camp kids came running out the back door of the house and into the yard, yelling, laughing and jostling one another. Jamis took one look at them and pulled a set of earplugs out of his pocket. After brushing Natalie's cheek with his fingertips, he headed toward the log cabin.

"Jamis?" She reached out and touched his arm. "Will you join us this one time for a huddle?"

He glanced at the faces of the children, debating. Then he shook his head and put the earplugs away. "One time, Nat. That's it. I'm serious."

"I'm sure you are."

He scowled at her.

The new kids were running this way and that. "Let's gather together!" she called. Amidst a lot of groaning and moaning, they all, including Sam, Ryan, Toni and Galen, eventually gathered around Natalie. Glancing into Jamis's eyes, she leaned in. "What do we need to do to make this the best summer ever?"

"This again?"

"Oh, great."

"Get used to it," one of her kids muttered, probably Galen.

"Close your eyes," Natalie said. "Everyone." But she kept hers focused on her husband's clear and loving gaze.

"Wish it, see it," Jamis said, loud and strong. "Make it happen."

* * * * *

Missy Charms gets the shock of her life in the next Mirabelle Island story, ALONG CAME A HUSBAND! *Be sure to look for it in June 2010 wherever Harlequin Books are sold.*

*Bestselling author Lynne Graham is back
with a fabulous new trilogy!*

PREGNANT BRIDES

Three ordinary girls—naive, but also honest and plucky…

*Three fabulously wealthy, impossibly handsome
and very ruthless men…*

*When opposites attract and passion leads to pregnancy…
it can only mean marriage!*

*Available next month from Harlequin Presents®:
the first installment*

DESERT PRINCE, BRIDE OF INNOCENCE

* * *

'THIS EVENING I'm flying to New York for two weeks,'
Jasim imparted with a casualness that made her heart sink
like a stone. 'That's why I had you brought here. I own this
apartment and you'll be comfortable here while I'm abroad.'

'I can afford my own accommodation although I may not
need it for long. I'll have another job by the time you
get back—'

Jasim released a slightly harsh laugh. 'There's no need for
you to look for another position. How would I ever see you?
Don't you understand what I'm offering you?'

Elinor stood very still. 'No, I must be incredibly thick
because I haven't quite worked out yet what you're offering
me.…'

His charismatic smile slashed his lean dark visage.
'Naturally, I want to take care of you.…'

'No, thanks.' Elinor forced a smile and mentally willed him not to demean her with some sordid proposition. 'The only man who will ever take *care* of me with my agreement will be my husband. I'm willing to wait for you to come back but I'm not willing to be kept by you. I'm a very independent woman and what I give, I give freely.'

Jasim frowned. 'You make it all sound so serious.'

'What happened between us last night left pure chaos in its wake. Right now, I don't know whether I'm on my head or my heels. I'll stay for a while because I have nowhere else to go in the short term. So maybe it's good that you'll be away for a while.'

Jasim pulled out his wallet to extract a card. 'My private number,' he told her, presenting her with it as though it was a precious gift, which indeed it was. Many women would have done just about anything to gain access to that direct hotline to him, but his staff guarded his privacy with scrupulous care.

Before he could close the wallet, his blood ran cold in his veins. How could he have made such a serious oversight? What if he had got her pregnant? He knew that an unplanned pregnancy would engulf his life like an avalanche, crush his freedom and suffocate him. He barely stilled a shudder at the threat of such an outcome and thought how ironic it was that what his older brother had longed and prayed for to secure the line to the throne should strike Jasim as an absolute disaster….

* * *

What will proud Prince Jasim do if Elinor is expecting his royal baby? Perhaps an arranged marriage is the only solution! But will Elinor agree? Find out in DESERT PRINCE, BRIDE OF INNOCENCE by Lynne Graham [#2884], available from Harlequin Presents® in January 2010.

Bestselling Harlequin Presents author

Lynne Graham

brings you an exciting new miniseries:

PREGNANT BRIDES

Inexperienced and expecting, they're forced to marry

Collect them all:

DESERT PRINCE,
BRIDE OF INNOCENCE

January 2010

RUTHLESS MAGNATE,
CONVENIENT WIFE

February 2010

GREEK TYCOON,
INEXPERIENCED MISTRESS

March 2010

www.eHarlequin.com

HP12884

REQUEST YOUR FREE BOOKS!

2 FREE NOVELS PLUS 2 FREE GIFTS!

HARLEQUIN®

Super Romance®

Exciting, emotional, unexpected!

YES! Please send me 2 FREE Harlequin® Superromance® novels and my 2 FREE gifts (gifts are worth about $10). After receiving them, if I don't wish to receive any more books, I can return the shipping statement marked "cancel." If I don't cancel, I will receive 6 brand-new novels every month and be billed just $4.69 per book in the U.S. or $5.24 per book in Canada. That's a savings of close to 15% off the cover price! It's quite a bargain! Shipping and handling is just 50¢ per book*. I understand that accepting the 2 free books and gifts places me under no obligation to buy anything. I can always return a shipment and cancel at any time. Even if I never buy another book from Harlequin, the two free books and gifts are mine to keep forever.

135 HDN EYLG 336 HDN EYLS

Name	(PLEASE PRINT)
Address	Apt. #
City	State/Prov.	Zip/Postal Code

Signature (if under 18, a parent or guardian must sign)

Mail to the **Harlequin Reader Service:**
IN U.S.A.: P.O. Box 1867, Buffalo, NY 14240-1867
IN CANADA: P.O. Box 609, Fort Erie, Ontario L2A 5X3

Not valid to current subscribers of Harlequin Superromance books.

**Are you a current subscriber of Harlequin Superromance books
and want to receive the larger-print edition?
Call 1-800-873-8635 today!**

* Terms and prices subject to change without notice. Prices do not include applicable taxes. Sales tax applicable in N.Y. Canadian residents will be charged applicable provincial taxes and GST. Offer not valid in Quebec. This offer is limited to one order per household. All orders subject to approval. Credit or debit balances in a customer's account(s) may be offset by any other outstanding balance owed by or to the customer. Please allow 4 to 6 weeks for delivery. Offer available while quantities last.

Your Privacy: Harlequin is committed to protecting your privacy. Our Privacy Policy is available online at www.eHarlequin.com or upon request from the Reader Service. From time to time we make our lists of customers available to reputable third parties who may have a product or service of interest to you. If you would prefer we not share your name and address, please check here. ☐

HSR09R

HARLEQUIN
Super Romance

COMING NEXT MONTH

Available January 12, 2010

#1608 AN UNLIKELY SETUP • Margaret Watson
Going Back
Maddie swore she'd never return to Otter's Tail…except she *has* to, to sell the
pub bequeathed her, and pay off her debt. Over his dead body, Quinn Murphy tells
her. Sigh. If only the sexy ex-cop *would* roll over and play dead.

#1609 HER SURPRISE HERO • Abby Gaines
Those Merritt Girls
They say the cure for a nervous breakdown is a dose of small-town justice. But
peaceful quiet is not what temp judge Cynthia Merritt gets when the townspeople of
Stonewall Hollow—led by single-dad rancher Ethan Granger—overrule her!

#1610 SKYLAR'S OUTLAW • Linda Warren
The Belles of Texas
Skylar Belle doesn't want Cooper Yates around her daughter. She knows about
her ranch foreman's prison record—and treats him like the outlaw he is. Yet when
Skylar's child is in danger, she discovers Cooper is the only man she can trust.

#1611 PERFECT PARTNERS? • C.J. Carmichael
The Fox & Fisher Detective Agency
Disillusioned with police work, Lindsay Fox left the NYPD to start her own
detective agency. Now business is so good, she needs to hire another investigator.
Unfortunately, the only qualified applicant is the one man she can't work with—
her ex-partner, Nathan Fisher.

#1612 THE FATHER FOR HER SON • Cindi Myers
Suddenly a Parent
Last time Marlee Britton saw Troy Denton, they were planning their wedding. Then
he vanished, leaving her abandoned and pregnant. Now he's returned…and he
wants to see his son. Letting Troy back in her life might be the hardest thing she's
done.

#1613 FALLING FOR THE TEACHER • Tracy Kelleher
When was Ben Brown last in a classroom? Now his son has enrolled them in a
course, so he's giving it his all, encouraged by their instructor, Katarina Zemanova.
Love and trust don't come easily, but the lessons yield top marks, especially when
they include falling for her!